"YOUR ONLY CHANCE LIES IN PREVENTING THE ASSASSINATION OF PRESIDENT ABRAHAM LINCOLN . . ."

"What?"

A burst of audio and visual static reduced reception to unintelligible noise. Then the paradox-generated interference was gone again, as suddenly as it had come.

"....Fourteenth of April at Ford's Theater—" *blast, crackle.*

"... you must be within two meters of the President ... just before the bullet smashes into Lincoln's brain. Your total window of opportunity will be three seconds."

FRED SABERHAGEN

AFTER THE FACT

BAEN BOOKS

AFTER THE FACT

A Baen Books Original

Baen Publishing Enterprises
260 Fifth Avenue
New York, N.Y. 10001

First printing, March 1988

ISBN: 0-671-65391-1

Cover art by David Mattingly

Printed in the United States of America

Distributed by
SIMON & SCHUSTER
1230 Avenue of the Americas
New York, N.Y. 10020

ONE

Central Illinois was about the flattest place that Jerry Flint had ever seen. Plowed fields, islanded here and there by clumps of trees and farm buildings, seemed to go on forever. The horizon was lost in an indeterminate haze more appropriate to Indian Summer than Spring.

Here and there along the interstate that stretched southwest from Chicago, grain elevators in tiny towns stood up like junior skyscrapers. Occasionally the highway would line up on one of them and rush straight at it for three or four miles, only to swerve at the last moment, bypassing both tower and town completely.

Jerry had intended to use the driving time to prepare himself for the interview facing him in Springfield, but found himself listening to the wind

1

rushing past instead. Before he was well out of Chicago he had begun to realize that there was not a whole lot in the way of preparation that he could do; since he knew next to nothing about the people who ran the Pilgrim Foundation for Historical Research, it was difficult to imagine what sort of programming or systems work they might want from him.

Tom Scheffler, a fellow student at St. Thomas More in Chicago, had told Jerry that he had worked for the man Pilgrim himself about a year ago, had been well paid for his labors, and recommended that Jerry give the Foundation a try.

Or had Scheffler said even that much? Jerry couldn't remember now but certainly Scheffler, a big kid from Iowa, had been generally encouraging. Scheffler was an undergraduate in computer engineering at the University, where Jerry Flint was now working on his master's in computer science. The two of them had shared one class and a couple of seminars, and over the past few months had become moderately well acquainted.

Jerry didn't have the impression that Scheffler was much given to jokes, at least no more than the average student. So now Jerry, looking back at the brief discussion the two of them had shared on the subject of the Pilgrim Foundation, began to find it rather strange, and even a touch ominous, that the big youth had seemed secretly amused—or even a bit excited by the prospect of Jerry's coming interview.

Their only important conversation on the matter, Jerry recalled, had been conducted between classes, in something of a rush.

When Jerry brought up the subject, Scheffler had shrugged and smiled. "Sure, if Olivia says it's okay,—and she told you to talk to me, right?—give it a try. The guy does pay well, I can testify to that. He wasn't 'the Pilgrim Foundation' when I worked for him, though."

"Oh? What did you do?"

Scheffler's inward amusement seemed to grow. "No computer stuff, really," he said at last, apparently groping for the right words. "My work involved some traveling," he added, finding them. "And there were some historical artifacts."

"Oh?" Jerry was squinting, scowling, trying to understand, and at the same time not wanting to be late for his next class. "This Pilgrim is a collector, then? In some kind of private business?"

"I'm sure he is. Look, I can't really give you any details. He'll have to do that. But I know Olivia, too, and if she's the one who's trying to recruit you, I'd say it was definitely okay." And with a wave of hands they parted company as each hurried on to his next class.

Olivia—Jerry knew her only by her first name —the person who had suggested that he talk to Scheffler about this, was something of a mystery herself. She was only a voice on the phone to Jerry Flint; she had started the whole business by phoning him one day out of the blue, and suggesting that as a bright student he might be willing to accept a summer job that would guarantee the financial support he was going to need if he wanted to go on and get a doctorate in computer science.

Did he want that? For Jerry that degree was life's big brass ring: not only was the subject matter incredibly interesting, but people with such advanced degrees in computer science were currently going directly from school into jobs that started at a hundred thousand a year. Still, it was a little odd that Olivia was also the one who recommended that he talk to Scheffler.

When Jerry, having been given a phone number to call in Springfield, came to talk to Dr. Pilgrim himself, he was assured that if he were hired, a grant could be arranged, above and beyond his pay for the coming summer, that would finance his schooling all the way to a Ph.D. in computer science.

Jerry's preliminary research in the university library had failed to turn up any reference to grants from a "Pilgrim Foundation." Of course the library's list might well be out of date. Nor could he even find a foundation of that name listed anywhere; but, he told himself, that that meant little; these organizations came and went.

So on the appointed day, with a week of spring break clear ahead of him, he rented a car and started driving south.

Jerry hadn't visited the state capital since a seventh-grade historical tour, and he was vaguely surprised that the place turned out to be a modest scale model of the metropolis to the north, complete with suburbs. There were no grain elevators here, but as Jerry drove in he observed a couple of buildings even taller than grain elevators. One of these, as he got close to it, turned out to be the hotel that he was looking for. At twenty stories or so it loomed far above everything else in sight.

There was no difficulty in finding a parking space on the street close to the hotel. Jerry climbed out of his little red rented Ford, and pulled on the suitcoat that had been riding on the back of the front seat. He tightened and straightened his unaccustomed necktie, and set out for the hotel lobby, leaving his bag in the car's trunk for the time being. Wondering if Dr. Pilgrim might possibly be waiting for him right in the lobby, he checked his image in a passing plate-glass window. Jerry had about given up wishing that he looked a little bigger, older, more mature. The key word for his appearance, he thought, was really *nondescript*. He could try raising a mustache, but it would probably be thin, and certainly the same commonplace brown as his hair. There was, of course, even less to be done about physical size. At five-seven at least he was a comfortable way from being a midget. And the karate classes he'd been attending for the last two years kept him in good shape.

As for being and looking older—well, that was certain to take care of itself in time. He was twenty-five now, and still sometimes taken for eighteen.

The hotel lobby was modern, and at the moment it was pleasantly uncrowded. Perhaps business was not that great. Jerry approached the desk. Yes, there was indeed a room reserved for Mr. Jeremiah Flint. Yes, prepaid too. There was also a message waiting for Mr. Flint, and Jerry received it along with his room key.

The note handed over by the desk clerk was handwritten in a distinctive but very legible script, black ink on a sheet of hotel notepaper. It read:

Dear Mr. Flint,

Please accept my apologies for not being on hand to welcome you on your arrival. An opportunity to conduct an experiment, one that I dare not pass up, has arisen. If you are able to come to the lodge across from the entrance to New Salem State Park before five o'clock, we shall be able to begin our discussions there, while at the same time you will be able to see something of the Foundation's work.

In haste,
A. Pilgrim

New Salem was only about twenty miles away, according to the desk clerk, who had the directions memorized—it was evidently a favorite tourist destination. As for meeting Pilgrim there before five, that was no problem; it was now only a little after noon.

An hour later, after settling in and having a cheeseburger in the hotel coffee shop, Jerry was back in his little red Ford, headed out of town again.

State Route 97 re-entered farmland only a couple of miles from the hotel near the center of town. Presently the highway branched, and the branch Jerry was following became even narrower. Jerry had gathered from a tourist brochure picked up in the hotel that New Salem was a small log-cabin settlement preserved and reconstructed more or less as it had been on reaching its peak of prosperity, sometime in the 1830s. That was about the time young Abraham Lincoln, working on a riverboat, had arrived in the settlement and taken up residence.

Now, scanning the farmland ahead on both sides of the highway, Jerry saw no sign of any community, historical or otherwise: just farms, hedgerows and islands of trees, leafing out with fresh spring green. Such groves of course might conceal something, but mostly what he could see was the black earth of Illinois, ready and eager to start producing crops. Here and there the fields were already dusted with preliminary green of one fine shade or another. Now and again the freshly turned fields alternated with pasturage. At intervals he could see a tractor laboring in the distance, tugging at some kind of machinery with which Jerry was not familiar. He was pretty much a city kid, or at least a suburban one.

But now, ahead and to his right, the agricultural expanse was interrupted by a long sweep of woodland that seemed to follow the course of a stream. As the woods drew nearer, the highway drifted right, sliding down along a heretofore invisible slope in the flat Illinois countryside. Then it suddenly drove more deeply, leveling off again under an arch of tall trees that lost itself inside a tunnel of bright new leaves.

Suddenly there were roadside signs, proclaiming the presence of New Salem State Park. There were log structures to be seen, and split-rail fences. The twentieth century had not entirely disappeared, but it was no longer unquestionably in charge; on that descending slope a border of some kind had been crossed.

On Jerry's right now, as he cruised the narrow highway at reduced speed, a wooded slope went up. On his left, beyond more trees, he could catch glimpses of a small river, banks already green enough for summer. That, according to his map, would have to be the Sangamon, where Lincoln had once poled his flatboat.

The motel was on the side of the road toward the river. It consisted of a modest lodge made of logs, and rustic cabins scattered back from the two-lane highway. A handful of cars were parked in the gravel lot.

Jerry pulled off the road and parked, went through the business of seeing to his coat and tie again, crossed a wooden porch and entered a log-walled lobby. To his eye, moderately experienced in academic appearances, none of the three or four people in sight looked like the head of a foundation. Anyway none of them took any interest in his arrival. After peering vaguely into a restaurant and a gift shop, and generally standing around looking lost for a minute or so, he approached another hotel desk and asked if there were any messages for him.

"I'm not a guest here, but—"

The woman behind the counter was rummaging in cubbyholes. "Mr. Flint . . . yes, there's a message for you, sir."

This time the note was on a small sheet torn from a pocket notebook. And the handwriting, though nearly as superbly legible as that of the first note, was different, smaller and rather feminine.

Dear Mr. Flint—

Sorry again not to be able to meet you. The experiment is keeping Dr. Pilgrim and my-

self both busy. If you would please come up
into the park and join us in front of the
Onstot cabin, we can begin your introduction
to our rather unusual enterprise. We hope
to see you in the park this afternoon.

Jan Chen
(for Dr. Pilgrim)

Whoever Jan Chen might be, there was something intrinsically pleasing, Jerry thought, about
her handwriting. The notebook sheet looked busi-
nesslike enough, but he thought he could detect
the faintest whiff of perfume.

Jerry decided that he would walk up the hill—
he'd done a good bit of driving already today, and
would certainly have to do some more. The park
entrance proper was a few hundred yards down
the highway, but directly opposite the motel parking lot a fairly well-worn though unofficial-looking
footpath pointed in the right direction before van-
ishing among the half-greened trees a few yards
in. Breathing spring country air, Jerry crossed the
highway—traffic just now was light to nonexistent—
and started up.

The slope he was climbing was not particularly
high, but almost until he was there the trees obscured his destination; Jerry wondered if the area
had been logged since Lincoln's time. A wasp
cruised past then hummed away again. There were
a few muddy places at flat spots in the path, but
nothing that his city-shod feet could not avoid.

As Jerry crested the hill, which he saw now was
really an extended ridge, a small log cabin suddenly appeared among the trees. Beyond it there

was another, and another beyond that. All at once he became aware that the twentieth century had disappeared completely. There was only an earthen path, trees, logs—and above the trees a sky for the moment innocent of jet contrails. The tang of woodsmoke reached Jerry's nostrils, and when he looked for it he could see a faint blue-white trickle rising from the tall stone chimney of the nearest cabin.

Jerry now noticed that mixed with the smell of woodsmoke came the aroma of cookery.

The door of the cabin stood ajar in the mild gray afternoon. Out of curiosity Jerry pushed it farther open—this building was an exhibit in a park that was open to the public, right?—and peered into the dim interior, which was lighted only by one small window on another wall.

A figure moved, near the broad stone hearth where a small fire glowed amid gray ashes. The figure was that of a woman, wearing a bonnet and a long dress—a dress about a hundred years too long. Her face as she turned toward the doorway was shaded by the bonnet, hard to see.

"Come in," the woman said.

Jerry stood dead still, one hand on the door's ancient-looking, handcarved latch of wood. "I—" he started to say, and then quit. *No*, he thought.

"Come in," she invited cheerfully. "Try some cornbread."

Blinking against the smoke and dimness, he managed to get a better look at the woman. She was about forty, fresh-faced and a bit plump. In one hand, protected by a thick homemade potholder, she was gripping a high-sided metal pan from which she now began to pry slabs of steaming yellow-golden stuff onto a large white platter that waited on the handmade wooden table. Other dishes on the table held more cornbread already cut into chunks of modest size. There was also, Jerry observed with faint but real relief, a package of paper napkins, very much of the late twentieth century.

"You had me going for just a minute," he admitted.

"Beg pardon?"

"I thought—you being in the costume and everything—oh, never mind. I wasn't sure what was going on." It was easy enough to chuckle now.

"Oh." The woman was still smiling at him, but not as if she really understood. "We're from the historical society. We're occupying several cabins here today, demonstrating what life was like for the original settlers."

"Oh. I see. You're doing a very realistic job." Accepting first a paper napkin and then a piece of cornbread, Jerry spoke in honest admiration of the evident skill required for baking over the open fire. He listened politely to some more information on cooking tools and methods, and then strolled on. Out of the cabin now, he could see that the path continued on to join a system of broad gravel walks. In that direction were scattered a dozen or more log buildings whose loose grouping extended more or less along the top of the wooded ridge.

Picking up another brochure from a tray mounted on a rustic stand where the official walks began, Jerry learned that there were about twenty buildings in all in the reconstructed settlement. On this gray weekday a very modest number of other tourists were about. Jerry walked forward. He was just thinking that it oughtn't to be hard to pick out a working scientist and his assistant when he saw them. There was no doubt in his mind, though they were still at a considerable distance.

TWO

Approaching the man he thought must be Dr. Pilgrim, Jerry walked past a water-powered mill that was, for the moment at least, motionless, a blacksmith shop manned by folk in historic costume, and half a dozen more cabins. Then he was drawing close to the people he thought he was looking for, and their machines.

The little machines, mounted on what looked like surveyors' tripods, were aimed at what Jerry supposed must be the historic Onstot residence. The man who was concentrating his attention so energetically upon what the machines were doing was a couple of inches shorter than Jerry, compactly built, and of indeterminate age. At least he was still young enough for his black hair to be free of gray. His coloring in general was rather swarthy.

13

Muscular, hairy forearms protruded from rolled-up shirtsleeves. The half-dozen pockets of the man's Banana Republic bush vest were stuffed with electronic cables, small tools, pencils, notebooks, and what looked to Jerry like camera accessories.

The young woman with him looked vaguely oriental, as if the name Chen might fit her. Her straight black hair, or most of it, was tied up in an expensive-looking scarf. She wore jeans and a tucked-in shirt, with large dangling earrings that were perhaps intended to show that she didn't really belong on a construction crew.

At twenty yards or so, before either of the pair had given any sign of noticing him, Jerry paused in his approach. He was making a last effort at trying to figure out just what the hell they might be doing, so that his first attempt at conversation would not appear too stupid.

They had the Onstot cabin triangulated with their machines, and they were either photographing it or making surveyor's measurements of it. Or maybe they were doing something that required both processes. A couple of passing tourists gazed at the workers in ignorant admiration, and passed up a close look at the Onstot cabin, being anxious not to interfere with whatever kind of special work was going on.

The setup reminded Jerry vaguely of the laser systems that construction crews sometimes used to make sure that things were kept exactly level or exactly perpendicular. At least two of these devices could have been cameras, and all three of them had what must be their battery power-packs on the lower shelves of their tripods.

Jerry in his years of engineering studies had never seen anything like it. But he had to give up for the moment on trying to figure it out. He resumed his advance.

Though the man was facing directly away, it was he who made the young woman aware of Jerry's presence. As if he might have received some extrasensory warning, the dark-haired man lifted his eyes suddenly from his instrument and turned around to look at the new arrival. A moment later he raised a hand in an abrupt gesture, signaling his helper that they were through for the moment with whatever they had been doing.

Jerry strode forward, armed with his most intelligent smile. "Dr. Pilgrim?"

"Yes." As on the phone, the voice had the precision of an actor's, slightly and indefinably accented— James Mason would come close, thought Jerry, who was something of an old-movie buff. "Yes," Pilgrim continued. "And you will be Jeremiah Flint." He appeared genuinely pleased to see his visitor, and not to resent the interruption of his work.

The doctor's handshaking grip was firm but brief. Then he turned his head toward his assistant. "Jan, let that go for now. Come and say hello. It may be that our computer problems are on the verge of solution."

Jan Chen approached. Jerry took his first good look at her through a fragrance of lilacs; the bushes flanking the Onstot cabin door were in full spring bloom. She walked with a grace that suggested a model's training; her eyes were as black as her hair, but her skin glowed like old ivory. It hardly seemed to matter that her face was a long way from Jerry's ideal of classic beauty.

"I see you found our messages," she said to him in a voice in which he could find no accent at all. She shook his hand in a business-like way. "Sorry that neither of us could meet you in person at the hotel—either hotel."

"That's quite all right. I was glad to come up here and meet you on site. This will give me a chance to see what kind of work you're doing."

Pilgrim was frowning at his watch. "Now that you are here, Mr. Flint—may I call you Jerry?"

"Sure. Of course. I was wondering what you were doing with these devices that—"

"Now that you are here, I think it will be best if we spend as much of the afternoon as possible in our discussions. Therefore we had better break this off—Jan, let us pack up the equipment immediately."

The young woman nodded, murmured something in agreement, and turned away to begin folding one of the tripods. Pilgrim seemed to have another of them already folded—he had got it taken down with what seemed to Jerry altogether unlikely speed. The battery pack and everything else stayed neatly in a bundle with the tripod when its long legs were collapsed. Jerry was unable to catch a manufacturer's name, if such a thing was showing, before the device had been snapped inside a cloudy plastic cover.

Jerry volunteered to carry one of the three machines, and equally burdened, the three headed out through the main gate of the village to the hilltop parking lot through which most visitors approached.

"Have you been here before?" Jan Chen asked him.

"No, first time for me." His school tour, long years ago, had never got this far from Springfield.

"For me too. But I have long been an enthusiast of Abraham Lincoln, and to be here where he lived is exciting." Despite her rather stilted turn of phrase, Jan sounded animated; this meant something to her. She turned to point back into the village, indicating one direction after another. "He was a boarder there, at the Rutledge tavern. And a clerk over there. And a storekeeper and postmaster down there. His first claim to fame was as a frontier wrestler in these parts."

Jerry caught at a name. It brought back vague memories of someone's poem. "Ann Rutledge? She was supposed to be Lincoln's girl friend, wasn't she?"

"Many think so—but we can't be sure." They had come to a stop in the parking lot, and Pilgrim had unlocked the side door of a new van and was beginning to stow equipment inside. Meanwhile his assistant was starting to glow with an inner excitement, which Jerry recognized as that of the true enthusiast unleashed upon a favorite subject. She went on to discuss in detail the lack of any real evidence connecting young Lincoln with the innkeeper's daughter.

Dr. Pilgrim, meanwhile, apparently bursting with his own brand of cheerful energy, stowed the last bit of gear in the van and slid shut the wide side door. "I would like to suggest, Jerry, that I ride back to Springfield with you. I presume you have a car. We will meet Jan there, unload our equipment, and continue our discussions in the office."

Jerry found the rush to get the gear packed away not too surprising; a lot of companies had proprietary secrets they were reluctant to reveal, at least until you were contracted to secrecy. Probably this equipment was something like that. Jerry knew a momentary regret that he was not riding back with Jan. That would almost certainly make it a more pleasant trip—but possibly a less productive one. And Pilgrim was definitely the man he had to talk to, to find out as soon as possible if this job offer could possibly be as good as Mr. A. Pilgrim had made it sound.

After waving Jan on her way in the van, he and Pilgrim started trudging side by side down the winding, forest-lined drive that led to the highway and to the small motel parking lot where Jerry had left his car.

"Interesting equipment you were using up there," Jerry remarked in a bright tone, opening conversation.

Pilgrim gave a little shrug. "Not really mine, in any proprietary sense. I have learned to use it, that is all." The words were said in a deprecating tone, as if to imply he might not be capable of learning more. "I am not really a technologist. The fact of the matter is, the Foundation needs help in several technical areas."

"I see. What were you doing up there today, if you don't mind my asking?"

Pilgrim might not have heard the question. "Your

own role, Jerry, if we are able to come to an agreement, would be—largely—in the area of computers. Of course, we might ask you to do another little job or two also. Specifically, I should like to establish a network comprising several of the newer Macintosh machines. They would be connected by modem with a larger computer, one of the new "parallel" devices, and possibly with several other machines as well. The Macintoshes are in the Foundation's office in town, where we are going now."

Jerry's only experience with parallel processing was course work, but he had found that course work intensely interesting. But what could an historical research project need with that kind of raw power? Intriguing. Maybe this job would be *better* than it had sounded over the phone.

"Then I would be working here, in the Springfield area, full time. Is that it?"

"Yes—allowing for the occasional field trip elsewhere. You would work here during the coming summer, putting in as much time as your school schedule allows. The Foundation will pay all of your living expenses while you are in Springfield —or on any field trip we might require you to undertake—plus modest salary. And it will guarantee in writing that, provided your job performance is satisfactory, it will pay all your further expenses toward your doctorate in computer science."

"That sounds like a great deal."

Pilgrim, looking straight ahead through the windshield, nodded minimally. "Indeed. All this, of course, contingent upon our agreement that you are the right man for the job."

"Of course. I should warn you that microcomputers aren't really my specialty. I have worked some with Macs, though."

Jan and the van were long out of sight by the time they had walked down to Jerry's car. On the drive back into town Jerry, by invitation, held forth on the various computer projects in which he'd already been involved. They made a fairly impressive list for someone of his age; he'd had to work his way through most of college, and most of the work he'd done had involved computers in one way or another.

He wasn't sure though, how much of it Dr. Pilgrim understood. The man in the front passenger's seat sat listening and nodding thoughtfully, and for the most part appeared to be keenly interested. But he didn't really say anything that would offer good evidence of his understanding. It wouldn't be the first time that Jerry had tried to inform a highly intelligent but non-technical audience about his work, only to discover later that hardly anything he'd said had been understood. There were computer people, who could understand, and then there was the rest of the human race.

In a few minutes they were back in town, where Pilgrim began giving navigator's directions. Presently, only a couple of blocks from Jerry's hotel, they were driving into a large square whose center was occupied by a hulking stone building of antique design, obviously preserved or restored. Several signs informed the visitor that this was the Old State Capitol.

Guess who, thought Jerry to himself, must have done something or other in the Old Capitol. Any lingering suspicion he might have entertained that Lincoln was not the chief industry in Springfield had by now vanished under a barrage of commercial signs. You had the Lincoln This, the Lincoln That, the Railsplitter Something Else. A few people, just to be different, had dedicated their enterprises to Ann Rutledge.

At Pilgrim's direction Jerry now turned into a lane of traffic that dove sharply into a fluorescent cave right under the Old Capitol, where signs informed him of several levels of modern parking. Here, in one of the reserved sections, Jan stood waiting for them beside the van.

In a couple of minutes the three of them had unloaded the equipment from the larger vehicle and were carrying it upstairs to the surface.

They emerged on a broad sidewalk, facing the Old Capitol across the street. The buildings lining the perimeter of the square were mostly of brick, two or three stories tall. Approaching one of these, Pilgrim used a key on an inconspicuous door set back slightly from the sidewalk, and led the way up some indoor stairs. The plastic-covered tripods now and then knocked lightly against stairs or walls. At the top of the first flight Jan unlocked the door to a modest suite of offices. There was no sign on the door to indicate who occupied them. Nothing fancy, Jerry thought, carrying his burden in. Except maybe for some of the computer stuff.

These rooms might last have been modernized in the 1960s. In the first room were a couple of desks and a few battered tables. On some tables near the windows, a couple of instruments similar to the ones Pilgrim had been using at New Salem were mounted on shorter tripods, lenses aimed out through the windows in the direction of the Old Capitol building across the street. There were also three of the new Macintosh computers in the room, one with a color screen, and quite a bit of cabling.

"Did you arrange this setup?" Jerry asked, gesturing at the computers, when the equipment they had brought in with them had been stowed in a closet.

"No, I am a user only. And I am afraid there will be no chance for you to consult directly with the engineer who arranged this system—if that is the right term for what has been done here." Moving energetically from one table to another, Pilgrim had started flipping switches. Now Jerry saw that there were four Macs, the last one almost hidden in a corner. One after another each sounded a musical chime-note as it came to life.

"As you can see," Pilgrim added, "part of the system is optical—would you like to take a look?"

More than ready to get involved, Jerry went to the eyepiece of one of the tabletop units—it looked something like a cross between a surveyor's instrument and a telescopic camera. The image it presented was one of the most peculiar he had ever seen—it looked like a clear, somewhat magnified optical picture of the granite of the Old Capitol, overlaid slightly off-center with a computer reproduction of itself.

He turned away from the eyepiece and looked around. "I don't quite get it."

"The Foundation's object, Jerry, is historical research. The capitol building there, for example, was taken down stone by stone a few decades ago, and then reconstructed *in situ*. There are of course slight differences between the positions in space of its stone blocks now, and the positions occupied by those same blocks in, say, the year eighteen fifty-nine. With the center of mass of the earth itself as reference—excuse me." A phone at the far side of the office had begun to ring, and Pilgrim gestured to Jan Chen that he wanted to answer it himself.

She was standing by, smiling brightly, and Jerry turned to her. He asked: "It sounds like you're somehow able to determine exactly where each stone was in the past?"

Across the room, Pilgrim was frowning and muttering at whatever the phone was telling him. Jan shook her head. "I'm not the one to ask about what can be done with the computers and sensing devices. Ask me something about the dates of the Old Capitol there, or about Lincoln, and I can tell you a few things."

"Sounds interesting. I probably will. You're the resident historian then."

"That is really Dr. Pilgrim. I am only an assistant." No accent in her speech, no, but a certain overprecision, noticeable more at some times than others, that made Jerry wonder if she might have been born in another country. She went on: "this whole area around Springfield is just so fascinating to me, Lincoln being something of a specialty of mine. Naturally I was very pleased to be able to come here and work on this project."

"You have a degree in history, then?"

"Last year, from USC. And you?"

Jerry started talking about TMU, and the joys and problems of living in Chicago. Jan, it turned out, was originally from San Francisco. The struggles involved in surviving student life and planning their careers gave them enough in common so that there seemed no danger of running out of things to talk about. Jerry had been ready to plunge right in, tracing cables, starting to figure out the existing network that had been set up with the optical devices and the computers; but talking to Jan instead was, for the moment, quite satisfactory. Certainly it would have been impolite to cut her off, when she was so obviously interested in his background and what he might be going to do here, for the Foundation.

At some point Jerry became aware that Pilgrim, his hand over the phone receiver, was clearing his throat in an urbane effort to get their attention.

"Jan, Jerry, I am sorry. But it appears now that certain dull details of administration are going to keep me occupied for the next couple of hours at least." He frowned at the gold watch strapped to his hairy wrist. " 'Time flies like an arrow.' " The way he said the phrase made it sound like a quote, though Jerry had no idea what it might be from.

Pilgrim went on: "Jan, I would suggest that you spend the remainder of the afternoon conducting Jerry on a small tour of Springfield. With emphasis of course on the sites where we shall be working. Make use of the expense account; take him to dinner also. Sooner or later I will catch up with you. You might also even show him where he will lodge should we come to agreement on the terms of his employment." Pilgrim smiled suddenly, favoring Jerry with an unexpectedly bright and winning look. "As of now that seems a distinct possibility."

THREE

Two minutes after Pilgrim had given them his blessing, Jerry and Jan were out on the street, Jan fitting on an expensive-looking pair of sunglasses whose effect was to turn her from a mod archaeologist into a tourist. Before leaving the office she had also picked up a purse, which presumably contained the plastic tools that would let her make use of the expense account.

"The sites we plan to work on this summer," she announced, "all have something to do with the life of Abraham Lincoln, as you may have guessed by now."

"I'm not surprised to hear it," Jerry admitted.

"What to see first?" Jan pondered, looking around the square, where modern shops and vehicles surrounded and contained the time warp of the Old

Capitol. "I think the Lincoln Home, that's only a few blocks away. Then we should have plenty of time to drive out to the cemetery before it closes and take a look at his tomb. It's only a couple of miles, just on the edge of town."

"Whatever you say," Jerry agreed. The more he listened to this lady's voice, the more he enjoyed hearing her talk.

They started walking. A block before they reached Lincoln's Home ("the only house he ever owned", as Jan enthused) they passed into a restored historical area of the city. Here the streets had been closed off to motor vehicles, and were lined by wooden sidewalks. Spacious yards of neatly mowed grass, looking unnaturally perfect, surrounded sizable frame houses that Jerry could believe had been built during the nineteenth century.

One of those houses, on the northeast corner of Eighth and Jackson, and marked with appropriate signs, was their destination. Lincoln's home was open to visitors on payment of a small fee. Jan insisted that the fee should be on the expense account.

Jerry had seen rooms like these in museums. Some of the furniture inside, Jan informed him, was original, the rest being authentic-looking reproductions. Only the Interior Department, who managed the show, knew which was which, and they weren't telling.

A hacker at heart, Jerry had developed the unconscious habit on first entering someone's house of looking around for computers. He caught himself doing it now; but naturally enough there was not even an electric outlet visible. Having registered this fact consciously, Jerry stood looking at a writing desk equipped with primitive steel-nibbed wooden pens, and a candlestick.

"I guess what you achieve doesn't always depend on your tools," he murmured, trying to picture Old Abe at the keyboard of a word processor.

"No! Not at all! Isn't that beautifully true?" Jan appeared to feel that he had touched on an important point.

"I don't suppose he wrote the Gettysburg Address at this desk, or anything like that."

"Certainly not the Gettysburg Address. But some very beautiful and logical prose. He was quite a successful lawyer."

"After he'd given up his career as an amateur wrestler."

"Oh yes."

A narrow stairway brought them to the upper floor, where from behind low anti-tourist railings they considered the Lincoln bedrooms—there had been four children when the family lived here, it appeared. Jan had little to say here, evidently wanting to allow Jerry to form his own impressions. Almost the last stop on the tour was the archaeological site in the backyard where the Lincoln privy had once stood; there was not much to see now, beyond a modest display of nineteenth-century glass bottles.

When they emerged from the house onto the wooden sidewalks again, Jan glanced at her wristwatch. "We've still got plenty of time to see the tomb. Oak Ridge Cemetery stays open until five."

"The tomb, and the house here, will be among the sites we work on this summer?"

"Oh yes. Definitely."

They were walking back toward the underground garage. Jerry said: "You know, maybe I missed an explanation or something, but I still don't get exactly what the Pilgrim Foundation is trying to do. I mean what is your historical research trying to accomplish exactly? And how?"

Jan sighed. "Lincoln is—endlessly fascinating." It sounded like a preliminary to an explanation, but nothing followed.

Jerry waited until he felt sure no more was coming. Then he said: "To me, 'interesting' would be a better word. Lincoln and his times are interesting, sure. But to me nothing in history can be as fascinating as what's happening now. Something you learn how to do, something that will really change the world. I mean, with all due respect, whatever you find out about Lincoln now is not really going to change much in our world."

Jan was not at all taken aback. "Modern technology can be applied to history."

"Well, sure. To research. But I mean . . . suppose you were able to discover that Lincoln was really George Washington's grandson. Or that he kept a mistress on the side. Whatever. People nowadays would pretty much shrug and say 'so what?' And the world would go on as before. I mean, as far as I can see, all this historical research just isn't going to change it any." Then, with the sudden feeling that he might be speaking too harshly about this lady's pet enthusiasm, he added: "Now come on, your turn. Tell me how I'm all wrong."

"You're all wrong." Jan was smiling, and to his

relief she didn't seem to have taken his argument all that seriously. Then, giving it thought, she became more serious. "Jerry, Lincoln had an enormous input on what our world is today. The United States is still one nation only because of him. And he's the man who killed slavery; he didn't do it all by himself of course, but far more of the credit must go to him than to any other person."

"Yes, I'm sure."

"And then, you see, there came along a fanatic— John Wilkes Booth. 'A Confederate doing duty on his own responsibility' is what he called himself. Booth crept into Lincoln's box at the theater, and shot him in the back of the head, just as the Civil War was coming to an end, in the spring of 1865. Only three months into his second term." Jan seemed to think that this last point was very meaningful.

"Well, yes, I suppose. Everyone knows it was John Wilkes Booth, right? But I mean, however Lincoln was killed—"

"Can you imagine how much better off our world might be now if he had been allowed to live at least four more years? If he, instead of Andrew Johnson, had been President until 1869?"

"No, can't say I ever thought about it."

"Andrew Johnson was rather better than the reputation that some historians have given him. But he simply was not in Lincoln's league as a politician."

"Somehow I don't think of Lincoln that way."

Jan smiled at him. "He was a politician, take my word for it. And he was a very effective leader, beginning to be recognized as a national hero,

with the war winding to a close. Andrew Johnson
made some effort to follow his policies, true, but
. . . Johnson was almost impeached." Jan seemed
to despair of being able to convey the magnitude
of the difference in the two men.

"Too bad we can't get Lincoln up out of his
tomb, then. We could use him now."

Jan smiled at him more brightly than ever. "It's
been tried."

"Huh?"

"Some years after the War, there was an attempt to kidnap his body and hold it for ransom.
No, I'm not making this up. That's why there are
twelve tons of poured concrete over him now."

The tomb, a gray stone structure rising out of a
green lawn, was bigger than most houses, even if
you didn't count the granite shaft ten stories high
that rose from the middle of it like a miniature
Washington monument. On the flat roof of the
tomb surrounding the central shaft were groups of
bronze soldiers in Civil War uniforms, posed in
dramatic attitudes, gripping weapons, waving their
bronze flag, beating their drums, pointing out the
enemy in the distance. Jan and Jerry walked into a
marble foyer, where Jan pointed out a scaled-
down replica of the seated Lincoln from the Me-
morial in Washington. There were park attendants
on hand in this room, and a few other tourists. Jan
led Jerry down a hallway of pink and brown marble to peer over a velvet rope into a chamber of
red stone.

The tomb itself, the single stone standing over
the actual resting place, was simple. On the wall

of rock behind it was carved: NOW HE BELONGS
TO THE AGES. And on the single stone the
legend read simply:

ABRAHAM LINCOLN
1809–1865

Information carved into the walls indicated what
auxiliary entombments there had been in this room.

MARY TODD LINCOLN
1818–1882

EDWARD (Eddie) BAKER LINCOLN
1846–1850

WILLIAM (Willie) WALLACE LINCOLN
1850–1862

THOMAS (Tad) LINCOLN
1853–1871

"Poor guy didn't have very good luck with his
family," Jerry observed. "Two of his kids died
before he did. One didn't live much longer."

"No." Jan was almost whispering, as if the family had been her personal friends. There was no
doubt that she was moved. "No, neither he nor his
wife had very good luck that way."

They drove out through the iron gates of the
cemetery shortly before closing time, and only a
few minutes later were back in the heart of town.
Jan dropped Jerry in front of his hotel; they had

agreed to meet in the lobby in an hour to discuss dinner arrangements.

As Jerry showered he thought to himself that he still had learned next to nothing about the Pilgrim Foundation, its organization, financing, goals and methods. Obviously its people somehow planned to glean something from the past by using their tripod machines and a computer network. But his hosts had been avoiding his questions on that subject all day. Well, probably they were waiting until he was confirmed as an employee and had signed something giving them legal protection against his disclosure of their secrets. That was all right with Jerry. He'd do the same, he supposed. But he was growing ever more curious and impatient.

Jan was sitting and waiting for him in the lobby when he came down, promptly on time. She had changed into what he supposed ought to be called an evening dress, of startling red. It looked beautiful on her, and there was nothing at all about it to suggest the nineteenth century. "I'm hungry," she greeted him. "Do you like Italian food?"

"One of my favorites."

Jan said she knew a good place within walking distance of the hotel.

He was moderately impressed when they reached the place; more evidence that the Foundation was not going to stint on its expense account. When they were asked if they wanted anything from the bar before dinner, Jerry hesitated at first. He was not ordinarily a teetotaler, nor very much of a drinker either. But when Jan immediately ordered a vodka martini he decided this wasn't part of the test, and went along—with a better conscience when she launched into a story involving Pilgrim's preference for something called *akvavit*. The story raised in Jerry's mind the question of just what relationship existed between Jan Chen and Pilgrim, other than that of employee and employer. So far he had no sense that there was any.

Food arrived, custom-designed pizzas, served with class upon good dishes. Chianti was available and therefore seemed called for as an accompaniment—Jerry had absorbed this as an article of faith during his early college years, and Jan expressed a willingness to be converted.

They ate, sipped wine, and talked. Jan, it appeared, had been born in California and had grown up in San Francisco. In Chinatown? Jerry wondered. But he didn't as yet feel quite sure enough of himself to ask her that.

He had spent the earlier part of his own childhood in one of the smaller, more distant and less affluent suburbs of Chicago. Then, when he was about ten years old, his parents, had been able to move to the more affluent Lombard.

"Every spring they have a Lilac Festival there— it's pretty famous. It reminded me of that today, when I saw the lilacs out at New Salem."

" 'When lilacs last in the dooryard bloomed—' ", Jan quoted. It was really marvelous, how daintily she could eat pizza, and what a respectable amount this technique allowed her to put away. "That's Walt Whitman. It has something to do with Lincoln too."

"Oh." Jerry felt a certain sadness. "I haven't had a lot of time to look into poetry."

His companion looked sympathetic. "In your

field I can understand that. It must keep you very busy. Poetry is one of Dr. Pilgrim's favorite things."

"I've been meaning to ask you. Does Dr. Pilgrim have a first name? I saw a first initial on the note he left for me."

Jan smiled. "If he does, I haven't heard anyone use it."

"Oh." Jerry smiled back. "Hey, is that lilac perfume you're wearing?"

"Actually it is." Now she was pleased to the point of giggling. It was a quiet giggle, as if it might concern secrets. Then, seemingly with her next breath, as if there might have been a transition but Jerry had somehow missed it, she was asking him: "Was there ever a moment—probably in your childhood—that you thought you had lived through twice? Or maybe more than twice? I don't mean *déja vù*, that's something else entirely. I mean twice in rapid succession, like bing-bing. Know what I mean?"

Jerry sat back in his comfortable chair, regarding his companion's ivory skin, face and slim neck and bare shoulders over the red dress. He had the sensation the martini and the wine were rapidly turning to water in his blood, that full sobriety had suddenly returned.

He said: "Funny you should ask. There was a moment just today . . . not exactly what you're asking about, but . . ."

"Yes?"

"Well, it was nothing, really. I had just arrived at New Salem, and I was starting to look for you and Dr. Pilgrim. Directly across from the hotel there's a footpath leading up into the park, and I went up that way and came on the log cabins without any warning. I looked into the first one, and there was a woman inside wearing a costume just like what Lincoln's mother must have worn. Making cornbread over a fire. And it shook me for just a moment. Like maybe I had really stepped into some kind of time warp—know what I mean?"

Jan was listening with calm interest. "I suppose she was one of those historical society people."

"Yeah." Jerry paused; then let it go at that.

"Most people—" Jan had to suppress a tiny, lady-like, chianti-hiccup. She began again. "Most people would not be really shaken, even for a moment, by such a trivial experience. And yet I get the impression, from the way you talk about it now, that you really were somewhat taken aback—if only for a moment. Now, why should that have been?"

Jerry popped a fragment of pizza crust into his mouth and followed it with another sip of wine. He chewed meditatively.

"Well?" Jan sounded genuinely interested.

"Well. Funny you should get me to talk about it. No one else ever has. There was one time, when I was a kid, when something happened that was really very strange, along the time-warp line. Or at least I have this memory of a strange thing happening, whether it ever actually did or not. Maybe some part of me is always on the lookout for something like it to happen again."

"Tell me about it." Jan Chen's voice was sympathetic, her eyes intent.

"I will. Though I've never told anyone else about it until now." He sipped his wine again. "Before my family moved to Lombard we lived farther out from the city, in a house we were renting on the edge of a small town—it was almost like living on a farm. I was only a little kid then, it was a lot of fun." He paused for a deep breath. "Anyway, one day the house we were living in burned down. Something wrong with the wiring. My dad—he's my stepfather, really—was at work, and my mother was visiting a neighbor."

"Excuse me. You were an only child?"

"Yeah. Anyway, I was just coming home from school. I was the first one, or almost the first one, to see the smoke and flames. The fire was just getting a good start. All I could think of was that my mother must be in the house somewhere. I wasn't even scared, except for her.

"There was a neighbor woman running across her yard toward our place, shouting my name. But I paid her no attention. I ran on into the house, yelling for my mother. First I looked in the kitchen for her, and then in the other lower rooms—it wasn't a big house; it only took me about five seconds to discover that my mother wasn't on the ground floor anywhere. All I could think of was that she had to be upstairs.

"There were flames on the stairs already, just getting a start there, but I hardly thought about that. By that time I was in a total panic. I ran up the stairs, yelling my head off. I had to get my mother out."

"You were a brave little boy."

"I was a crazy little boy, maybe. I'm telling you this like I remember it. What my memory of today tells me happened."

"I understand." Jan nodded. Her concentration was more intense than ever; her dark eyes had widened subtly as she listened.

"My mother wasn't upstairs, either. There were only a couple of rooms up there, and it took me only a few moments to make sure she wasn't home. But still, by the time I got back to the head of the stairs, the fire had spread. There was no getting down those stairs anymore. It would have been like stepping into a furnace."

"You could have crawled out of a window," Jan whispered. It was the same almost reverential whisper she had used in Lincoln's tomb.

"I might have. Except, as I remember, it was still winter and we still had these big tough storm windows on. And the window sills were high, well above the floor. I'm not at all sure I could have got out of one before the smoke got me, or the fire, the way those flames were spreading. Anyway, at the time I'm not sure I even thought about windows. Oh, one more thing. When I was running up the stairs, my left arm and my left shirtsleeve got burned. Pretty badly. But I didn't feel the pain that much right away. You know how it can be when you're excited?"

"I know."

"But once I was upstairs I started feeling the burn. Still not real bad. All I could think of—standing there at the top of the stairs and knowing I couldn't go down them—was that it had all been a great *mistake*. It had been *wrong* for me to come upstairs. I should have known better. If my mother had been in the house when the fire started, she would have noticed it burning and got out. She never slept during the day. There had been no need for me to come up here looking for her."

"So what did you do?" His soft-voiced listener, posing with unconscious art in the soft light of the candle on their table, was leaning her pale chin upon one slender wrist.

Jerry sipped his wine. "I guess," he said, "I decided not to come upstairs after all. That's how I remember it."

"I'm not sure I understand."

"I know damn well *I* don't. Everything that I've told you happened, I remember it happening, as surely as anything in my life has ever happened. And yet, there I was, downstairs again, standing just inside the front door, a good ten or twelve feet from where the fire was just getting started on the stairway. And neither my arm nor my shirt were burned at all.

"The stairs were no longer a mass of flames, at the moment they looked almost safe, just as they had when I—came in the first time. I could have run up there, but I didn't, because I had just been upstairs, and I was sure my mother wasn't there.

"I backed out of the house, away from the flames, and just as I went out the door I saw the stairs inside start to go up like a torch." He fell silent.

Jan occupied herself for a few moments in looking thoughtful. Then she asked encouragingly: "There's more?"

"A little more. Yes. The neighbor lady, who had been running across the yard to keep me from going into the house? Well, she was still running across the yard when I came out. She ran up to me and grabbed me a moment later, and pulled me back farther from the burning house.

"She said: 'Where's your mother?' and I said: 'She isn't home.' Later, quite a long time later, someone asked me how I'd known that. I don't remember what I answered."

Frowning lightly, Jan asked an unexpected question. "How big were these yards? I mean specifically the one the lady was running across."

"Not all that big. I couldn't possibly have had time to go inside, and search the entire house, and come running out of it again before the neighbor lady arrived on our doorstep. And yet that's exactly what I did. As I remember it."

Jan's smile was conspiratorial, but it looked honest. "And now there are two of us who know you did."

FOUR

Coming out of the Italian restaurant some inde-terminate time later, emerging into the mild spring night, Jerry had put strange memories out of his mind. He felt suddenly inspired to burst into song, if only in a muted way.

But after singing only a few words he came to a sudden stop. "What're we going to do tomorrow? But never mind that, what're we going to do now?" He felt enthusiastic, ready to explore new worlds. Had he had too much to drink? No, hardly that. Not really. Just one martini and a little wine.

" 'Tomorrow and tomorrow and tomorrow,' " Jan quoted brightly, " 'creeps in this petty pace from day to day—' "

"You're quoting again. You definitely have a habit of doing that."

"When one works constantly with Dr. Pilgrim, one tends to get into the habit." Jan gave no sign of having been at all affected by the wine she had consumed.

"I suppose one might do that, if one has any stock of quotations at all upon which to draw. Of course if one is studying for a degree in computer science, and trying to hold down a job at the same time, one hasn't had time to read all those books that one is supposed to read."

Dr. Pilgrim's assistant shook her head, sighing tolerantly. Somehow she and Jerry had come to be holding hands as they strolled the city street. There were only a few passers-by. Spring moths swarmed the brilliant street lamps.

"This is a bank building," said Jan suddenly, tugging at Jerry's hand, bringing him almost to a stop in front of what was indubitably a bank. "Springfield has little banks. Chicago has big ones where you can find what you need no matter what. If you really need a bank, Jerry, I think a man in your situation should look for one in Chicago. Remember that."

"Is that Walt Whitman too? Or I suppose Lincoln recommended Chicago banks."

"Lincoln had some interesting ideas on banking. But that's beside the point."

"Jan." Now Jerry did come to a full stop. "Did you have a whole lot more to drink than I did, or what?"

"Oh no. Oh, no, no, no." She was vastly, but apparently soberly, amused.

"Then I don't get it. What you were saying

about the banks. There must have been something I missed, or . . ."

"Don't worry about it now. Maybe someday you'll want to remember it." She smiled as if she were pleased with him.

Whatever. They strolled on. "Jan, what're we going to do tomorrow, really? I don't want to screw up my chances for this job, I think I'll like it. I mean even apart from the financial . . . Hey, Pilgrim was going to see us again tonight, isn't that what he said?"

"Yes, I think he will."

"Do you think I'm too drunk to see the boss tonight? I am feeling a little light-headed."

"Not this once," she assured him, taking his hand again. "This once it will be perfectly all right."

"At least I don't have t'drive anywhere tonight. And there's no hurry, is there? It's days and days before I have to get back to Chicago." He paused to glare sympathetically at the silhouette of the Great Emancipator, here confined to a window as part of his twentieth-century career in advertising.

"We'll do our best to keep you busy."

"I bet you will."

"Look," said Jan, looking ahead herself and gesturing lightly in that direction.

About five parking spaces ahead of them, nestled up to the metered curb, was the unmarked Foundation van. Dr. Pilgrim was in it, or at least most of him was, for he was sticking his dark curly head out of one of the side windows. A moment later he had slid quickly from the vehicle and was approaching on foot.

To Jerry's relief, the boss looked reassuringly tolerant of his employees' condition. Maybe, Jerry thought hopefully, he and Jan didn't look as intoxicated as he was beginning to feel. He really didn't deserve to feel like this, he hadn't taken *that* much wine . . .

Pilgrim appeared almost but not quite ready to join them in their revelry. "Some people here who would like to talk to you, Jerry," he said, after a quick exchange of looks with Jan. "One more little item to be taken care of before you retire to a well-earned rest. Are you game for one more small adventure? But of course you are."

"Some people?" asked Jerry. "Who?"

"My backers. You have already spoken with one of them, this most attractive lady, on the phone." Pilgrim was holding open the side door of the van for Jerry to get in. "The gentleman is Mr. Helpman." At least the name sounded like that to Jerry.

Jerry got in, taking the nearest empty seat, a captain's chair approximately amidships. In the chair beside his own there waited a youthful-looking lady he had never seen before, a well-proportioned and well-dressed lady who looked as if she would be tall when she stood up, and who was definitely attractive, though her face just now was mainly in shadow. Meanwhile from one of the seats in the far rear a black man of indeterminate age, well-dressed in suit and tie, was looking at Jerry with an air of hope.

Pilgrim, still outside on the sidewalk, slid shut

the door through which Jerry had gone aboard, leaving him in the van with the two strangers. At the same time the lady at his side asked him: "How are they treating you so far?"

"All right. Fine." Then he scowled at his questioner. "Excuse me, but who are you?"'

"My name is Olivia. You spoke with me on the phone."

"Yeah. I thought I could recognize your voice. But I still don't understand—"

"All will be explained to you eventually. Provided—" Olivia sighed. It was a worried sound, or maybe she was only tired. "Have they talked to you about going on a trip?" In the back seat Mr. Helpman nodded silently, seconding the question.

"Trip? No, I understood that we were going to be working here around Springfield." Jerry noted with satisfaction that he was still capable of plain, coherent speech.

"Fine. That's fine." Olivia swiveled her chair, turning her back to confer with Helpman momentarily, in whispers so low that Jerry could not hear them.

Then she faced Jerry again. "You may tell Dr. Pilgrim that his project has my provisional approval. And good luck to you." With a last hard-to-interpret look at Jerry, and a quick decisive movement, the lady called Olivia opened the door on the street side and got out. Helpman followed her quickly, slamming the door behind him.

For a few moments Jerry, feeling befuddled, had the whole interior of the van to himself. He supposed he might have been able to use the time to good advantage, thinking, if he had known where to start. But the whole business was so—

—and then Pilgrim and Jan were back, piling into the van, Jan taking the captain's chair where Olivia had been, while Pilgrim settled himself in the driver's seat.

They were both looking at Jerry with concern. "Well?" Pilgrim demanded.

"Well, she said to tell you that whatever you're doing has her provisional approval. Is she your banker, maybe?"

Pilgrim, relieved by the message, nodded with an odd smile. "In a manner of speaking she is." He faced forward and got the engine started.

"I can walk back to the hotel from here," said Jerry.

Jan, having taken Olivia's place in the luxurious armchair beside him, shook her head. She said: "There's just one more thing we'd like to show you tonight."

" 'Always a little farther, *it* may be' " quoted Pilgrim from up front, where he was driving joyously and skillfully. " 'Beyond that last blue mountain barred with snow . . .' "

Jerry had ceased to listen to him. Jan was much more interesting than the doctor's quotations, and also more accessible, being seated where he could swivel easily to face her. She now engaged Jerry in what seemed to him an unusually witty conversation—in which he managed to hold his own quite well—while Pilgrim drove them through the darkened streets of Springfield.

"This—this's been like no other job interview

I've ever had," Jerry pronounced with feeling at one point. He meant it as a sincere compliment to Pilgrim and especially to his most delightful aide who sat almost within reach, still wearing that enchanting red dress.

"Nor ever will have again, I should imagine," Pilgrim agreed cheerfully. The boss was still apparently unable to perceive anything improper in the speech or behavior of his prospective new employee. "Glad to have you aboard, as the cliché goes. In fact you literally cannot imagine what a burden your successful recruitment has lifted from my mind."

"Then I'm hired? Really hired?"

"Oh, most definitely you are hired."

"You might almost say," said Jan from beside Jerry, "that you are already on your way to work." Then she giggled, as if she were beginning to give way at last to the chianti. Pilgrim, his face unreadable, glanced back at her once and then faced forward to the road.

They sounded like they were joking, but they must be serious about hiring him, Jerry reflected. If they really didn't want him they'd be dropping him off at his hotel now, instead of taking him—where were they taking him, anyway? And hey, wait, how could he really be practically on his way to work?

They were, he noticed, definitely heading out into the country again. They were driving through solid darkness now, except for passing headlights.

These, along with the headlights of the van itself, revealed a narrow highway. But the next time

Jerry interrupted his talk with Jan to look ahead, the highway had been replaced with a gravel road. And now there were no other headlights to be seen, in either direction. Roadsigns had now ceased to exist also, being replaced by wooden fenceposts and wire beyond the tall grass and fringe of weeds that overhung the edge of the road.

Jerry was just starting to doze off, seatbelted into his comfortable chair, when the van slowed to a stop. Pilgrim opened the driver's door into an enormous silence.

"Our local headquarters," said Jan. She sounded like a cheerful nurse, and she was acting like one now, helping Jerry out of his seatbelt and then out of the van. Standing on grass and gravel, he felt somewhat disconnected from his own arms and legs. Looking up, he beheld more stars, many more, than anyone ever saw in Chicago.

The van had stopped in a driveway, close to the front of an isolated structure that appeared to be a farmhouse. It was a two-story frame building painted white, looking ghostly in the night. There were no lights in the house when they arrived. But now Jan tripped lightly up the wooden steps and opened the front door and reached inside, turning on a light over the porch. Meanwhile Pilgrim, surprisingly strong, had taken over the job of supporting Jerry. Jerry found himself being walked up the steps as if two bouncers instead of one five-foot-five researcher had him by the elbows. Not that the job was done discourteously.

Once inside the house, the two senior officials of the Foundation turned on some more lights, and guided Jerry through it. He was blinking rapidly by this time, and his eyes didn't really focus all that well any more. At first he didn't see anyone else in the house, but he thought there must be other people around somewhere, because he heard a door close softly, several rooms away, while Jan and Pilgrim were both still with him.

His two escorts were conferring in low-voiced haste; he couldn't hear what they were saying, but whatever it was, it was all right because both of them were smiling when they turned back to Jerry.

"The best thing will be for you to get some rest," Jan was assuring him now, "before we do anything else. There's a room back here that's going to be yours when we get you all moved in. Wouldn't you like to lie down for a while?"

Jerry didn't answer for a moment, because just now, out of the corner of his eye, he had seen something strange: a diminutive figure, like a masked and somewhat deformed child, passing briefly through his range of vision at the end of a hallway. Now he was seeing things.

"Jerry? I say, wouldn't you like to lie down?"

"Oh. Course I would. Specially if you come with me." Then Jerry could feel his face turning red for having said a thing like that. At the same time he chuckled.

Jan, more than ever the skillful nurse, was not perturbed. "I'll see you settled into your room. Then for the time being you'll have to rest."

"Busy day tomorrow," Jerry agreed helpfully, as she assisted him down the hallway. He was demonstrating proudly that he was still capable of thought. There were no strange little monsters in sight now. Probably by the sheer power of his will he could keep them at a distance.

His last remark for some reason evoked a laugh from Jan. It was the freest laughter he'd heard from her yet, a pleasant, ringing sound.

"That is for sure," she agreed, "a very busy day." And she marched him on, with Pilgrim leading the way. They passed a room whose door, white-painted wood with an old white doorknob like the other doors inside the house, had been left ajar, and Jerry glanced in. He was able to see very little except a white, free-standing screen that reminded him of doctors' offices and hospitals.

"Here we are," said Pilgrim, leading, and they went on past that doorway and into the next one. Jerry was dimly aware of a narrow white bed, coming closer to him with little lurching motions, in time with his own unsteady strides. Then the bed unexpectedly clipped him at knee level and he toppled over onto it. The landing was beautifully comfortable, even though somehow in the course of falling he had turned over so that he was now lying on his back.

His eyes had closed of themselves. When he opened them again, Jan and Pilgrim were still there. A bottle had just clinked on glass, and they were holding little glasses with clear liquid in them, raising the glasses to each other, in the act of toasting something.

"To success," said Dr. Pilgrim softly, and with a gesture included in his toast a picture that happened to be hanging on the wall. Jan hoisted her glass a notch in that direction too, before she tossed the contents down.

Jerry looked up at the wall between his two fellow workers. By now he certainly had no trouble recognizing the face in that dark frame, though it was younger than you usually saw it, and wore no beard. Abraham Lincoln, in one of his usual sloppy suits. Was it a photograph or a painting? Did everyone in his time dress like that?

"And now, Jerry, one more drink for you." Jan's arm went very nicely around his neck and shoulders, to raise his head. 'Are you sure I need another?' he wanted to ask as he swallowed obediently. Some milky stuff, quite pleasant. He hoped it would be good for hangovers.

A moment after that the support of Jan's arm was gone, and Jerry's eyes were closed again, and he could hear himself snoring. It would be all right. A little nap, just a little, and he would spring up again and show these people that he wasn't really drunk.

"Like a light," he distinctly heard Jan commenting. He could hear her and someone else who must be Pilgrim hovering at his bedside a moment longer, and then there were the soft sounds of feet retreating. They both went out, darkening the room and shutting the door on him, but the door wasn't completely closed. He could tell that by the gentle incompleteness of the sound it made. Then both of them were gone, somewhere down the hall.

In another moment, Jerry knew, he would be sound asleep. It wasn't that he minded sleeping—

but to be practically carried in here like this—that was somewhat humiliating. He felt an urge to sit up, get up, assert himself in some minor way, do something of his own volition. Show them—show them how tough he was. That was the idea. After that he would be willing to take a nap.

It wasn't really hard to get back on his feet, just as sometimes in a dream it was very easy to do things that should be hard. Things in dreams, he had noticed, tended to be very easy, or else utterly impossible.

He was standing at the white door of his room, and pulling it open, before he realized that this wasn't the door leading out into the hall. This one instead opened into an adjoining bedroom, where a white hospital-type screen blocked out most of the light that would otherwise have shone in here from the hallway. In this dim room there was a fair amount of what looked like hospital equipment.

This room too contained a bed, but the figure under its white sheets wasn't Jan, that was for sure, damn it all anyway. And it was far too long a figure to be Pilgrim. Yes, a long and bony figure—really a familiar one in these parts—with dark hair and a darkly bearded face that showed as little more than a mass of shadows above the sheets.

Stupidly, without any real intention of doing so, Jerry took one more step closer to the bed, and then another. He stood looking down at that shadowed face for what seemed to him a long time. He began to feel a cold sensation in the pit of his stomach—but the feeling, like everything else, was too remote to be of any real importance. Then the figure on the bed stirred lightly, as if in sleep, and

Jerry turned away from it hastily and stumbled back into his own room.

He had one thought: if it were only wine that had befuddled him, what he had seen just now ought to have shocked him sober. So what had overcome him was more than wine. And that meant—

The last thing he saw clearly was the white bed from which he had arisen, swinging up to claim him, with finality this time.

FIVE

Coming back to life was a slow, gradual, and painful process. Jerry's head was throbbing with what felt like the patriarch of all hangovers. To make matters worse, at some time during the night someone had stolen his soft white bed, substituting for it a bag of some coarse, malodorous fabric that crackled each time he moved as if it were stuffed with very crisp and durable dried leaves.

Somewhere outside the barricade of his eyelids, light had reappeared. It was daylight, he supposed. But that was no cause for rejoicing. He was in no hurry to behold what daylight might reveal. In fact he was rather afraid to find out. He couldn't really remember what had happened to him last night.

He had been through a job interview, of sorts.

Oh, he remembered that much, all right. He, Jerry Flint, the graduate student from the big city, had driven down to Springfield to talk to some people about a job, and had made a total and utter ass of himself. That much he could remember with bitter clarity, though a great many of the details were still mercifully obscure. And then just at the end of the evening, before he had passed out totally, he had looked in the bed in the next room of the converted farmhouse, and thought that he saw—

Jerry groaned. With eyes still shut, he extended a leg to find the edge of the bed. He needed a bathroom, and the need was going to become urgent very soon.

His exploring foot could locate no edge, and in another moment or two Jerry had realized that this was because there was no bed. By now one of his eyelids had come unglued and opened, and with this advantage he could see that he was indeed lying on the floor. An unfamiliar floor. Between him and its rough-hewn, unfinished planks there was only the thickness—the thinness, rather —of a stained mattress that really did crackle with his every movement, as if it contained cornhusks.

It seemed that the folk of the Pilgrim Foundation were blessed with an exquisite sense of humor, as well as pots of money. Not only a cornhusk mattress, but they had also changed Jerry's clothes for him. He was now wearing some kind of handmade gray shirt—it felt like good linen—and shapeless trousers that looked somewhat the worse for having been rolled in dust and leaves. Over his shirt he had on an embroidered vest, that came down past his waist. There were stockings—unfamiliar ones—on his feet, and a kind of enlarged bow tie loosely looped around his collar.

In a far corner of the room, which was barren of all furniture except the mattress, stood a pair of leather boots. The heels were too low for cowboy boots, but they were high-topped and laceless. Beside them, resting on some kind of brownish folded garment, was a high stovepipe hat of approximately the same color. A shapeless bag the size of a small suitcase, made of cloth fabric except for its two cord carrying handles, rested beside the clothing.

This was the same size and shape as the room in which Jerry had fallen asleep—but no, it wasn't the same. It might have been the same room once. Last night's room had had two doors, and two windows, and here were two doors and two windows in the same locations. But these windows lacked screens or shades, as well as nearly all their glass. Green leaves, as of dense bushes, were crowding in from outside; he must be on the ground floor. Through the broken windows came in the smell of lilacs and the song of robins.

For a minute or so he stood unsteadily in the middle of the room, turning round and round in a kind of hopeless stupidity. He stared at the faded and weathered wallpaper—last night the walls had been painted—and at the white-painted woodwork. Yes, as far as the general architecture went, this looked like the same room in which he had fallen asleep last night. But last night's house had been decorated and comfortably furnished, and this one was long abandoned.

When Jerry stumbled over to the door to the room adjoining and pushed it open, there was no one in there either. This chamber was as barren as the one in which he had awakened, and its windows were broken too. Outside the broken windows, birds were singing cheerfully. No doubt they had a good idea of where they were.

The need to find plumbing, or some emergency substitute, was fast becoming an imperative. Jerry, wary of the splintery floor, got his feet into the boots. They fit him perfectly, and felt as if they had been already broken in. Then he went down the hallway looking for a bathroom.

He needed only a few moments to decide that he was wasting his time. There wasn't a bathroom in this house, not on the ground floor anyway, and if there was one upstairs it couldn't be functional. So he would just have to go outside. Somewhere. . .

He reached a back doorway, from which the door was missing. Untended fields surrounded the house for as far as he could see. In a back yard overgrown with weeds were a couple of ramshackle outbuildings, including a privy partially screened from the house by tall hollyhocks—barren of flowers this early in the year—and more spring-blooming lilac bushes. The door of the privy squeaked open on what looked like homemade hinges when Jerry pushed it in, and a field mouse scurried out of his way. The smell inside was very old, but still pungent enough to be the final trigger for his nausea.

Emerging some time later from the wooden sentry-box of the abandoned latrine, Jerry felt considerably better, though his head still ached and his hands trembled. At least he was back in the world again, and prepared to deal with it.

In a great silence he walked completely around the deserted house, confirming that he had the place entirely to himself. Then he stood for what felt like a long time in the back yard, looking things over. He shaded his eyes with a hand when he looked east against the morning sun. There were no other houses nearby in any direction; there was what looked like another farmhouse, about a mile to the south, but that was too far away for him to be able to make out any details.

Whoever had concocted this joke had known what they were doing, and had spared no effort or expense.

From where Jerry stood he was able to see a part of an unpaved road that passed close in front of the house. There were no phone lines along that road, no utility poles of any kind. He could see part of a split-rail fence, much like the ones at New Salem. There was no traffic passing. He watched for what felt like a considerable time—his wristwatch was missing—and not a single vehicle came by.

When he gave up at last and re-entered the house, his first sickness and confusion had passed, and he could look at things more thoughtfully. Now Jerry noted the complete absence of light switches. Not surprising when there were no incoming wires visible. Nor were there any electric outlets in the barren walls, any more than there was running water in the kitchen. He'd passed a hand-levered pump in the back yard.

Next he toured the house, upstairs and down;

everything he saw confirmed that the place had been abandoned for years. Almost all the windows were gone, all the rooms suffering from exposure to the weather.

Returning at last to the room in which he'd awakened, he looked again at the tall hat waiting for him on the floor. This time he tried it on. It fit him nicely. The folded garment turned out to be a coat. He was afraid that it would fit him too, and threw it down on the mattress without making the experiment.

Then Jerry went down on his knees beside the carpetbag and started taking out the contents. Most of it was clothing. There was a spare vest and trousers, along with several sets of odd-looking underwear, of the same general style he'd already found himself to be wearing, and socks and handkerchiefs. There were two clean shirts, much like the one he had on, with detached collars packed in a separate interior pocket of the bag.

Another small pocket in the bag held a straight razor, folded shut, and a small pouch made of a material that felt something like plastic but wasn't. In the pouch Jerry discovered a bar of soap, and a small brush he could dimly recognize as a shaving aid, probably because it had been packed in proximity to the razor.

Yet another small interior pocket held a small blue-steel revolver. Jerry, who was no firearms expert, fumbled around gingerly with the thing, turning the cylinder and gently thumbing back the hammer and slowly letting it down again. Peering at the cylinder he could see cartridges occupying five of the six chambers. Something about them looked peculiar even to his eye, amateurish with regard to firearms.

In the same pocket of the bag there was a folded letter, still in its envelope; envelope and letter were creased and worn. In faded, water-spotted blue ink the letter was addressed to one James Lockwood, at some illegible location in Missouri. The handwriting, Jerry thought, was probably feminine. And it looked, he thought, oddly like Jan Chen's.

He opened the letter and started to read. There was no date or any other heading.

My Dearest Jim—

That was about all he could make out; the body of the letter had been soaked worse than the address. He would try to decipher the rest later, when he had time. Or he would mind his own business. These things weren't his.

Working quickly, he repacked the bag with all the items he had taken out of it. Then at last he grabbed up the coat from where he had thrown it down, and tried it on. The coat proved to fit him as well as did the garments he was already wearing, but the cut of it was very strange, different from that of any suit coat Jerry had ever worn. It came down halfway to his knees, and hung on him as unpressed and shapeless as the trousers.

Now Jerry started on the coat's pockets, with which it was well supplied. They contained a handkerchief, basically clean, and a small folding pocket knife. There was also a great deal of paper money, in several colors and varieties, with every variety claiming to be dollars. Most of the notes bore the name of one bank or another, in different states. And then there were gold and silver coins. Counting it all up as best he could, Jerry figured that he was in possession of something close to a thousand dollars altogether, if this money was real.

But of course it couldn't be, not really. The money, like the clothing and the gun, had to be part of the big joke that was being played on him. Yes, of course it did.

His fingers were shaking more and more as he stuffed the cash away awkwardly into the unfamiliar pockets of the coat.

There was a key—a single key—resting by itself in one of the inner pockets of his coat. An old-fashioned large key, with a comparatively simple bit. From the moment he saw it, Jerry had the feeling that it was important.

And there was a locket in one of his coat pockets, with a painted miniature likeness inside. The likeness of a comely young woman with brown hair, wearing a high nineteenth-century collar; he didn't know her. She was certainly not Jan Chen, or the one-name Olivia either. Was she perhaps the woman who had written the indecipherable letter to Jim Lockwood?

Jerry's head ached, and so did his throat. Remembering the pump in the back yard, he went back to it, and with much squealing and clanking of metal made it work. For what felt like a long time there was no result. Then water, rusty at first, gushed from the spout, and Jerry soaked his head in the yellowish irregular stream, and swallowed a much-needed drink.

All right. Joke or whatever, he was here, and he would deal with the world as it came to him.

If this was a joke he could go along with it. He put on his coat and hat—the first people who saw him dressed like this were going to laugh at him, but so what—and went out of the front door of the house to stand on the edge of the road. Between the ruts there were some horse-droppings that didn't look all that old. The road itself was not modern gravel, but what looked like clay, in places no more than mud. Here and there puddles still lingered from the last rain. Split-rail fences of the type Jerry had seen at New Salem marked off fallow fields on either side.

In one direction, toward Jerry's left, there were some buildings in sight, a mile or two away. In the other directions, nothing that looked like a habitation. Carrying his carpetbag, he started walking to his left, which he decided had to be north, assuming that the rising sun still marked the east.

These untended fields were deriving no benefit from their fences, but the wooden rails provided perches for a profusion of songbirds. The day was warm and clear, but not yet hot. All Jerry could think of was that if he kept walking long enough on a road, someone would come out of a house, drive up in a car, or descend in a helicopter, and start to explain the joke.

The more he thought about this tremendous joke, the more explaining he could see that it was going to take. But on the other hand if he once admitted that this might not be a joke—

His mind had reached a place where logical thought seemed to be of little benefit. Therefore he rested his mind as best he could, and kept on walking.

Another human being came in sight at last, a man, way off across the fields, driving horses as he walked beside them—no, the animals that he drove were mules. They were hitched up to something, pulling it.

Jerry had been walking for about a mile when he became aware of another engineless vehicle, this one overtaking him from behind. He heard the thunk of hard wheels on uneven ruts, the quick hooves of a horse, the jingle of harness.

Jerry stepped off the road. He turned and made himself smile as the driver of the wagon pulled to a stop beside him. The driver, a man of about forty, was dressed in a costume very similar to Jerry's, with minor variations. "Headed for Springfield?" he called down cheerfully.

"Yes. I certainly am." Jerry took the question as an invitation, tossed his carpetbag into the small cargo compartment at the rear of the buggy—or whatever this four-wheeled two-passenger vehicle ought to be called—and climbed up awkwardly onto the single high seat beside the driver. In a moment they were under way again, in a hard-jolting but still remarkably quiet ride.

Holding the reins in his left hand, the driver extended his right to shake. "Winthrop Johnson. M'friends call me Win."

"Jer—Jim Lockwood." He had a letter in his pocket, didn't he, to prove his identity? If it should ever come to that. Whatever the game, he had to play the cards he had been dealt. "Thanks for the ride."

"Don't think a thing about it. Suppose you haven't been walking far?"

"No, no. Not far." Jerry took off his hat, scratched his head, and rubbed his eyes. Already the buggy's motion was beginning to revive his queasiness; but he had no wish to go back to walking. "Truth is, last night some friends and I got into a bottle. Went a little deeper than I planned."

"Hahaa." It wasn't really a laugh, more a drawn-out sound of sympathy. Win Johnson shook his head; he was obviously a man of worldly understanding. "I've been down that road myself more than once. There've been mornings when I didn't rightly know where I was when I woke up."

"I appreciate your sympathy." Jerry allowed his eyes to close again. "How far is Springfield?"

Johnson squinted up toward the sun; there were certainly no road signs to consult. "Should be there by dinner time, or so they told me. This road's a new one to me—maybe you've been over it before?"

Jerry shook his head.

"Well then, we'll just be explorin' together. I'm a land agent for the railroad, and have been talking to some surveyors. Don't believe I caught what your line is?"

Jerry considered. "I travel," he said after a moment.

"Hahaa. Between jobs right now. Wal, m'friend, I don't know if Springfield is a-going to be the best place to find a new one. Chicago, now, I'd say your chances are bound to be better there. Things will be a little slow all over, I'm afraid, now that the war is winding to an end."

"An end," Jerry repeated. He was barely able to keep himself from asking: *What war?*

The other nodded. "Grant's troops entered Richmond on the third. Can't be long now before Lee surrenders. That should just about finish her off."

"On the third." Jerry thought he was going numb all over. "What's today?"

"Well, the fifth. Wednesday."

Jerry was riding with his eyes closed again. He told himself that when he opened them, he would be riding in an automobile. But he couldn't convince himself of that, not while the damned buggy kept bouncing so. Not while he could smell the horse, and hear the beat of hooves. Grant and Lee. Richmond. Sure.

"Hate to see a man suffer so," said the voice of Winthrop Johnson. "Here, have a hair of the dog?"

Jerry opened his eyes to see, almost under his nose, the jouncing right hand of his companion extending a small metal flask in his direction. With a kind of desperation he accepted the flask and put it to his lips. The taste of the stuff inside was fiery, but still surprisingly good, and the net result of a couple of small swallows actually beneficial.

"What is that?" he asked, gasping lightly as he handed the flask back.

"Peach brandy." His benefactor seemed somewhat surprised by the question.

"It's very good—no, no more, thanks. One hair of the dog is plenty."

"Not from around these parts of Illinois, are you, Jim?"

"No, no. Back east."

"Thought so, listenin' to the way you talk. I'm from Indiana, myself. You from New York, maybe?"

"That's right."

"Thought so. I can usually pin a man down by the way he talks."

The countryside flowed past the buggy at a slow pace, but still faster than his feet had been able to make it move, and with infinitely less effort on his part. His brief stint of walking had been enough to convince him that this mode of transportation was in every way an improvement.

At intervals Win Johnson's rig passed a couple of heavy wagons, laden with farm produce and laboring in the same direction. Two young women costumed in ankle-length dresses and pinned-on hats went by going the other way, in a light two-seater carriage pulled by a graceful gray horse. Jerry, numb with wonders, observed them in their Scarlett O'Hara costumes almost without surprise. Johnson tipped his hat lightly to the ladies, and Jerry caught on just in time to tip his own hat just before the other carriage passed.

Why was he going to Springfield? Chiefly, he decided, because he had to go somewhere. He couldn't have simply waited in an abandoned farmhouse for something to happen. But God knew what was going to happen to him next.

With half his mind Jerry continued to make wary conversation with Win Johnson, while with the other half he got busy trying to reconstruct the exact circumstances of his departure from what he considered the normal world—the late twentieth century, in which era he had spent his life up until now. This just didn't feel at all the same as his childhood escape from the burning house. No, this experience was vastly different. Apart from the subjective difference, this time he had been outfitted.

But how had it happened? Everything had seemed perfectly normal when he'd arrived in Springfield. He'd registered in a real, modern hotel, one with plumbing and electric lights and elevators. Then he'd driven out to New Salem, where there were split-rail fences just like these, and at about that point things had started to go subtly wrong. After he'd met Dr. Pilgrim and Jan Chen the deterioration had speeded up.

After visiting New Salem, and the Foundation office, he'd gone out to dinner with Jan. He could still sense pizza and wine in aftertaste. But damn it, there had to be something besides wine to explain why he'd passed out. He hadn't consumed that much. He just didn't, ever, drink enough to knock himself out. He never had. Certainly he wouldn't have done so in the course of an extended job interview.

It could be, it could very well be he supposed, that someone had put something other than wine in his glass. Certainly Jan Chen had had the opportunity. Jerry hadn't been taking any paranoid precautions—hell, he hadn't even been paying attention. But why should she, or anyone else, have drugged him?

Because, the obvious answer came, Jan Chen and Dr. Pilgrim, and probably Olivia and Mr.

Helpman too, had determined that he was going to wake up here. Wherever "here" might be.

Have they spoken to you about your going on a trip of any kind?

But basically he couldn't believe it. No, somewhere there was a real explanation. A better one at least than the one he couldn't swallow, involving as it did the armies of Grant and Lee. This place through which he was riding now was some kind of extended historical area, an expansion of New Salem. And . . . and Jerry couldn't really believe that either, but at the moment he had nothing better.

Somehow the hours passed, and with them the miles of the seldom-traveled road, with never a utility pole in sight, or even a contrail in the sky. Instead there was the smell of the open land in the spring, and the feel of the open air. There were also a great many flies, drawn perhaps by the smell of horse. Once Johnson pulled off the road and whoa'd the horse, and the gentlemen relieved themselves in the tall roadside grass, beside a copse of trees. There were whole sections of mature woodland here, much more of it remaining than in the Illinois that Jerry knew.

They climbed back into the buggy and drove on. The burden of Johnson's conversation was what a smart man ought to do after the war, what turn the climate for business was going to take when peace became the normal state of affairs once more. Johnson was not so much anxious to convince Jerry of any course of action as to use him as a sounding board. What did Jerry think of petroleum as an investment?

"I think it might do well."

Eventually the woods thinned out considerably, and they passed some dwellings that were not attached to farms.

"Looks like we made it," Johnson remarked unnecessarily.

The unpaved road was gradually becoming an unpaved street. The capital city of Illinois was even muddier than the countryside, and Jerry's first general impression was that of an extended rural slum. Not only dogs, but pigs, goats, and chickens appeared unfettered on every road. But the houses were clustering more closely now, and the gardens grew closer together. Now the streets were tree-lined; elms speckled with green springtime buds made graceful gothic arches, spanning some streets completely.

"Where can I drop you off, Jim?"

"Eighth and Jackson." Jerry had been pondering how best to answer this question when it came, and now he gave the one Springfield location that he was able to remember.

"Right you are. Remember what I said, Chicago's probably the place for you to try."

"I'll remember, thanks. And thanks for the ride."

"Don't mention it."

Jerry jumped out of the buggy when it slowed almost to a stop at the proper corner. He remembered to retrieve his carpetbag. Win Johnson clucked to his horse and rolled away.

Long afternoon shadows were falling across Eighth Street. There was one building in sight that Jerry could recognize, the house on the northeast corner of the intersection. He stood in the dusty street with his carpetbag in hand, staring at that house, for some time after the sounds of Winthrop Johnson's horse and buggy had died away. That was Abraham Lincoln's house on the corner, and if Jerry only went up to the door of it and knocked . . . but no. If Grant and Lee were fighting in Virginia, Abraham Lincoln couldn't be here in Springfield, could he? President Lincoln would have to be in Washington.

Unless, of course—it hit Jerry suddenly that Lincoln had been shot, just as the war was ending. Of course; Jan had talked about that at some length last night: the tragic loss that Lincoln's death had been to the country and the world. The peculiar intensity of her talk came back to Jerry now, though at the moment he couldn't recall all the details of what she'd said.

Now he seemed to remember that she'd even kept on talking to him about Lincoln after he'd passed out. And then—or was it earlier—he'd seen that unbelievable figure in the bed in the next room. And before that, the little monster running across the bedroom hall.

No, those visions must have been hallucinations, brought on by whatever drugs they'd dosed him with. Jerry couldn't possibly have seen what he now remembered seeing. That would be as crazy as—

Looming to the northwest above the springtime trees and the common rooftops, the bulk of the Old Capitol building made a half-familiar sight, rising above nineteenth-century frame houses. Jerry walked toward it almost jauntily, swinging Jim

Lockwood's bag. There were moments when he was almost dead sure he was dreaming, ready to give in and enjoy himself without responsibility.

There was nothing dreamlike about the square, lined with shops and stores, when he reached it. On the east side, just about where he remembered Pilgrim's offices being located, was a totally different structure called the State Bank building.

He had found the bank. And now there was something—what was it?—that he had to do.

He walked the wooden sidewalks, liking the sound his bootheels made, attracting no particular attention among men who were dressed in much the same style as he was, and women gowned more or less like the two in the passing carriage. Some people, including all of the blacks in sight, were in much poorer clothing.

Letting himself move on impulse now, Jerry made his way to the front door of the bank and entered. He had taken the big key from his pocket, again without quite knowing why, and now he put it down silently on the polished wood of a counter, under the eyes of a clerk who wore garter-like metal clips pinching in his voluminous shirtsleeves, and held a wooden, steel-nibbed pen in hand.

The clerk scrutinized first the key and then Jerry. He did not appear to be much impressed by what he saw in either case.

"Not one of ours," the clerk finally remarked.

The compulsion, whatever its cause, had vanished now. Jerry was on his own. "Just thought it might be," he got out with a clearing of his throat. "I found it. It . . . belonged to my uncle. It was in a box of his things that got sent to us . . . after Gettysburg."

The other at last picked up the key and silently turned it over in his fingers. He looked at Jerry for a long moment, then said, "From one of the Chicago banks, I'd say." The clerk's accent was different from Winthrop Johnson's, and sounded even odder in Jerry's ears. Indefinably American, and yet harsher than any regional dialect Jerry had ever heard.

Jerry took the metal object back. "I'll ask around when I get there. Thanks." It was only on the way out of the bank building that he remembered consciously: Jan Chen advising him, somewhere, sometime, to go to a Chicago bank.

The railroad depot was not hard to locate, being only a few blocks away—nothing in Springfield appeared to be much more than a few blocks from the center of town. Inside the wooden depot a chalked schedule, and a tall wall clock with a long pendulum, informed him that he had two hours before the next train to Chicago. Jerry purchased a ticket for the considerable sum of ten dollars and then returned to the town square. There was an unmistakable restaurant open there, and he listened to people talk cheerfully about the war being over while he enjoyed some of the best chicken and dumplings he'd ever had.

Some of the diners around him were consuming what seemed to Jerry an amazing amount of hard liquor with their meals. Quantities of wine and beer were disappearing also. Remembering last night, he contented himself with a mug of beer, and found it tasty but somewhat warm.

His dinner cost him less than a dollar, a bargain as compared to the price of the train ticket. Well-fed but feeling deadly tired he walked back to the station. Departure at night, by gaslight and lantern, was a scene of many sparks from the wood-burning engine. The engine smoked every bit as much as Jerry had expected it would, and the conveyance jolted noisily along. The sunset had completely faded now, and the countryside outside the window at Jerry's elbow was as dark as death.

The only light inside this coach was a poor lantern, hung near the ceiling in the rear. Maybe there were first, second, and third class coaches, and he'd got into fourth class by mistake. Jerry buttoned his coat, whose inside pockets held his money, slumped in his seat, and fell into the dreamless sleep of great exhaustion.

SIX

The train carrying Jerry labored its way into Chicago shortly after dawn. It looked like the start of a grim day in the city, which was wrapped in an atmosphere composed of coal soot and mist in about equal parts. The railroad station was a darkened brick cavern, smoky and bustling at that early hour, crowded with human activity.

Walking stiffly, he made his way out of the station amid the throng of other overnight passengers, all of them blinking as they emerged into the more-or-less full daylight of the street outside. The streets of downtown Chicago were marginally better, or at least less muddy, than those of Springfield. The boots of an army of pedestrians sounded on the wooden sidewalks with a continuous hollow thumping, a sound regularly punctuated by the sharper tap of crutches. Here and there Jerry noted the different impact made by the crude shaft of a primitive artificial leg.

In the street, as inside the station, soldiers in blue uniforms made up a large part of the crowd. Most of the uniforms were faded and worn. Young men with missing legs or arms, some still in uniform, were a common sight. There must be, Jerry thought, a military hospital or demobilization center near.

Stretching his stiff limbs and rubbing sleep from his eyes, he lugged his carpetbag to a small restaurant a couple of blocks from the station, where he ordered breakfast. He would have paid a princely sum for cold orange juice, but nothing like that was on the menu. At least the coffee was hot and invigorating, surprisingly good. The prices were reassuringly low—incredibly so, in fact, and he fortified himself with hotcakes, ham and eggs.

He ate his breakfast sitting beside a window that gave him a good view of the street outside. The volume of street traffic was impressive, made up of horse-drawn vehicles of all shapes and sizes. This, like the Chicago he remembered, was an energetic city, though so far Jerry had seen no building more than five or six stories tall. Were there any? He wondered.

Many of the men in the restaurant—the place was fairly crowded but there were only one or two women among the patrons—were reading newspapers. Jerry beckoned to a ragged newsboy on the street outside and bought a paper through the open window.

Half of the front page of the Chicago newspaper

was filled with advertisements, the other half with news, mainly about the war. The armies of Grant and Lee, it seemed, were still pounding away at each other in Virginia, though from the tone of the reporting, clearly the writer expected final victory soon. It was further reported that hopes were widespread that the "great rebellion" would be crushed completely out of existence in only a few more days.

Jerry sat for at least a minute just staring at the date on the newspaper. Seeing it in print made it official, and therefore somehow more believable. Today was Thursday, April 6, 1865.

Still he sat there, time and again looking up at the world around him, then dropping his eyes to stare at the paper again. Only now, this morning, after a night of exhausted sleep aboard the train, was he able to win the struggle with his outraged sense of logic, his engineer's scientific propriety, and finally come to grips with his situation. No longer was he going to be able to pretend to himself that any part of this could be a fake, a trick. And he wasn't crazy—or if he was, there was nothing he could do about it. However it had been managed, every test he could apply indicated that he was really there, in the last days of the Civil War. Whatever that damned Pilgrim had done to him, for whatever purpose—and Jan Chen, that damned, lying, sexy woman—

But first things first. He was a long way from being able to take revenge on Pilgrim and his helper now. Unless some rescuing power should suddenly intervene to save him, and he saw no reason to expect that, he was going to have to somehow find his own way back to his own time.

The trouble was that he had no indication of any place to start. Of course the letter to Jim Lockwood, whoever he might be, might be a clue, if Jerry could understand why it had been given to him.

Still sitting at his breakfast table, he dug the single page of the letter and its envelope out of his pocket once more, and tried again to read the water-damaged writing. He had no better success than before.

As he put the letter back in his pocket, his hand once more encountered the bank key and he pulled it out. It was much bigger than the keys he had commonly carried in the twentieth century. The hard, precisely shaped metal lay in his hand feeling large and solid and enigmatic. Jerry could not shake the intuition that it had to be of great importance.

Putting away his change as he left the restaurant, Jerry let his hand remain in his pocket, resting on the one key. The same irrational compulsion to *use* the key that he had felt in Springfield, was now stirring again, though less wildly this time.

Carpetbag in hand again, he set out, with the odd feeling that once he started walking he would go in the right direction.

On his short walk from the railroad station to the restaurant he had noticed only one bank, one with a conspicuous painted sign. Now he was walking toward that sign again. Probably the establishment under that sign would be the most logical place to go, for someone arriving on a train, who had been advised to patronize a Chicago bank.

And Jerry suddenly recalled that he, on the night of wine and pizza, had been mysteriously advised to do just that.

Sauntering into the bank lobby, Jerry tried to adopt the air of a man of wealth—it wasn't really hard to do, now that he had realized how many stacks of hotcakes the money in his pockets could buy. The air inside the bank was blue with smoke. Half the men in the lobby seemed to be smoking cigars; but unless there were compelling reasons, he didn't really want to go that far in trying to project an air of affluence.

Brass cuspidors stood beside almost every counter and under every table in the bank, the floors and carpets around these targets being heavily stained by poor marksmen. The mellow brightness of gaslights augmented the smoky daylight that entered through high narrow windows to shine on the wood panelling of the walls.

Jerry set his bag down on the tobacco-stained carpet. He had brought his newspaper with him from the restaurant, and he opened it now and used it as a cover, observing the activity in the lobby past its edges, now and then turning a page. It took him a few minutes to identify the counter where safe-deposit business was being transacted, and the clerk who handled it.

Unhurriedly he loitered closer and observed more closely. When, finally, he was able to catch a glimpse of one of the keys being presented, he decided that it was a good match for the one he was carrying in his own pocket.

Jerry read for another minute or two, then un-

hurriedly folded his newspaper under his arm again
and strolled up to the counter.

The clerk accepted the key calmly. "And the
name, sir?"

Jerry had had the time to get his cover stories
and his excuses, if any should be required, as
ready as he could get them. "Lockwood," he announced. "James Lockwood."

The clerk, his eyes in a permanent squint, moved
his shirtsleeved shoulder to let the gaslight fall
more fully on the pages of the register he had just
opened. "Yes, Mr. Lockwood. Sign here, please."

The book was turned and pushed across the
counter to rest in front of Jerry. He felt no more
than faintly surprised to see that the open page
already contained several specimens of Jim Lockwood's signature, presumably one for every time
he'd visited the box. More surprising somehow
was the fact that in several places another name,
this one signed in a definitely feminine hand—
though for once not that of Jan Chen—alternated
with Lockwood's. Jerry read the lady's name as
Colleen Monahan. The most recent visit by Ms.
Monahan, it appeared, had been only yesterday.

Jim Lockwood's penmanship looked nothing at
all like Jerry Flint's usual hand, but he committed
the best quick-study forgery he could, and then
held his breath, waiting to see if it would sell. But
it seemed that he need not have worried, for the
clerk scarcely glanced at the book when Jerry
pushed it back across the counter.

"This way, sir." And the man was lifting open a
gate in the counter to let Jerry through. He was
now facing the entrance to a kind of strongroom,

walls and door of heavy wood reinforced with plates of iron or steel. Together they entered the strongroom, where Jerry's key in the clerk's hand released one of a row of little strongboxes.

"Would you prefer a booth, sir, for privacy?"

"Yes. Yes, I would."

In another moment, Jerry, clutching in both hands a small metal box that had the feeling of being almost empty, was being shown into one of a row of tiny partitioned spaces, the door of which he was able to pull closed behind him. The booth was open at the top, enabling its occupant to share in the light from the windows and the gas-jets of the lobby.

Jerry set down his metal box on the small table provided, opened the catch, and swung back the lid.

There were two items in the box, one a mere folded piece of paper, the other a large, old-fashioned, stem-winding pocket watch, with chain attached.

Paper first. The timepiece did not look all that informative, but with paper there was hope. He took the small sheet up and unfolded it to read a note.

Dear Jim Lockwood—

Things have gone a little sour. Whatever day you get this, bring this note when you come out and meet me outside the bank. If I am not there come back every hour at ten minutes after the hour in banking hours.

Our employer is concerned about your health.

Colleen M.

The handwriting of the note, he thought, matched that of the alternate signature in the book kept by the clerk. Jerry sighed and folded up the note and put it in his pocket.

Next he picked up the watch. It was ticking, evidently wound and functional. To Jerry's inexpert eye the timepiece, looking serviceable but plain, did not appear to be of particularly great value. Its case was of bright metal, hard enough to be steel. There was a round steel protective cover over the face, and Jerry thumbed a little catch and swung the cover back. Then he caught his breath.

The surface he was looking at was not like any watch face that he had ever seen before. It was more like a small circular video screen; and even more like a miniature round window into a small three-dimensional world.

The video turned itself on while he looked at it. In the window there now appeared, in full color and apparent solidity, the face of the man Jerry had known as Pilgrim. The lips of the image were moving, and now—suddenly, when Jerry held the watch at just the right distance—the voice became audible. But image and voice alike were being blocked out at intervals, by bursts of roaring static and white video noise.

"—paradoxes of time travel," Pilgrim's voice was saying, "caused in large part by"——*crash, whirr*— "may prevent your seeing or hearing this message in its entirety. Therefore I attempt to be creatively redundant. We here at this end, Jerry, can only hope and pray that you will find this message, and that enough of the content is going to come through to enable you to"—*whizee—fizzle—zapp!*

Long seconds passed. When the picture came back again, Pilgrim's head was in a different attitude.

"—and one time only," Pilgrim's voice resumed in mid-sentence. "Then this message will self-destruct." His swarthy face frowned. "Let me emphasize once more, Jerry, that your only chance of being able to return to your own time, and finding your own history intact when you do so, lies in preventing the assassination of President Abraham Lincoln."

"*What?*"

Pilgrim's image proceeded imperturbably. "Within a few days of your own arrival in the world of eighteen sixty-five, the President is shot to death by—"

Again there was interruption, audio static accompanied by visual effects that momentarily reduced the picture to unintelligible noise. The effects of video distortion in three dimensions were especially chaotic. After several seconds, the interference was gone as suddenly as it had come.

"—have until the fourteenth of April, Jeremiah, at Ford's Theater in Washington. Unless—" *blast, crackle.*

And, yet again, static had cut off the flow of information. But in another moment Pilgrim was back again, coming through as loud and clear as ever. "—chosen you for this mission because of this almost unique ability which you possess. Without this power to avoid some of the effects of paradox, your mission would be truly hopeless. With it, we can hope that you have at least a fighting chance of success."

"A fighting chance!" Jerry was raging in a whisper at the image. "Are you crazy? What are you talking about? Are you—?"

"—you must be at the side of the President, within two meters to have a high probability of success. Within three meters, to have any chance at all. And you must be there in the moment just before the assassin's bullet smashes into Lincoln's brain. Your total window of opportunity will be approximately three seconds long. During that three-second period, just before the bullet strikes, I repeat, you must activate the beacon."

"Activate the what?" Jerry murmured unconsciously. His own face contorted in a scowl, he was frozen in absolute attention on the message. Pilgrim had indicated—hadn't he?—that it was going to self-destruct.

Meanwhile Pilgrim's hands had come up into sight on the small screen. The view closed in on them. They were holding a watch that looked very much like the one Jerry was holding, except that the timepiece in the image possessed a real face and hands.

The closeup held, while Pilgrim's off-screen voice continued: "The hands must first be set, thus, at exactly twelve." His fingers demonstrated, opening the glass face of the watch and moving the hands directly. "Then the stem must be pulled out, to the first stop. This is the first stage of activation, and I repeat it will in effect give you the advantage in speed of movement that you will need."

"Repeat? You never—"

"Then, at the precise moment, just as the assassin pulls the trigger of his weapon, pull the stem to the second stop. This will activate the beacon."

"*What* beacon?"

"That's all. Until you need it on the fourteenth, this device will seem to be an ordinary timepiece. Need I emphasize that you must not lose it? You can wind it, by omitting to set the hands at twelve, pulling the stem out and turning it in the normal way."

Now the image of the watch disappeared from the small screen, which was filled by Pilgrim's face. He said, with emphasis: "Once more: The activation of the beacon must be accomplished *only during the proper three-second interval*. Pull the stem out to the second stop a second too late, and you will strand yourself permanently in the nineteenth century. Pulling it a second too soon will doubtless have the same effect, with the added drawback of causing irreparable harm to much of what you know as Western Civilization.

"But, do it at the right moment, and you will save the life of President Lincoln. You will also be restored to your own world, under conditions which ought to earn your country's eternal gratitude."

There was a sudden sharp whiff of a strange, acidic odor in Jerry's nostrils. There was, briefly, a shimmering in the air immediately surrounding the watch. Jerry almost dropped it, although his hands holding the instrument could feel no heat. In a few seconds the shimmering was over and the smell had dissipated. Jerry was left holding a device that looked exactly like the one Pilgrim had held during the demonstration. The face was solidly visible, and the hands agreed at least approximately with those of the sober clock on the wall of the bank lobby, which he was able to see over the partition of the booth. And the instrument he held was ticking.

Stunned, Jerry mechanically tucked the watch into the watchpocket of his vest, and after a couple of tries managed to get the chain attached to a buttonhole in what he considered had to be the proper way.

Still somewhat dazed, he closed up the safe-deposit box, now empty but for the cotton batting, and carried it out of the little partitioned booth, to hand it back to the incurious clerk.

You must be there in the moment just before the assassin's bullet smashes into Lincoln's brain. Your window of opportunity will be approximately three seconds long . . .

Oh, must I? You son of a bitch, Pilgrim. I'd like to see to it that something smashes into your brain. I didn't ask you to dump me into this drugged dream, this, this—

The fate of Western Civilization? More immediately graspable: his chance to get home. Pilgrim had said that it would be his only chance. Maybe that wasn't necessarily so, but the bastard could probably arrange matters that way if he wanted to.

And it would happen in Washington, on April fourteenth. He recalled the date on the newspaper he was again carrying under his arm. This was April sixth. He had eight days.

He was just outside the bank, on the wooden sidewalk, with no idea of which direction he ought to go next, when a gentle hand in a soft gray glove placed itself on his arm, making him start violently. The young woman who had come up to him had chestnut hair, and calm brown eyes under her flower-trimmed hat. The face on the locket? No, he thought, not at all.

"Don't be startled, Jim," she said in a low, husky voice. She was smiling at him pleasantly. "Someone might be watching us. You don't know me but I'm your friend. Because I'm in the same boat you are. I used to work for Lafe, but I've given it up too."

Jerry opened his mouth to say something, and closed it again.

"Walk with me. Smile." Her hand on his arm turned him gently on the busy sidewalk, and they walked together, at a moderate pace. He noticed vaguely that they were moving in the direction of the railroad section. "I'm Colleen Monahan. I'm working directly for Stanton now. It's all right. He sent me to see to it that you get back to Washington alive."

SEVEN

After hurrying Jerry down a side street near the railroad station, Colleen Monahan brought him up some wooden steps to the front door of a cheap-looking rooming house only a few blocks away. In the dim hallway inside the door the smell of stale cabbage overlay a substratum of even less appetizing odors. Next she led him up a dark, uncarpeted stair; there were four short flights, with a right-angled turn after each one. From somewhere nearby came the voices of a man and woman quarreling.

The upper hallway where they left the stairs smelled no better than the lower one. In another moment Jerry's guide was unlocking the door to a small and shabby room.

"Our train leaves shortly after dark," she announced, locking the door after Jerry as soon as he had followed her into the room. "If you want to change clothes before we start, there's a few things in the wardrobe there that might fit you." The more he heard of Colleen Monahan's speech, the more easily Jerry could detect a trace of some accent in her voice; perhaps it was a genuine Irish brogue. And probably it would be more than a trace when she spoke with feeling.

"The train to Washington?" he asked.

"Of course. What did you think? I said I'd get you there alive."

It was said in a matter-of-fact way that made the implied danger all the more convincing. "I bet," Jerry said carefully, "that lots of people arrive there alive every day."

Standing in front of a small wall mirror, Colleen had unpinned and taken off her hat. Now she turned to face him. "Not with Lafe Baker trying to stop them, they don't," she said. The short reply had the sound of practical advice, delivered calmly. Now, as Jerry approached the room's single window, intending to look out, she added: "Better be careful. And hand me over that safe-deposit key while I think of it. You won't need it any longer."

Jerry pulled out the key, tossed it in the air and caught it. "How'd you recognize me?" he asked softly. "Lots of men go in and out of that bank."

"I paid the safe-deposit clerk to pass me a signal. What did you think?"

After giving her the key he edged up to one side of the window and moved the curtain gently. The window gave an elevated view of backyards, woodpiles, and privies, the scene decorated by a few lines of laundry. If someone somewhere out there was watching the room, Jerry couldn't see them. He let the dirty curtain fall back.

Turning to the tall wooden wardrobe, he took a look inside; only a few clothes were hanging there, but about half of them seemed to be male attire, somewhat shabbier than Jim Lockwood's. "You mentioned changing clothes. Do you think I ought to?"

"You ought to know better than I," she answered shortly. "Maybe the men chasing you don't know what you're wearing now; maybe they haven't been after you every inch of the way here from Missouri. I can tell you it's damned likely they will be after you from now on. And I've promised the old man in Washington to bring you there alive."

He closed the wardrobe doors again. Pilgrim had arranged for him to be guided to this woman, obviously, but he had never said anything to Jerry about her. Beyond what she was telling him herself, Jerry had no idea of who she really was and how much she might know.

Cautiously he asked: "What's going on in Washington?"

"Sit down and rest yourself. Don't be waitin' for a special invitation." Colleen herself was already occupying the only chair, so Jerry sat down on the bed—the mattress was a grade quieter than cornhusks if not really any softer. His hostess continued: "What's goin' on? Stanton and Watson, Lord bless 'em, are finally ready to clean house. Old Lafe is goin' to be on his way out—provided we can get you there alive to testify. Mr. Stanton won't act until he can hear the facts from you personally."

Stanton. Oh yes. Jerry could definitely remember Jan Chen, somewhere across the vast gulf of time, telling him that was the name of Lincoln's Secretary of War. The name of Watson, on the other hand, meant nothing to Jerry, unless it was going to turn out that Sherlock Holmes was alive after all. Nor could he recall ever hearing of someone known as Old Lafe.

Unable to stand the uncertainty any longer, Jerry asked: "What do you hear from Pilgrim?"

"Who?" She had heard him perfectly, but the name obviously meant nothing to her—or else she was a suberb actress.

Jerry sighed. "Never mind. So, Old Lafe is going out."

"He won't be got rid of lightly," his informant went on, shaking her head grimly. "He is efficient, when he wants to be, as we all know. But now the stories about his corruption are mounting and mounting, and the war is winding down. He can be dispensed with now. But Lafe Baker won't disappear without a fight, as we both know. And how are things out in Missouri?" She flounced her body in the chair, adjusting the long skirt. She was better dressed, Jerry realized, than anyone would expect an occupant of this boarding house to be.

He only shrugged in answer to her question.

"I trust you got the goods on him." There was hopeful hatred in the question.

Jerry looked her in the eye, trying to appear impenetrable rather than ignorant. "I want to get to Washington," was all that he could find to say, at last. "Alive." The problem of someone there knowing Jim Lockwood, and wanting him to give testimony about something, would have to wait.

"Right, don't tell me, I don't want to know."

Colleen had gone behind a professional mask. "Wouldn't do any good. Even if you told me, I wouldn't be able to testify first-hand. I forgot to ask you if you'd had anything to eat."

"I've eaten well. You? And how about the train tickets? I've got money."

Colleen smiled. "That was to be my next question." She pulled an apple out from somewhere and began to munch on it. "Won't be needing any tickets between here and Detroit. We're going that far on a private car. I'm Sarah James and you're John James. We're married, of course. I don't think Lafe's people are going to be looking for a married couple. That's why Stanton sent a woman as your escort." Then she straightened herself firmly in the chair, as if to discourage any idea of intimacy the mention of marriage might have suggested.

"A private car." That was impressive, thought Jerry. If it was true. "How'd you manage that?"

"The men who own the railroad are only too glad to be able to do a favor for Mr. Stanton." She stated that as if it should be an obvious fact, and Jerry did not press for any elaboration.

His companion, chewing thoughtfully on a piece of apple, studied him and then remarked: "You don't look all that much like the picture I'd formed of you from Mr. Stanton's description, though there's no doubt it fits. Strange how you can get a picture of someone in your mind and then it's wrong. By the way, did you bring the note?"

Jerry dug from his pocket the note he'd taken from the safe deposit box, and passed it over. Colleen looked at it and was satisfied. "Reckon you're all right," she said.

Silence stretched out for a few moments, threatened to become uncomfortable. Jerry asked: "Have you been in this line of work a long time—Colleen? Mind if I call you that?" And he was thinking how different she was from Jan Chen, presumably in some sense her colleague. He wondered if they knew or had ever heard of each other.

"I've been at it long enough to know my way around. And for now you'd better start to call me Sarah." It was something of a reproach.

"Of course."

The two of them sat talking in Colleen's room until it began to grow dark, when she suddenly asked him: "Have you the time?"

He dug out Pilgrim's watch and flipped open the metal faceplate. "A little after six."

"Then we must go." From under her bed Colleen pulled out a small bag, evidently already packed. Jerry, carrying his own heavier carpetbag, followed her out the door. There was no light in the room to be extinguished.

This time Colleen Monahan led him on a circuitous route through the evening streets. Here and there lamps glowed in the windows of houses, and a man was carrying a short ladder from one gas streetlight after another, patiently climbing again and again to light them one by one.

Colleen looked over her shoulder frequently; Jerry, imitating her, could see no evidence that anyone was following them.

Pausing beside a high board fence, Colleen took one final look around, then dodged suddenly through a hole in the fence where several boards were missing. Jerry, staying on her heels, found that they were now in a railroad yard, a couple of blocks from the lighted station. The ground underfoot here was a maze of track. Kerosene lamps behind colored glass made what he supposed were effective signals. In the middle distance a couple of trains, lighted by lanterns and showering sparks, were moving sluggishly. Switch engines grumbled and snorted in near-total darkness, dragging the cars industriously.

Their baggage bumping against their legs, Jerry and his guide picked their way across one siding after another, moving in the general direction of the station. Chicago was evidently already well on it's way to becoming a great railroad center.

"What are we looking for?" Jerry whispered when Colleen paused at last, obviously uncertain of exactly which way to proceed.

"We're looking for the man we're going to meet," she whispered back.

"Who's that?"

"A friend. I'll know him when I see him."

She moved on, with Jerry continuing to follow her as silently as possible.

Ahead of them an uncoupled passenger car waited on yet another siding. A dim figure emerged from behind it, looking in their direction. Colleen waved, and the man ahead returned her gesture, his arm almost invisible in the gathering gloom.

As they approached, the man waiting in the shadows tipped his cap in a remarkably humble gesture. Jerry could see now that he was black, wearing what Jerry took to be a kind of railroad uniform.

"Mistah and Missus James? I'm Sam." The speaker touched his cap again, this time in a kind of half-military salute. "We expectin' you heah. Lemme take you bags."

"Never mind that, we'll manage," said Colleen. Despite the interference of her long skirts, she was already halfway up the steep steps leading into the car. "Let's get moving."

"Yas'm. We'll be moving any minute."

Someone would have to locate and attach an engine first, thought Jerry. But he kept quiet. In a matter of moments they were all three inside the car, where he received his next surprise. He wasn't sure what kind of an interior he had been expecting, but these quarters were furnished better than Lincoln's Springfield home, and Lincoln had not been a poor man when he lived there. Kerosene lamps with ornate shades were hidden behind shaded windows that let out practically no light. Thick carpets covered the floor, except for a layer of steel plates in the near vicinity of the woodburning stove. The heating stove, secured by steel tie-rods to the floor of the coach, was standing cold and empty in the mild spring night.

Not only the furnishings but the layout were more like those of a house than a railroad coach. In the rear, where the three had climbed aboard the car, was a kitchen-utility room, complete with cookstove, ice-box, woodpile and pantry. A narrow door standing open on a small closet revealed inside a primitive flush toilet, with overhead water tank. There was a scuttle of coal beside the cookstove, in whose iron belly a small fire was burning.

From this room Sam conducted his guests through a narrow passage leading forward along the left side of the car. At its front end the passage opened into a single large parlor, luxuriously furnished, with two softly upholstered sofas, matching chairs, and a few tables. Kerosene lamps secured near the corners of the ceiling provided lighting, and elegant curtains had been drawn on all the windows, making this a private world.

Colleen paused for just a moment, as if the place were somehow not what she had been expecting, but she was determined not to show it. Then she carried on. "Sam, can you fix us something to eat? I saw a pantry back there."

"Yas'm. I got a fire goin'. Supper comin' right up."

Jerry and Colleen sat on soft furniture in the parlor of the millionaires' train, looking at each other.

"Lord," she said with feeling, "some folks know how to live. Don't they, though?" Continuing a running commentary, she jumped up to investigate an unopened door, that must lead to the central room or rooms, bypassed by the narrow hallway.

". . . I just hope that one day I—" She opened the door and fell silent. Jerry looked over her shoulder. Here was another cold stove, bolted down and vented through the roof like the others. The room also contained a wide, curtained four-poster bed—as well as a chamber pot, barely visible underneath, a washstand, another sofa, and a small table and chair. Some railway car, Jerry thought.

Somewhere outside the curtained windows, one of the switch engines was slowly rumbling its way closer; men's voices were calling just outside the private car. Presently there came the jolt and jar of coupling. Jerry had ridden twentieth-century trains a couple of times, but those had been electric powered commuter specials, plying smoothly on short trips between Chicago and the suburbs. This, he expected, was going to be another new experience.

Colleen, still struggling not to be overly impressed, stood in the bedroom doorway. "This is very fancy indeed."

"Just so's it's fast."

"I expect it'll be that too."

With another jolt, the string of cars that now included theirs got slowly into motion.

Colleen moved to one of the parlor windows and parted a fringed curtain slightly to peer out. "We're coming almost to the station . . . there's the train we're joining . . . they're putting us right behind the tender. That's good, most of the smoke will blow past us." There now began a slow deliberate lurching forward and back, a grinding and banging, as more cars were coupled and uncoupled.

"This is the sixth of April," said Jerry, hanging on to the heavy parlor table for support during this lengthy procedure. "I must be in Washington before the fourteenth."

She looked at him. "I'm sure we will be, barring a train wreck. Or something worse. But what happens on the fourteenth?" When he did not answer she looked at him and added: "All right, I shouldn't ask."

Presently Sam returned, bearing waiter-style on one raised hand a tray of covered dishes, linen napkins, fine china, and crystal glasses. His two clients had seated themselves at the parlor table and were just beginning to enjoy their dinner when the train got under way. Sam had provided hot soup, fried oysters, fresh bread and cheese, red wine and hot coffee.

"Thank you for providing such elegant transportation, Mrs. James," Jerry toasted his companion with a gesture of his wineglass. During recent minutes he had noticed that she was indeed wearing a plain gold ring on the third finger of her left hand; he wondered if it was the real thing, or part of her costume for this assignment. But that was none of his business.

"It's my job," she answered modestly, having glanced around to make sure that Sam was out of sight before she spoke. With the steady volume of noise that the cars made in motion, anyone who tried eavesdropping from around a corner was going to be out of luck.

"So," said Jerry pleasantly. "I think that safe-deposit box was a good idea."

"Yes indeed," his companion agreed calmly.

Jerry hesitated, considering. He wanted to probe for more information, about Stanton, and in particular about the mysterious Lafe Baker, who was evidently hoping to arrange Jim Lockwood's death. And about the testimony Jim Lockwood would be expected to provide, if and when he reached Washington alive. Yet he was afraid to ask questions, fearing to give himself away.

"How's Stanton?" he asked at last.

"Him? How is he ever? Sickly little muck of a man with his gold-rimmed glasses and his great gray beard. Bullies and blusters those folk who are afraid to stand up to him. But he gets his job done, and two or three other men's work beside, I'll be thinkin'. When he finds corruption he'll not put up with it, in Baker or anyone else."

"And where is Baker now?"

"Ha, wish I knew. But we're here, locked in on a moving train, and it's not about to keep me awake tonight worryin' about it." Colleen looked again toward the corner of the passageway where Sam had vanished. "I wonder if our friend would bring us a tot of something to keep out the chill." She looked at Jerry with sudden suspicion. "You're not a drinkin' man, now are you? I mean heavy?"

"No. Not so it becomes a problem. Almost never. I remember one occasion when wine got me into trouble—but right now I could use a tot of something too."

Swaying to his feet with the motion of the train. Jerry made his way halfway across the parlor to an elegant little cupboard he had noticed earlier. The doors of the cupboard were unlocked, and when they were opened they revealed not only the bottles he had been hoping for, but a good selection of fine glassware as well. With a little gesture Jerry pulled out one bottle labeled brandy. There was no ice, of course, but what the hell, sometimes you had to rough it.

When he and his charming companion—really, she wasn't at all bad looking—had toasted each other, he remarked: "I see there's a sofa in the bedroom. Perhaps I'd better sleep in there. It might look a little strange to Sam if he found me out here on one of these." And with his free hand Jerry patted the cushions beside him.

"I think perhaps you're right. The *sofa* in the bedroom it should be for you." The emphasis upon the second word in the last sentence was not all that heavy, but it was definitely there. "And now, if you don't mind, Mr. James, I'm very tired." Colleen looked uncertainly for a moment at her empty brandy glass, then smiled briefly and put it down—Sam would take care of it—and swayed to her feet against the motion of the train.

A few minutes later, going back to the kitchen-utility room to take his turn with the water closet, Jerry observed Sam, who was bedded down wrapped in a blanket on the floor beside the cookstove. The supper dishes had already been washed and stacked in a rack to dry. To all appearances their attendant was dead to the world.

Jerry paused for a moment, studying the sleeping man. A slave? No, surely not, here in the north. But had Sam perhaps been a slave at some point in his life, his living human body bought and sold? Almost certainly. The thought gave Jerry an eerie feeling.

Coming forward in the car again a few minutes later, Jerry once more passed the sleeping Sam, who did not appear to have moved a muscle. Moments later he entered the parlor and came to a dead stop.

Here in the parlor only one of the high-hung kerosene lanterns was still burning, the light somehow turned down to dim nightlight intensity. The door leading to the bedroom was closed. Seated in an armchair directly beneath the lantern, Pilgrim was waiting, his strong, compact body swaying lightly with the motion of the train. He frowned at Jerry but at first said nothing, as if he were waiting to hear what Jerry had to say.

Recovering from his initial surprise, Jerry at last moved forward again, to lean with both fists on the parlor table.

"Well?" he demanded. "Is the joke over? Had enough fun?"

The dark man in the chair sat with folded arms, shaking his head slowly. His face remained saturnine. "Would that it were all a joke, my friend. Would that it were."

"I think you better tell me just what the hell is going on."

"I shall do my best." Pilgrim drew a deep breath and expelled it. Not far ahead, another train's engine whistled sharply. "You have been drafted to carry out a rescue operation. At the moment it is not going well."

The train swayed, rounding a curve, and the flame in the dim lantern swayed lightly with it. "Whatever it is you drafted me for, since you're here now, I suggest you take over the operational details yourself, and send me home."

"I should be delighted to take over, as you put it, and myself do everything that needs to be done. In fact nothing would please me more. But that is, I regret, not possible."

"Really."

"Yes."

"Let me see if I can begin to understand this. Your message on the talking watch indicated that the object of the rescue operation is Abraham Lincoln. And that if he can be saved from assassination, then there's some chance of my resuming a normal life."

"That is roughly correct."

"Good. Meanwhile, your aide, little Jan, spent most of an evening back in Springfield feeding me drugs and telling me how important Lincoln was to history, how different everything would be if he hadn't been shot. Which means that if I save him, I'll be resuming my life in a different twentieth century. Or are you telling me there would then be two different futures?"

Pilgrim was shaking his head with a slow emphasis. "Understand this from the start. *There is only one future.* There is only one world."

"Then how can we expect to save Lincoln, and not change—"

"Trust me. It can be done."

"Trust you!"

"Jeremiah, my time for answering questions is severely limited; I advise you to seek information that will be of practical benefit. As for my taking over, as you put it, I repeat that is impossible. A tangle of potential paradoxes prevent it. I can help you, advise you—up to a point—but that is all. If it were possible for me to do the job you have been assigned, I should not have gone to all the trouble of finding and recruiting you."

"You're saying I'd better trust you because you're not going to give me any choice."

"At this point I cannot. Not if you want to return home."

Jerry fumed in silence for a moment. Then he demanded: "Who's this Lafe Baker that Colleen Monahan is telling me about? Why does he want to kill Lockwood, and why did you set me up here as someone who's likely to be killed?"

"Colonel Lafayette C. Baker is head of the War Department's Secret Service. He is becoming, even in this corrupt and brutal era, something of a legend in the realms of corruption and brutality. Now that the war is effectively over, his employer, Secretary Edwin McMasters Stanton, is ready to be rid of him.

"As for why you now bear the identity of James Lockwood, you must realize that we were severely limited in our choices of a persona in which to clothe you. Lockwood himself is dead now, as you have probably suspected. You do not look very much like him, and Stanton of course will know on sight that you are a fraud. So you must avoid meeting Stanton."

"Thanks. Thanks a lot. He'll be waiting for me at the station in Washington, I suppose."

"That is possible."

"Wonderful. Now what is all this crap about my having a three-second window of opportunity in which to act?"

"I regret," said Pilgrim, "it is all too regrettably true that—"

The train swayed again, the lamp-flame swaying and dimming too. Jerry leaned backward from the table, needing a momentary effort to maintain his balance. When he looked for Pilgrim again, the chair was empty and the man was gone.

EIGHT

Jerry spent some time walking about looking for Pilgrim. He covered the interior of the car from one end to the other, without result. Sam in his nest of blanket on the floor had shifted position at last, but he was still asleep. And when Jerry entered the bedroom, Colleen was snugly asleep in the big bed, covered to the chin and snoring gently. He wondered if Pilgrim was still watching him from some other dimension or something. Well, tonight it wasn't going to matter to Jerry a whole lot. He was dead tired; having someone watch him sleep wasn't going to bother him.

Silently he fastened the small bolt on the inside of the bedroom door. One lamp in the bedroom was still burning dimly, and Jerry went to it and fiddled with a little wheel on the side, as he had observed other people doing with lamps. The little wheel had something to do with adjusting the length of the burning wick, but he couldn't get it right. At last he gave up and simply blew out the flame; afterward, in nearly total darkness, he could still smell the hot metal and the kerosene.

The speeding train roared and swayed hypnotically through darkness. Groping his way around, he removed his coat and boots, making sure he had his revolver within easy reach. Then he stretched out on the sofa, which was comfortably soft but a little short for even Jerry's modest height. His last waking thought was that he was a taller man in this world than he had been in his own.

Jerry awakened to bright daylight outside the bedroom's curtained windows; he could feel and hear that the train was just stopping somewhere. A glance toward the bed showed him that his roommate was still asleep. He supposed Thursday had been a tiring day for her as well.

Cautiously Jerry arose from the sofa and moved to a window, where he parted the curtains and squinted out. They had reached some kind of a city or town, and baggage was being unloaded from the train. A few passengers appeared to be waiting to get aboard. Two clocks were visible, one in a brick tower in the middle distance, the other through the window of the nearby depot—both said one minute after eight.

The timepieces reminded Jerry of the device Pilgrim had so craftily arranged for him to possess, and so earnestly warned him not to lose. He pulled it out of his watch pocket and looked at it now. The watch was ticking as steadily as before, but now it said seven-fifty. That meant that either the two clocks outside were wrong in unison, or . . .

Could something be wrong with the hardware Pilgrim had provided for the mad attempt to rescue Lincoln? Jerry, the student of science and engineering, didn't see any reason why not. If anything could go wrong, it would. That was all he needed, one more complication on top of—

There was a slight sound from the direction of the bed, and Jerry turned to see Colleen sitting up halfway, propped with pillows, and looking at him. She was holding the blanket up as high as her shoulders, which, he was just able to see, were demurely covered by what looked like a flannel nightgown.

"Good morning," he offered.

"And a good morning to you." She freed one hand, without letting the blanket slip more than an inch, and used the fingers to rub her eyes. "Where are we?"

"I don't know. Stopped at a station. I was just wondering if we're still in the central time zone."

The puzzled look Colleen gave him in response warned him to let that question drop for now.

She was ready to change the subject anyway. "If you would turn your back," she requested.

Silently he went back to the window, hearing her get out of bed behind him. That sound was followed by the rustle of voluminous layers of clothing, most of it being put on, he presumed. His mind returned to the latest oddities of time. How likely was it that both of these town clocks would be wrong together?

"You can turn back now," Colleen's voice announced. He turned to behold his roommate with yesterday's dress on, and pins in her mouth, busy in front of a wall mirror doing something with her hair. At that moment there came a tapping at the bedroom door, and Sam's voice sang out announcing that breakfast was ready in the parlor.

That at least was cheerful news. "We're getting the royal treatment," Jerry remarked.

"I told you, we're supposed to be great friends of the president of the railroad. In a way we shall be, if we give a good report of him to Stanton."

Breakfast was good. Excellent, in fact. Jerry was now firmly convinced that everyone in this century who could afford to eat at all took the business seriously.

Sam, in and out of the parlor with serving dishes, gave up his first cheerful attempts at making, or provoking, conversation when he sensed that the reigning mood was one of reserved silence. Jerry had begun to develop the unreasonable feeling that the man was putting them on, acting the part of a black servant out of some old movie.

Before breakfast was over, the train had lurched into motion again—only to grind to a halt a few minutes later at the next town.

Today was April seventh. Most of the remainder of the day passed very slowly. Armed with a time-table and Pilgrim's watch, Jerry charted the crooked progress of the railroad across Indiana and part of Michigan. There were many more stops than he had hoped, more, even, than he had expected. A number of the towns boasted steeple clocks visible from the train, no two of which were in agreement with each other. The watch in Jerry's waistcoat pocket ticked on steadily—he had remembered to wind it on retiring—but on the average its time grew farther and farther divorced from that displayed in the cities through which they passed.

Colleen sat most of the morning knitting quietly, but after Sam served lunch, she put her needlework aside restlessly and began speaking about the small town in Indiana where she had grown up. One of her brightest memories was how exciting it was when the railroad first came through.

"One of these towns here?" He was reasonably sure that they were still in Indiana.

"No, no. Far to the south."

She mentioned a brother, and Jerry asked: "Is he in the army now?"

"He died at Vicksburg."

"Uh . . . sorry to hear it," Jerry replied awkwardly.

She acknowledged his sympathy with a slight nod. "I have another brother with General Sherman in Georgia."

"Older or younger?"

"Oh, younger. I'm the oldest in the family. Twenty-four. What about yourself?"

"Twenty-five."

"I meant, about your family." She blushed just slightly.

"No brothers or sisters," he said shortly. Jerry suspected that as an only child he had missed out on a lot of happiness.

"You meant there never were? Ah, that's too bad. It must have been a lonely way to grow up."

"I had a lot of cousins around when I was small," he said truthfully. "That helped."

She hesitated very briefly before she added: "And no wife now, I suppose?"

"No wife."

"That's just as well in our line of work. You'll leave no widow."

"Is that why you let yourself get into it—I mean, did becoming a widow—"

Colleen nodded, and before he could very well express his sympathy again she had turned to the window, as if to keep him from seeing her face. Jerry wanted to ask her more questions about herself, but, not being ready to answer the same sort of questions, he forebore.

As he served the evening meal's first course, Sam announced that the train would reach its final stop, Detroit, early the next morning. He suggested that reservations for Mr. and Mrs. James for the next train east be made by telegraph from the next stop. Jerry thought that a good idea and gave Sam money for the telegram.

During the night Colleen tossed in her bed, crying out with nightmares. Jerry, awakened on his sofa, went to comfort her.

He took her by the arm, wanting to wake her gently. But she pulled free and rolled away across the wide bed, whimpering. In the midst of her broken murmers, Jerry thought he made out a name: Steven.

Suddenly Colleen rolled back toward Jerry, clutched his wrist, and pulled him onto the bed. He lay there, atop the covers, with an arm over her covered shoulder, comforting her as best he could.

Slowly Colleen came fully awake, the moans of

her dream-struggle turning into a soft and hope-less weeping.

"Hey, it's ok, it's all right." Jerry kept reassur-ing her gently as he lay there with no urge to do anything but soothe her. Gently he stroked her hair.

Presently she ceased weeping, and soon after that she said: "You're a good man, Mr. James. Perhaps the best I've met in this business. Now go back to the sofa."

She was patting his arm gently, but her voice, though it still trembled, had an edge to it.

"Yes ma'am," said Jerry, and went back.

Their train carried them into Detroit right on schedule, early on the morning of Saturday, April eighth. In the railroad depot of that city they said goodbye to their millionaires' quarters, and to Sam, who had fixed them a sizable hamper of food to take along when they boarded their next train.

Switching trains was accomplished without any special difficulty, but the loss of their private car meant goodbye to any chance for open conversa-tion, and though it eased the problem of how to keep his background obscured, Jerry had mixed feelings about that. It meant, as well, goodbye to other privacy, and that he did not like at all.

On the plus side, he now began to overhear a lot of interesting conversation, conveying useful information to the visiting alien. The other passen-gers on this train were all white—Jerry gathered that blacks rode in the baggage car when they rode at all—but otherwise quite a mixed bag. This train was vastly inferior to their private accommodations, but luxurious compared to the local that Jerry had ridden out of Springfield. Their coach boasted a water closet at each end, as well as sinks. There was even a cooler for drinking water, tin cup attached by a slender chain.

Here, as in the private car, the layout was somewhat compartmentalized. The rear compartment, about a fourth of the car, was for ladies only, but Colleen, like most of the other women, chose to stay with her male companion as much as possible. Seemingly there were no unaccompanied women aboard.

She rode beside Jerry in a double seat, while around them children wept, shouted, laughed, and otherwise made a racket, and adults dozed, chatted, or endured the trip in silence. The roaring train surrounded them oppressively, raining considerably more soot and sound upon them than they had been exposed to in the private car.

The clocks in the passing towns kept getting further and further ahead of Jerry's watch. By now Jerry had begun to wonder whether any regular time zones had yet been established. These people seemed to be setting their watches and clocks by the local sun! Not that he cared much; he had more immediate problems to worry about.

At a whistlestop just east of Cleveland, Colleen touched Jerry on the arm and pointed unobtrusively out through the grimy window beside her.

"Some of Lafe's people," she murmured, so softly that no one but Jerry would have had a chance of hearing her.

Jerry looked out the window with great interest,

just in time to observe a couple of tough-looking men in civilian suits and bowler hats stop a young man on the platform. He had put down his carpet-bag and they were showing what might be badges —Jerry couldn't really tell from where he sat—and obviously interrogating their victim.

Colleen added in the same low tone: "Only looking for bounty-jumpers, most likely."

Now he was really lost. Damn Pilgrim, anyway. He asked: "And how are bounty-jumpers best recognized?"

"They won't be recognized at all, I'd bet, if it's to be left up to those two," Colleen sniffed. She appeared to regard Lafe's agents and their victim with about equal disdain. The train pulled out before they saw the conclusion of the incident.

The day wore on, passengers feeding themselves from whatever food and drink they had brought with them. A garrulously extroverted young soldier, recently discharged and radiant with joy as his Pennsylvania home drew ever nearer, went from seat to seat aboard the coach offering to trade some of his hardtack biscuits for a share in more palatable fair. Jerry and Colleen shared some of the contents of their hamper with him, but declined to try his biscuits, which he had been carrying wrapped in a long-unwashed fragment of blanket.

When darkness had fallen and it was time for berths to be made up, the ladies retired to the female compartment in the rear. Overnight passengers, it appeared, were expected to supply their own bedding, and sure enough, the bottom of the hamper packed by Sam revealed two folded blankets.

A uniformed porter came around to fold the men's berths down from the wall, causing the daytime seats to disappear as part of the same transformation. The only railroad-supplied bedding was the slightly stained mattress pads that came down with the berths, triple-deck constructions with each shelf jutting independently from the wall.

The night of April eighth passed uneventfully, and Colleen dutifully rejoined her husband next morning somewhere in Ohio. At the first stop that the train made after sunrise, people in their Sunday best came aboard carrying palm branches. Jerry stared at them uncomprehendingly.

"Palm Sunday," Colleen beside him commented.

"Oh." Sunday, the ninth of April, he thought. That leaves five more days. Am I really going to do what Pilgrim tells me? Do I have a choice? If this is Palm Sunday, next Sunday will be Easter. And Friday the fourteenth will be Good Friday, won't it?

Colleen gazed after the happy Christians moving past them through the car. "Were your folks religious, Jim?"

"No. Not much."

"Mine neither. But there are times when I think I'd like to be. Are yours still alive?"

"My mother is," he said, abstractedly, truthfully. "My father—my original father kind of walked out, I understand, when I was very small."

"Stepfather bring you up?"

"Yep. I always think of him as my father. He's still around."

As if unconsciously, two-thirds lost in her own

thoughts, Colleen reached to take his hand. No one had ever taken his hand in quite that way before, he thought. Almost—he supposed—the way a loving wife might do it. For some reason Jerry was moved.

The remainder of Sunday passed as had the days before, in soot and sound and roaring motion. How many such days had he now spent in this alien world? He was starting to lose track.

The train that bore him was beginning to seem itself like a time machine—or an eternity machine perhaps, a mysterious and inescapable conveyance whose journey never ended. Eventually the lamps were once more lighted, the berths made up again. Men and women retired in their separate compartments.

Jerry's was a middle berth tonight, with one man snoring below him and another overhead. Bootless, hatless, and coatless, his belongings tucked around him, he dozed off wrapped in Sam's gift of a blanket. His coat, with revolver carefully enclosed, was folded under his head.

He was awakened in the small hours of the morning, by the sound of heavy gunfire.

NINE

Jerry had his revolver in hand and his boots on when his feet hit the narrow aisle between stacks of berths. Most of his bunkmates were already on their feet, milling around and cursing in the near-darkness, and a good proportion of them were also armed. The train had ground to a stop by now. Armed male passengers were looking out of windows.

This was no train robbery, though. Squeezing himself into position at a window, Jerry could see that huge bonfires had been built along both sides of the track. Men on horses were racing madly by, waving their hats and yelling, whooping up a giant celebration.

Jerry caught the words shouted by one rider who shot past at top speed: "—Lee's surrendered!—"

Now the door at the men's end of the car was standing open and someone had thrown a bundle of newspapers aboard. Someone else had got the lanterns burning brightly. Bottles of whisky and flasks of unknown fire were being passed from hand to hand, and Jerry choked down a swig.

Presently he got to see a newspaper, dated Monday, April tenth. The lead story on the front page read:

NEWS BY TELEGRAPH
THE END

THE OLD FLAG VINDICATED
LEE AND HIS WHOLE ARMY SURRENDERED YESTER-
DAY

The Official Correspondence Between Grant and
Lee
On Thursday, the President paid another visit
to Richmond. Accompanied by Mrs. Lincoln,
Senators Sumner and Harlan, and others . . .

Celebration was spreading aboard the train. Exploding, Jerry decided, would be a better word for it. Amid the noise the women, wrapped in shawls and blankets, were coming forward from their sleeping compartment demanding to know what was going on. Men, some of them utter strangers, shouted victory at them, hugged and kissed them. Women screamed in joy and prayed when they heard the news, thanking Providence for the end of casualty lists.

The train whistle shrieked again and again, but so far the train remained standing where it had stopped. Jerry could see lights in windows out there, some kind of a town nearby, no one sleeping in it now. Men were leaning out the open windows of the train, firing revolvers into the air, bellowing to add their noise to that of the celebration going on outside.

Jerry had turned to face the rear in the crowded aisle, wanting to see Colleen as quickly as possible when she appeared from the women's quarters. But so far she hadn't come into sight. He swayed on his feet with the jolt that came as the train at last made an effort at getting into motion again.

The jolt was repeated, this time with more effect. The movement drew more cheers from those aboard, as if it were another military victory.

"Mistah Lockwood?"

There was a tug on Jerry's sleeve, and he looked down into the face of a small black boy. "What is it?"

"Youah wife, sah. She want you back in the baggage cah. Two cahs back."

Baggage car? All Jerry could think at the moment was: *She's found out something. Maybe Baker's people are on board.* "Lead on," he said, pausing only to grab his coat and hat from inside his berth.

He followed the boy back through the narrow corridor that bypassed the women's section of the coach, and then outside through its rear door. There was no enclosed vestibule between cars, only one roaring, swaying platform coupled to another, a standing space beaten by the wind of the train's passage and sprinkled with the sparks and soot and cinders of its power.

"What—?" The boy had disappeared, somewhere, somehow. Jerry wrenched at the handle of the door leading into the next car, but if his guide had gone that way he had locked the door behind him.

There were two ladders close at hand, one on the end of each car, each ladder a series of rungs riveted or welded to the body of the coach, leading up to the train's roof. And now at the bottom of the nearer ladder, a few feet away, a dark figure stood, gripping a rung with his left hand, holding a gun in his right, aiming it at Jerry. The gunman was mouthing words of which the train noise would let Jerry hear only a shouted fragment.

"—sends his regards—"

Had Jerry been at all familiar with the reality of firearms, had he ever seen at first hand what they could do, he might have been paralyzed by the threat. As matters stood, he reacted before fear could disable him.

At the karate dojo they had sometimes, in leisured safety, rehearsed responses to this situation. Rehearsal paid off now. Jerry raised his own empty hands—the first step was to make the attacker think you had surrendered. Then a fraction of a second later he lashed out with a front snap kick, catching both wrist and gunbutt with the toe of his right boot.

There was an explosion almost in Jerry's face. Powder fragments stung his skin, while the flash and the bullet went narrowly over his left shoulder. The gun itself went clattering away in darkness.

Immediately after impact Jerry's right leg had come down to support his weight again, so now he had both feet as solidly planted as anyone's feet could be on the rocking, jouncing platform. Jerry was no black belt, and the straight overhand punch he threw at his opponent was not as hard as some he had sent at the wooden *makiwara* in the practice dojo. But still it landed with considerably more force than the man might have anticipated from someone of Jerry's size and build, even had he seen it coming.

Hit on the cheekbone by a stunning impact, the disarmed man let out one surprised sound and staggered back, his first inadvertent step carrying him off the platform at the top of the steep iron stairs that led down to the ground. While the train was in motion those stairs were barricaded, but by nothing more than a low-slung length of chain, whose links now caught the tottering man at the back of his thighs. For a moment his arms waved frantically. He tried, and failed, to grab at the handrailing beside the steps. Then he was gone.

By now the figure of another man had appeared on the platform, and Jerry turned instinctively to meet the new threat. Dimly he could see that the arm that came swinging up at him held a knife. He blocked the blow somehow, but the man's other fist, or something he held in it, clouted Jerry on the side of the head and he went down, momentarily dazed. Now at last he remembered the pistol in his own inside pocket, and managed to pull it out. It was kicked out of his hand before he could fire. He tried to roll over on the narrow platform, but his opponent was crouching over him, knife poised for a downward thrust.

Another gunshot punctuated the steady roaring of the train. The second enemy sprang away, and in a moment had vanished up the ladder to the roof. One more shot rang out even as the man was climbing, and Jerry thought he heard the ricochet go whining away from heavy steel.

Colleen, wrapped in a blanket over her night-gown, stood in the open doorway of the forward car, a stubby-barreled pistol in her hand. In a moment she had moved forward to crouch over Jerry. "You hurt?"

Before he could answer he had to get to his feet and take an inventory. Everything was function-ing. Amazingly, he thought, there was no blood. Along his left forearm the sleeve of his coat had been ripped by his attacker's knife, but the blade had not pierced the shirtsleeve or the skin beneath.

"Let's get inside. This's only a two-shot." And Colleen, gesturing with her pistol, tucked it back into the folds of her blanket. "Damn it all, I should have known right away. Little nigger boy came to tell me you wanted me to stay put. I should have known."

Inside the train again, in the light of the kero-sene lamps, he could see the anger in her eyes, and could tell that some of it at least was directed at him, Jim Lockwood, the experienced agent, who had just fallen for what must have been some kind of a crude trick. But she was angry at herself too.

"What do we do now?" he asked, humbly.

She looked at him in surprise, then shrugged. "Keep going, get to Washington fast as we can. Got a better idea?"

"No."

Inside the coach the celebration was still in

progress, and if anyone aboard the train had heard the sounds of gunfire out on the platform, no one would have thought twice about them. But eventually the excitement tapered off, and most of the passengers returned to their berths. A few stayed up, singing patriotic songs in drunken voices. Jerry, back in his berth, dozed fitfully, hand under the pillow of his rolled-up coat, where his gun would be if he had managed to retain it. He had refused Colleen's whispered, reluctant offer to loan him her reloaded "derringer", as she called it. He thought, but did not want to admit aloud, that she could probably use it much more effectively.

Sleep was difficult to attain. Each time Jerry began to doze off, he woke up with a start, certain that someone had just intruded on his berth to aim a gun at him. But there were no real intruders, and eventually he slept.

The tenth of April dawned without further serious incident. Berths were turned back into seats, and the day began to drag by, like the other dull days of the trip before it. In Pennsylvania Jerry and Colleen changed trains again, the interior of the new coach being almost indistinguishable from the one they had just left. If anyone on the old train had noticed the loss of one or two passengers during the night, no one so far was making a fuss about it.

One after another the cities and towns of the victorious North crept slowly past the windows of the train. Each town no matter how small was decked out in bright bunting. American flags were everywhere. And it seemed that each settlement had found at least one cannon of some kind with which to fire salutes to passing trains. And everywhere, in every town, the churchbells rang. They seemed to go on ringing from morning to night without interruption. Jerry could not always hear them, he could usually hear nothing but the train itself, but again and again he saw the bells dancing in their little church towers of wood or brick as the train rolled past.

It all proclaimed that the War, after four years of blood and death, was over.

All that Jerry could overhear among the other passengers confirmed it: the fighting had essentially ground to a halt, though still it had not officially or entirely ceased. In scattered places there were still Rebel soldiers in the field, and some of them were still capable of offering resistance. But the Confederate government had fled from Richmond days ago, just before the city fell, dissolving itself in the process; and now that Grant's arch-opponent Lee had surrendered in Virginia, the back of organized resistance had been broken. Lee himself at Appomatox had scotched any idea of a prolonged guerrilla war, by saying to his men that if anything of the kind should happen he would feel bound in honor to give himself up to the Federal authorities as being in violation of the surrender agreement he had signed.

It was necessary to change trains yet once again—for the last time, Colleen and the timetable promised. The next set of cars were more crowded. And, perhaps because they were now getting close to Washington, the talk aboard became ever more political. Jerry had it confirmed for him that Stanton, Secretary of War, was indeed a great power in the land; Stanton's name was mentioned even more than that of Lincoln. And Andrew Johnson, Lincoln's Vice-President, was evidently at best a non-entity. All Jerry could hear of Johnson were a few snickers at the way the man from Tennessee had disgraced himself by taking too much to drink before last month's inauguration ceremonies.

And then at last, on Tuesday the eleventh of April, Jerry realized that the train was passing through Maryland, and Washington was very near.

TEN

The church bells of the city of Washington cried peace and victory with a thousand voices. The great national celebration, begun on Palm Sunday, was continuing. Not only continuing, it seemed to be picking up steam.

The train that would convey Jerry and Colleen Monahan into Washington had halted at a watering-stop, and they, along with a number of other passengers, had got out to stretch their legs, and enjoy the feeling of solid silent earth beneath their feet once more. There was no town here, only three or four houses in the midst of Maryland woods and fields. The train, currently six or eight wooden coaches long, waited with most of its windows open. Birds sang amid spring foliage in a nearby grove; the stationary engine grumbled to itself as it drank from an elevated watering-tank beside the track.

"How far from here to Washington?" Jerry asked in a low voice, squinting ahead along the track. They must be entering the South, he thought; here even the April sun was strong enough to make the distant rails shimmer.

"Just about ten miles. Why?"

Jerry didn't answer right away. He had been evolving a plan in his own mind, and he decided this was the time to put it into effect.

When he spoke again it was to try another question: "Will Stanton have anyone meeting us in Washington?"

The two of them were strolling trackside, now far enough from the other passengers to let Colleen answer plainly. "Don't see how he could. He won't even know what train we're coming in on. No one but he and Peter Watson know he sent you to Missouri, or sent me to warn you and bring you back."

Colleen had previously mentioned Peter Watson a couple of times, saying enough to let Jerry identify the man as some kind of high-level assistant at the War Department. Now he said: "Some of Baker's people obviously know about me now. And about you. Who we are, what train we're on."

"Looks that way."

Jerry had stopped walking, and was standing looking up and down the track. "We leave the train here," he said at last, decisively.

She took his meaning at once. "All right, if you think best. What about our baggage? Just leave it aboard?"

He hesitated. "I don't see how that would help. If anybody's watching us they'll know we've gone, whether we take the bags along or not. And it'll just take us a minute to get the things off the train."

"If Baker still has an agent on the train, and he sees us go?"

"If he follows us, we'll have a chance to see who it is. If he doesn't, he'll lose us." Jerry raised his eyes, looking for branching trackside wires. "There's no station here, no telegraph. He won't be able to send word on ahead."

Colleen nodded. "Then let's get moving."

Within two minutes the two of them had retrieved their bags from the train, and were hiking a path across a muddy field, in the general direction of the nearest house.

"We'll hire a wagon here," Jerry decided. "Or else we'll walk until we find a place where we can hire one."

And after they had found new transportation, Jerry added silently to himself, would come the next step. It might be trickier, but somehow he would accomplish it.

Over the past few hours he had been thinking over his situation as intensely as the hypnotic jolting of the train would allow. In Washington, as Colleen had just confirmed, only Stanton himself, and probably his aide Peter Watson, were able to recognize Jim Lockwood on sight. Jerry's trouble was that he was not Jim Lockwood, and the best he could expect from his first meeting with the Secretary of War was to be thrown into a cell. There would be no prospect of getting out any time soon. *Habeas corpus* had been suspended for several years now, and the leaders of Lincoln's administration seldom hesitated to jail suspected traitors and subversives first and investigate them later. At best, Jerry would certainly be prevented from stationing himself inside Ford's Theater on Friday evening, three days from now.

"Getting off the train is not enough," said Jerry presently, casting a look back to see if they were being followed. "We're going to split up here."

Colleen was taken aback for a moment; this was the first time since she had met Jim Lockwood that he was making a serious effort to take charge. But her male partner's assertion of authority really came as no surprise. She only looked at her companion thoughtfully and did not argue.

Jerry, who had his own argument ready, brought it forth anyway: "Baker's people know the two of us are traveling as husband and wife. Don't they?"

Colleen, still thoughtful, nodded.

"Then it makes sense for us to split up. You go on ahead as fast as you can, in the first wagon we can hire, and make your report to Stanton. I can give you some money for traveling expenses if you need it. I'll get to the War Department my own way, in good time."

"Traveling expenses? I could walk there from here in three hours. And why don't you go first?"

"I may get there first." Jerry, walking quickly, looked back again over his shoulder toward the train. A couple of the leg-stretching passengers were looking after the two deserters but so far no one appeared inclined to follow them. "But I want you to start ahead of me."

"All right." But Colleen was plainly somewhat puzzled and reluctant.

The second of the local houses that they tried proved to have a well-equipped stable, as well as a man eager to carry passengers into the city for a fee. Presently Jerry was waving Colleen on her way.

Now, he thought, would be the ideal time for him to hire a horse, as she had suggested before they parted. If he only knew how to ride one.

Rather than take that risk Jerry walked on, along the road Colleen's driver had taken. Luck was with him; in about ten minutes he overtook a wagonload of produce whose driver had stopped at roadside to mend a broken harness. For a few coins Jerry bought passage, and climbed into the rear of the wagon, where he would be able to lie almost concealed among the burlap bundles of early asparagus, the crates of eggs and chickens. He gave his destination as somewhere near Pennsylvania Avenue—from his schoolboy visit to the modern city he remembered enough of the geography to know that White House and Capitol would both be in that area. That meant that necessarily there would be crowds into which an alien visitor might safely blend.

He could remember someone, somewhere aboard the roaring confusion of trains between here and Chicago, claiming that there were two hundred thousand people in the city of Washington now. The listeners on the train, Jerry remembered now, had seemed impressed by that number.

When the wagon had jolted on for a while—in blessed lack of soot, and relative silence—Jerry raised his head to look about him. And sure enough, there in the hazed distance was the dome of the Capitol at last. For a moment he could almost believe it was the modern city that lay before him.

During the long hours spent staring out the windows of one jolting railroad car after another, Jerry had considered that once he had escaped from Colleen he might hide out in the suburbs until Friday. Either in the actual suburbs of Washington—they had to exist in some form, he thought—or on some nearby farm. But he had never been satisfied with that idea. A stranger who didn't know his way around, particularly one who behaved in any way oddly, would be bound to be conspicuous anywhere in countrified surroundings. In the center of the city, though, say between the White House and Capitol, right in the middle of the crowd, there ought to be more strangers, including foreign diplomats and visitors, than anyone would bother counting. This was, after all, the capital city of a sizable nation.

There would also be plenty of Baker's men in town, Jerry assumed—but the point was that even if some of those men could recognize their fellow secret agent Jim Lockwood, they still wouldn't know Jerry Flint from Adam. And no one would be passing around photographs.

Except, of course, that the two men who had tried to kill him on the train had known whom they were after, and they might be able to recognize him again. One of those men, at least, had fallen from the speeding train and might well be dead now, or at least in no shape for action. And Jerry doubted they could be here already—but if they were, they were. Trumping all other arguments, he, Jerry, was basically a city man, and he trusted the instinct that urged him to seek out a crowd in which to maneuver.

Staying low in the wagon, surrounded by the bundles of asparagus and the crated chickens, Jerry didn't see much of the city as it grew up around him. The sound and rhythm of the horse were soothing after days of trains—anything would be soothing after that, he thought. He could hear the gradual increase of the traffic round him, music, human voices, roosters crowing. Once a squad of blue-clad Union cavalry came cantering close past the wagon, the faces of men neither old nor young looking down at him incuriously. Then the cavalry was gone.

It was something of a dirty trick he'd played on Colleen, Jerry mused, leaning back on a sack of produce and watching the formation of spring clouds overhead. He could only hope she'd had no more trouble with Baker's people. At best she would be reporting to Stanton a success that would fail to materialize, and Jerry felt rotten about that. But he considered that he had had no choice. He was committed to serve that tricky snake who called himself Pilgrim, in some plan that Jerry didn't really understand at all. How could Lincoln's life be saved by transmitting a signal, operating a beacon of any kind, at a moment when the fatal bullet was already on the way to its target? And supposing Lincoln's life could be saved in such a way, wouldn't a lot of familiar history necessarily be lost?

The tops of some relatively tall buildings, three

and four stories high, were now coming into sight above the piles of produce that surrounded Jerry. At last the wagon stopped. The farmer's bearded face came into view, as he twisted round from his seat to stare at his passenger in silence. Jerry sat up straight; a quick glimpse of the Capitol dome assured him that he was at least somewhere near the destination he had bargained for.

He scrambled to his feet, handed over another coin as had been agreed, and hopped out of the wagon with his carpetbag. The wagon rolled away. A few passers-by, black and white, cast curious glances at the young man who had thus arrived in their midst, and now stood on the sidewalk dusting himself off. But no one said anything. Surveying the crowd, Jerry saw more blacks here than he had seen anywhere en route; some of them looking happy as if they were high on drugs, others wretched. All of them presently in sight were very poorly dressed.

Jerry hoisted his bag and walked off briskly, joining the flow of pedestrians where it was thickest. Here, he noticed, the sidewalk was made of brick. Washington was quite the metropolis.

He circled around the block, first clockwise and then counterclockwise, making sure to the best of his ability that he was still not being followed. Then, after one false start, he made his way to Pennsylvania Avenue, which as he remembered ran between the Capitol and the White House, which last structure now seemed blocked from view by red-brick office buildings under construction. The Washington Monument came into view, surprising Jerry by being in an obviously unfinished state, much shorter than he remembered it.

His next surprise was the sight of a horse-drawn rail car, carrying a crowd of passengers down the middle of Pennsylvania Avenue. He soon discovered that brick sidewalks were by no means universal here; they had been laid down in a few places, but as in the towns and cities of Illinois, wood or mud prevailed everywhere else. Here too poultry and livestock were in the streets, pigs rooting in the mud.

Above all here in Washington, there were many uniforms, more than anywhere else. Bodies of troops marched or rode horses through the streets, others appeared standing around or joining in the general flow of pedestrian traffic.

Long hours on the cars spent listening to others' conversations had provided Jerry with a great many fragments of information. One pertinent item he had filed away was that Willard's Hotel was the most prestigious place for a traveler to stay in Washington. It stood on Pennsylvania Avenue, no more than a couple of blocks from the White House, just across the street from a large structure called the Armory, and a little over a mile from the Capitol at what appeared to be the other end of Pennsylvania. Standing on the sidewalk outside Willard's now, Jerry considered that if the lobby was any indication the place had to be overcrowded. All the better, from his point of view. He had money—at least Pilgrim had not stinted on that. If he couldn't bribe his way into a room, he couldn't, but he thought that it was worth a try.

A sign outside the hotel boasted that all its rooms were equipped with running water. After five days—or was it six?—of steady railroad travel, that decided matters.

Making his way in to the desk, Jerry learned from a clerk that it was very doubtful that there were any rooms available. But at that point a twenty-dollar gold piece laid unobtrusively on the desk worked wonders. On impulse he scratched his name on the register as Paul Pilgrim, of Springfield, Illinois.

The upper room where Jerry found himself was small, but otherwise luxurious. It did indeed boast running water in a small sink, and a flush toilet in an adjoining private closet, but hot water was something else again; maybe only the luxury suites had that piped in. No great problem for the wealthy guest. A few more coins brought a procession of black men to Jerry's door carrying a portable tub, along with hot kettles and steaming pails. In a few minutes the tub, resting on his thick bedroom carpet, was filled and steaming.

Jerry spent a few moments in unpacking his bag. Then he stripped and shaved and soaked in the hot tub, trying to ease the endless jounce and chatter of rails out of his joints, to remove from his skin the layers of grease and grime and soot.

Out of the tub and dressed in clean, if wrinkled clothing, he made arrangements with the porter concerning laundry. When he went downstairs at last, he remembered to check the local time by a clock in the lobby. Then he carefully, for the first time, reset his watch, opening the face and moving the hands exactly as Pilgrim's video tutorial had directed. Exactly how knowing the exact local time might help him on Friday night, he could not be sure. But he felt better for having made at least a vague commitment to exact timing.

Just off the lobby of Willard's was a magnificent and crowded bar, where Jerry now repaired for a beer. This struck him as the perfect means of sluicing the last of the railroad soot out of his throat. As he enjoyed the first gulp he realized that there was something peculiar about the crowd of men around him; and a moment later he understood what it was. In the whole bar there were, to his initial amazement, no uniforms. Then he read a faded notice on the wall, warning everyone that in Washington liquor service to members of the military was illegal. That was something to keep in mind; it meant that there would have to be a lot of back rooms, somewhere.

After that one cold delicious beer he took himself to dinner, which at Willard's seemed to be a more or less continuous affair; the entrance to the dining room had been busy since he first saw it. Crowds of a density that made Jerry feel secure surrounded him as he sought and obtained a table, and after days of subsistence on what amounted to box lunches, a serious meal improved his morale enormously.

After he had eaten, he strolled through the lobby, wondering if after all he should try a cigar. At last he did buy one and got it lighted. When it went out he was content to chew on it a little—if the enemy who were looking for him now had spent much time observing him on the cars, they might well be convinced that the man they were looking for didn't smoke.

Jerry was restless, unable to stop walking. The lobby soon proved too confining, and he went outside. The cigar was starting to make him queasy now, and he threw it into the muddy street. Judging by appearances, anyone who objected to littering here would be put away as a lunatic.

The crowds on the sidewalk were tending irresistibly in one direction, toward the White House. Jerry wondered why.

Mr. Lincoln was at home again, he heard somebody say. Home from where? he wondered. Oh yes, there had been something about the President visiting the fallen Rebel capital. Richmond, as Jerry recalled, was not very far away.

And now, just over there, a few yards away beyond that high iron fence, Mr. Lincoln was at home. Gradually the impact of that simple statement grew on the visitor. Jerry shuffled forward with the crowd. For the moment his problems were forgotten.

The sun was down now, and the evening cool and misty, like the last part of the day that had gone before. Far down Pennsylvania Avenue to the southeast, the new-looking dome of the Capitol was somehow being illuminated as dusk faded into night. They must, Jerry supposed, be using some kind of gaslights.

Earlier he had been able to catch an occasional glimpse of the unmistakable White House. And now as he drew closer he could see, just ahead,

what must be part of the grounds behind an iron
fence. For the moment the building itself remained
out of sight behind a gray bulk of stone; when
Jerry got close enough to read the sign in the faint
gaslight of the street lamps this stone mass turned
out to be the Treasury Department. Jerry couldn't
remember whether the Treasury building had been
standing here or not when he had visited this city
as a schoolboy in the nineteen-seventies.

And now the President's House itself was coming into view, considerably smaller than Jerry's
twentieth-century memories proclaimed it, and
more isolated in its park-like grounds. The crowd
was flowing slowly and spontaneously toward it.
Some of the people walking toward their President's house were carrying lighted candles, Jerry
saw now, as if this were some vigil of protest
organized in the late twentieth-century. But the
mood tonight was not protest, it was one of quiet
rejoicing. Gates in the iron fence stood open, and
guards, both military and civilian, stood by, letting
the people in. A crowd was gathering freely on the
north lawn; and the nonchalant ease with which
this was allowed sent something like a shock of
horror through Jerry.

A number of people around him were singing
now, singing softly and joyfully, groups of them
working away on different songs, none of which he
could recognize. Only now did he gradually become aware of how high a proportion of black
people there were in this particular crowd. In a
way the blacks were difficult to see, making only a
shadowy part of the throng, ever ready to move

aside, to disappear when jostled. But they were there, ineluctably.

Lighted candles had been placed in many of the windows of the White House too, as if this gathering on the lawn had been anticipated or invited. And now there was a murmuring in the crowd. Directly over the north entrance—Jerry was sure the entryway he saw now was a simpler construction than the one he remembered seeing in his own century—a light of extra brightness appeared in a window, the exactly central window on the upper floor. The glow of a lamp held there illuminated the faces of the crowd below.

And now the window was being swung open to the nation and the night. There were people standing just inside, in what appeared to be a hallway. Someone's arm held the kerosene lamp up higher, and now a murmur of applause ascended through the night from the crowd below.

Abraham Lincoln, holding some papers in his hand, was standing in the window, in the bright lamplight. There could be no mistake about who he was.

Jerry, aware presently of a strange sensation in his lungs and ears, realized presently that he had suspended breathing. It needed almost a conscious effort to start the process up again. Meanwhile across the surface of his mind there flowed the memory of how as a child, visiting Disneyland, he had sat between his parents watching the robot Lincoln there. That robot was a thing of plastic and metal and electronics that stood up from a chair, facing the tourist audience, and with occasional lifelike movements of arms and head, a

natural-seeming shifting of its weight, delivered a
speech of Lincoln's words in a recorded voice—
whose voice? Yes, that of the actor Royal Dano.

At moments this evening's experience was ee-
rily similar. "We meet this evening," the tall man
in the window began—and then he had to pause
for a moment while the arm beside him adjusted
the position of the lamp, so he could read his
speech. Lincoln was wearing reading glasses,
whereas the robot had not. Dano's voice in the
character of Lincoln, Jerry decided now, had been
very much like the real thing, high and clear, with
a kind of rustic accent. Lincoln continued: "Not in
sorrow, but in gladness of heart."

Another murmur, almost the start of a cheer,
ran through the crowd, there was some jostling for
position, and Jerry missed the next words. For a
short time the President's voice dropped below
audibility.

The next words that Jerry was able to hear
clearly were: "Unlike the case of a war between
independent nations, there is no authorized organ
for us to treat with. No one man has the authority
to give up the rebellion for any other man. We
simply must begin with, and mold from, disorga-
nized and discordant elements. Nor is it a small
embarrassment that we, the loyal people, differ
among ourselves as to the mode, manner, and
means of Reconstruction."

Jerry was trying to work his way forward through
the crowd, in an effort to hear better; it wasn't
easy, for a lot of other people were doing the same
thing, and the bodies toward the front, almost
under the overhanging portico, were closely packed.

Around him there were murmurings: not of approval of what the President was saying, nor of disagreement either. Actually it sounded rather like the beginning of inattention. So far the President was not giving these people what they wanted tonight; what they had come here this evening to get, whatever that was.

Now he was talking about Louisiana. "Some twelve thousand voters in the heretofore slave state of Louisiana have sworn allegiance to the Union, assumed to be the rightful political power of the state, held elections, organized a state government, adopted a free-state constitution, giving the benefit of public schools equally to black and white and empowering the Legislature to confer the elective franchise upon the colored man. Their Legislature has already voted to ratify the Constitutional amendment recently passed by Congress, abolishing slavery throughout the nation. These twelve thousand persons are thus fully committed to the Union, and to perpetual freedom in the state—committed to the very things, and nearly all the things, the nation wants—and they ask the nation's recognition and its assistance to make good their committal."

Lincoln's audience this evening approved of him in general, and they wished him well. But he was losing them as an audience, paragraph by reasoned paragraph of his speech. It was dull business that he had written out to read to them tonight, not words of triumph or inspiration. Urgent business, doubtless, but dull. Tonight it was enough for almost everyone but him to savor victory. The war at last was over.

Now the President's voice was coming through clearly again. He was saying something about very intelligent blacks, including the former slaves who had fought in the Union ranks, being allowed to vote.

There was grumbling in the crowd at that. "Damned radical after all!" was one of the comments Jerry heard near him. "Democrats were right. He'll have the niggers voting in the next election. Voting straight Republican."

ELEVEN

On the morning of Wednesday, April twelfth, Jerry awoke from a confused dream in a state of disoriented terror. He lay for an indeterminate time staring at the white plastered ceiling above him before he could recognize it as that of his room in Willard's, and remember how he had come to be here lying under it.

Next he tried to gather his thoughts, to sort out the dream he had just experienced from the hardly less probable reality of the last few days. In his dream he had been somehow forced to play the part of a gate-guard at the White House. He knew he was only playing the part, because the job was not properly his and at any moment his false position was likely to be discovered. Worse than that, he could see that the assassins were already approaching, a horde of them on horseback, moving

147

in a compact mass like the Union cavalry he had seen in the streets.

Jerry ran forward, trying his best to block the killers' entry, but there was no gate in the iron fence for him to close, only a great gaping gap with broken hinges hanging at the sides. The mounted men ignored Jerry's feeble efforts to hinder them and charged on past, raising sabers and carbines as they swept on to kill Lincoln, who was standing in the White House window holding an anachronistic flashlight.

Now, as Jerry lay in bed regarding one of Willard's plastered ceilings, and listening to the rumble of wagon-traffic in the street outside, the dream-terror gradually faded into a very conscious horror at the truth. In this earlier and in some ways so much more innocent version of America, the President appeared to be readily accessible to any enemy. It was unbelievable to Jerry, raised on the idea of celebrities as casual targets, that the man had already survived more than four years in office in this bitterly divided country.

Someone in the restaurant last night had been talking about Lincoln's customary bodyguard, a fanatically devoted friend of his from Illinois named Ward Lamon, who was apparently of gigantic strength and went armed to the teeth day and night. Jerry supposed such a watchdog might have had a great deal to do with Lincoln's survival up till now. But another of the people in the restaurant had commented that Lamon had just been dispatched by Lincoln on some confidential mission. That, Jerry supposed, was going to make things easier for John Wilkes Booth on Friday night. And

perhaps the absence of such a protector would
make things simpler for Jerry too. At least he
could hope.

And at least he had the name of the assassin—
John Wilkes Booth. He could have remembered
that even if Pilgrim had not reminded him. He
could remember too that Booth had been—or was—
an actor.

The trouble was that last night almost anyone,
with only a minimum of luck, would have been
able to work his way to within a few feet of a
well-lighted and helpless Presidential target. Jerry
had no idea where Booth was at this moment on
Wednesday morning. But if the murderous actor
had been in town last night, he had missed a great
opportunity.

And Jerry had to stop him Friday, or else . . .
but the old doubts arose again. Why should he,
Jerry, trust Pilgrim's assessment of the situation?
Pilgrim had already tricked him at least once, and
rather viciously.

Easy enough to say that he ought not to trust
Pilgrim, but what was he going to do instead? Walk
into a police station and tell them he'd been kidnapped from the twentieth century? Or settle down
here to spend his life—probably a short, unhealthy
one—as a petroleum salesman?

The bottom line for Jerry at the moment was
that he was following Pilgrim's orders because he
really had very little choice. He would at least
pretend to go along with Pilgrim's plan, until some
reason to do otherwise, some better chance of
getting home, presented itself.

Thoughtfully Jerry got up, dressed himself in

clean clothes—his laundry had been returned on schedule—and descended to the lobby. The ground level of the hotel was as crowded as it had been yesterday, and no one appeared to be ready to take time out from his own affairs to pay any attention to an out-of-town businessman named Paul Pilgrim, of blessedly nondescript appearance.

Looking at the throngs milling before him, he could see that there might be many others who would be considered more interesting than himself. For a moment he wondered if there might be any other time travelers on the scene. There were uniforms in plenty, of course, but still civilian clothes predominated. According to the jokes Jerry had overheard yesterday in the barbershop and the bar, seekers of political office were continually swarming into Washington from all across the nation, the eternal bane of the President in particular, and of everyone else in government who had in some degree the power to hand out patronage. The federal government of 1865 might be small and primitive by the standards of Jerry's time, but no doubt it was huge and bloated by the prewar standards that these people around him could remember. Jerry suspected that civil service examinations did not exist in this world, and that the opportunities for enrichment at public expense were tremendous.

Over breakfast—it was huge, and very good; there seemed to be no lesser kind of meal obtainable at Willard's—Jerry turned his mind to practical matters. As he visualized the situation, getting into the theater Friday evening was only the start of what he had to do. He would have to be as close to Lincoln as possible, preferably standing or sitting right beside him when the assassin approached. Obviously there were considerable difficulties. And the more Jerry thought about them, the larger those difficulties loomed.

For one thing, other people might be approaching this accessible President all the time, and how was Jerry supposed to recognize Booth when he saw him? At this moment he had not the faintest idea of what the man looked like. Other questions popped up in bewildering numbers, as soon as he began to consider the situation seriously. Was Lincoln going to be accompanied to the theater by any bodyguard at all? Evidently not by the formidable Lamon, and probably not by any competent substitute. But there might be someone on the job, someone who would interfere with Jerry's effort to get close to the President, even while failing to stop Booth.

Presumably there would be other people in the President's theater party too. His wife, doubtless. What was the old sick joke? Oh yes: *Besides that, Mrs. Lincoln, how did you like the play?*

But who else would be there? And what was the general layout of the theater? And where was the President going to sit? Hadn't Pilgrim's recorded briefing mentioned a box seat?

This was Wednesday morning, which when Jerry thought about it was none too soon to start finding out the answers. Maybe he would get another briefing from Pilgrim before he was expected to go into action, but maybe he wouldn't.

Immediately after finishing his breakfast, Jerry stopped at the desk for directions to Ford's Theater. Relieved to find how near it was, he started out on foot, picking his way across muddy intersections where no one had yet thought to install traffic signals. Turning off Pennsylvania, he walked five blocks east on E Street to Tenth, then half a block north. The theater was there, on the east side of the street.

There was no marquee or other sign projecting over the sidewalk, only a tall, wide front of red brick containing five arched doorways at ground level. There were also five windows in each of the next two stories above. Smaller buildings crowded up close against Ford's on either side, and none of the structures looked more than a few years old.

Jerry approached the theater more closely. On the front wall posters advertised the current show, OUR AMERICAN COUSIN, starring Laura Keene. A additional strip of pasted paper reminded passers-by that the performance of Friday, April fourteenth, would be the last.

There was nothing to be gained by waiting around out here on the sidewalk. Jerry squared his shoulders, ran through once more in his mind the story he had decided on, and started testing the five front doors of the theater to see if any of them were open.

The second door from the right proved to be unlocked. He walked through it into a dim lobby. No lamps were lit, and, after he had closed the front door behind him, the only daylight entered here indirectly, from a window inside a small office at one side. Men's voices, low-key and faint, were coming from the direction of that office. Jerry had opened and closed the street door quietly, and he thought it probable that no one in the office had heard him come in.

Ahead of him a dark stairway led up into heavy gloom. He badly wanted to see the layout of the theater, and decided to take a chance. If he should be discovered wandering about inside, he had his story ready.

From the top of the broad, carpeted stairs he emerged into the relatively lighter gloom of a large auditorium. He was standing now in a large, curving balcony, looking at a stage directly ahead of him where two small gaslights flamed, providing the only illumination in all the great space of the theater's interior. Jerry moved forward slowly, until he could lean his hands on the railing at the front of the balcony. Now, where in all this vast space was Lincoln going to sit?

Probably in a box seat, for greater privacy. From where Jerry stood he could see eight box seats, four right and four left, four high and four low, all of them directly overlooking the half of the stage nearest the audience.

On Jerry's left as he faced the stage, a man's head and shoulder suddenly appeared, leaning out over the railing of the highest and farthest box on that side. In a moment the head and shoulder were joined by a beckoning arm. The man, who obviously wanted Jerry to come to him, bore a strong resemblance to—

Anger, relief, and hope rising in him together, Jerry pushed off from the railing and strode rapidly to his left along the curving front of the balcony. He was headed toward a door—when he looked for it he could see it—that must give access to the upper boxes on that side. In a moment he had pulled the door open and was groping his way forward through a darkened little vestibule.

"Shut the door behind you," whispered Pilgrim's voice from somewhere very close ahead. Then Jerry could see the man standing in a small doorway that led directly into the box seat closest to the rear of the stage, the same one he had been waving from. The two gas lamps set above the stage shone in past heavy red curtain to half-illuminate the compartment. Jerry moved forward silently.

"Have a seat," Pilgrim, wearing a twentieth-century shirt and khaki pants, pushed a small chair toward Jerry with his foot. Then, sighing as if he were tired, he retreated to let himself down again in the chair from which he had waved to Jerry. He added: "I had hopes that you would show up here, at some time before the big event. We need to talk. And here, at this hour, is an ideal spot."

Jerry considered several swear words, and then rejected all of them as a waste of breath. He kept his own voice low. "We need more than that. We need for you to get me out of here and back where I belong. I didn't ask to be—"

Pilgrim raised a thick hand, gently gesturing. "In good time, in good time, you may register your complaints about my conduct. You have a legitimate grievance; but others involved in this situation have more reason than you to complain of being treated unfairly."

"Including you, I suppose?"

"Forget about me—for the moment. Later I

may want to talk about myself. For now, what about Mr. Lincoln?"

"What about him? He was dead and buried a century before I was born, and it wasn't my fault what happened to him."

"Not quite a century—but it wasn't your fault. I agree. Not up until now. But what happens Friday night will be your fault. If you fail deliberately."

For a moment Jerry could find no words. In the effort he made a whispered sputtering. "Fail? *Fail?* I didn't sign up to do anything here. You kidnapped me here and then started giving me orders. Recorded orders. Garbled lectures from a talking watch. Guessing games and a disappearing act on a train. Why should I—" Jerry paused, quietly strangling on his anger.

"Nevertheless." Pilgrim, who had listened with an air of attentive sympathy, rubbed his forehead and stared out into the gaslight, which came between the dull red curtains of the box to turn his face and hairy forearms faintly orange and yellow. From the position he had taken he could see most of the interior of the theater, but it would be very difficult for anyone outside the box to see him, unless he leaned farther forward in his chair.

He went on: "Nevertheless, you are here now, and what happens to Mr. Lincoln now depends on you. There is information, vital information, I must try to give you while I can. My time is limited here, as it was on the train. I can sympathize with your anger; in your place I should be angry too. After matters are decided on Friday night I can bring you home, and I will do so—if all goes well. Before then I cannot. Now, will you listen to me?"

"I'm listening. It better be good."

"It is good. It is better than you think. To begin with, you have inherent powers of a rare kind, that you have hardly begun to realize as yet."

"Sure. And where did I get these powers from?"

"They are usually inherited. Your father—I understand that he disappeared early in your childhood—was probably a timewalker."

Jerry said nothing. He had come to a stop.

Pilgrim was watching him, perhaps with understanding. Pilgrim said: "Inherited. And danger calls them forth. Not ordinary danger, even of the degree that you confronted on the train. It might be more accurate to say that only death itself can activate them."

Jerry was silent, his long-nursed anger slowly quenching in an inner chill. "You mean . . ."

"You have spoken of your powers to Jan Chen. But we were practically sure you had them, even before we set out to recruit you."

Twice Jerry began to say something, and each time reconsidered. At last he said, in an altered voice: "You mean the time I ran into the burning house, when I was a kid."

"I mean exactly that. I can only approximate those powers mechanically. Perhaps I can help you by augmenting them, in a way. But without your help I have no chance of doing what must be done here Friday night. You, with my help, can do it. You can save Mr. Lincoln, if you will."

Jerry was silent for a few moments. He had the feeling he was losing the argument, had lost it already, even before his cry for justice had been fairly heard. "You've tricked me once already," he said finally. "Why should I believe anything you tell me now?"

Pilgrim gave him a hard look. "I tell you you are going to stay here, trapped in this century, unless you help Mr. Lincoln. Do you have any difficulty in believing that?"

"You bastard."

The swarthy man accepted the insult calmly. "I have been called much worse than that. You can spend the remainder of your life here, as I say. Forget about being a computer engineer, forget a great many other things as well. Or, you can do what I ask of you Friday night—and then return to your own time, with your future education financed as we had agreed. Not to mention the feeling of a job well done."

Jerry shifted in his chair. "You think you can manipulate anyone."

"I usually have fair success." It was said modestly.

"I think I just might knock your teeth down your throat. That would be a job well done."

"No." Pilgrim's answer was mild but prompt. "I will not tolerate a physical assault, especially by someone as well-trained as yourself. I make allowances for your anger in being tricked into this expedition—but I will not go that far in making allowances. By the way, that little skirmish on the train was well fought, if perhaps a touch too boldly; I was afraid that we were going to lose you there." Pilgrim was leaning back in his chair, quite relaxed, arms folded, watching Jerry. Everything in his attitude said very convincingly that his teeth were not subject to any knocking that Jerry might attempt.

"You were watching me on the train?"

"It is much easier to *watch* from another time-frame than it is to interfere. Thus, your re-establishment in this one, not to mention my bastardly schemes, became necessary to help Mr. Lincoln. I had to find some way to bring your rare inherent powers into play."

"Oh yeah, my rare inherent powers. I had almost forgotten. Tell me about those."

"I shall try." For a moment Pilgrim looked almost humble. "You have seen that time can be manipulated. That we can sometimes travel through it, if you will. Some people, one in a million, can do something similar without the aid of technology— just as some are lightning calculators who on their good days can emulate the performance of a computer. You are one such. At the vital moment on Friday evening you ought to have more than one swing at the ball."

"What's that mean?"

"You will be able to back up, a matter of a few seconds or a minute, and start over."

"I will?"

"At least once, perhaps as many as three times. I hope no more than that; it is possible to get caught up in something like a closed programming loop."

"You're saying if I fail, I'll—I'll somehow be able to try again?"

"That is my fond hope. And the ability may save us all. You see, Jerry, there are usually great, and often prohibitive, paradoxes involved in any attempt to manipulate the past. Sometimes the difficulty can be overcome by making an abstract of the past, and manipulating that—but there are reasons why that approach is ruled out in this case. There is only one timeline, one universe, one past, and we must live with it, or try to change it at our peril."

"Why do we have to try to change it?"

Pilgrim ignored the question. He said in a business-like way: "You came here to this theater today to scout the ground, did you not? With a view to going along with my plan on Friday night?"

"Yes. All right, I admit I did that. I couldn't see anything else to do."

"A courageous and logical decision. Now." Pilgrim pointed straight out across the stage. "The box directly opposite, the counterpart of this one on the right-hand side, is the Presidential box where Lincoln will sit on Friday night. At this moment on Wednesday, no one in this city but you and I, not even Lincoln himself, knows that he is going to decide to attend the theater on Good Friday. But he will attend; unless of course you should be so foolish as to warn him. That would defeat all our plans utterly."

"All *your* plans. My only plan is to go home."

"I am afraid such a warning would defeat that modest ambition also."

"Huh. The talking watch seemed to be trying to explain something along that line. But I'm not sure I got the message. A lot of it was too noisy for me to understand."

"The noise of paradox, my friend. I am not going to attempt to explain the theory of time-travel and of paradoxes to you now. But the simple difficulty in transmitting a message is as nothing to the problems that would ensue were I to attempt to interfere directly in the matter of the attack upon Mr. Lincoln. Without, that is, the beacon signal that you will transmit to me as guidance. You still have your watch, I trust—? Good. History must be allowed to run smoothly in its time-worn bed."

"Then exactly what do you plan to do to help him? Lincoln?"

"Save him from being shot. On Friday evening, unless we interfere, John Wilkes Booth will enter the vestibule leading to the Presidential box yonder, across the stage. After blocking the vestibule door behind him to prevent interference, he will quietly step into the box itself, so quietly that none of the four occupants will at first turn around.

"He will shoot Lincoln in the back of the head, wounding the President fatally. Then Booth will leap from that box to the stage, breaking his leg in the process. Still he will manage to hobble to his horse out in the alley and escape."

Jerry looked. "I don't wonder he breaks his leg. Isn't it about twelve feet?"

"It is. I must warn you now not to underestimate Booth as a physical opponent. He is a good rider, an excellent shot and swordsman, and famed for his athletic feats on stage. He would not break his leg were it not for the fact that one of his spurs catches on a flag."

"Hooray for Booth."

"I am pleased that you are willing to rise to the challenge posed by such a worthy opponent."

"That's only because I haven't discovered a choice yet. Suppose I get within three meters of Lincoln at the fatal moment, and I do send the beacon signal you want. What do you do then?"

"Leave that to me."

"I expected you to say that. Anyway, suppose we somehow do save Lincoln. Isn't that going to turn history out of its bed rather drastically?"

"There are limits on what I am allowed to explain to you now."

"Very convenient."

"On the contrary. But it is so." Pilgrim once again became practical. "On Friday night no one will occupy this box where we sit now. Perhaps I will be able to establish here an observation post. In one way or another I will be watching events closely. But I *cannot* interfere until you, who are now an established member of this time-frame, trigger the beacon for me."

"I bet."

If Pilgrim was perturbed by his agent's lack of enthusiasm he gave no sign, but pressed on. "Remember the white door that you opened to enter the vestibule outside these boxes. There is a corresponding door on the other side of the theater, through which Booth must pass on his way to destiny. When he has passed through that door, he will immediately block it against outside interference. You must pass through that doorway also, before he barricades it."

"How am I supposed to do that?"

"It is up to you to find a way. You might consider concealing yourself in the Presidential box ahead of time, or in the darkened vestibule just behind. But I do not think that approach would work."

"Thanks for the helpful advice. By the way, who is Colleen Monahan? Is she another of your conscripted agents?"

"Colleen Monahan does not, I devoutly hope, even suspect that I exist. She is Secretary Stanton's agent, as she told you. And Stanton is Lincoln's loyal servant, according to his lights."

"Then I can trust her? Am I going to meet her again?"

"I can only guess at the answers to both questions, insofar as they depend upon the actions of individuals with free will. Certainly you must not trust her with any knowledge of my plans—or of your origins. Beyond that, it is your decision. Any other questions? I am going to have to leave you at any moment."

"Don't run off. Am I going to have a chance to talk to you again, before . . . ?" But Pilgrim was already gone. As on the train, his chair had emptied itself into thin air. Just like that.

A few moments later, feeling somewhat shaken, Jerry groped his way through the dim lobby downstairs and tapped on the half-closed office door. The voices inside, which had been still droning away, broke off as if startled.

A moment later the door was opened wide by a youthful-looking man with blue eyes, curly hair and large sideburns. He said in a salesman's voice: "You startled me, sir. What can we do for you?"

"The door to the street was open—I believe I may want some tickets, for Friday."

"Certainly, sir—how many tickets did you have in mind?"

"It would be a fairly large theater party." Jerry frowned, as if in thought. "I wonder if I might have a look at the auditorium before I decide on a location."

"Well, we have a good selection of seats—seventeen hundred of them to choose from. By the way, I am John Ford, the owner."

"Jeremiah Flint."

"Pleased to meet you, Mr. Flint. You're from out of town?"

"Illinois."

"I see. This is Tom Raybold, who works for me." The second man in the office was standing up now, moving forward to shake hands. His face had something of an odd expression, as if he were afraid that it was going to start hurting at any moment. "Tom, why don't you show Mr. Flint the auditorium?"

"I'll see to it right away."

Jerry, standing in the doorway waiting for Tom Raybold to pull his coat on over his shirtsleeves, looked around the little office. On a table just in front of him was a litter of old playbills and posters, once in ordered stacks, now undergoing entropy. A printed name caught his eye as he glanced down, and he looked more closely. One of the bills, dated in March, advertised the notable actor John Wilkes Booth, starring in THE APOSTATE. Unfortunately there was no picture.

A minute later Jerry was back in the auditorium, getting his second look at the place, this time with the official guidance of Tom Raybold, ticket seller and general executive aid.

Meanwhile another man, a carpenter with a thin

brown mustache and thin short beard, had come into the cavernous space and was banging away at something near the foremost row of seats.

"Ned!" Raybold called out. "Are you going to have that finished before tonight?"

"Reckon I will." The man's voice wheezed with the tones of a lifelong drunk, though Jerry guessed his age at no more than an ill-preserved thirty. He went back to his hammering.

"I understand," said Jerry to Raybold, "that the President comes here sometimes."

"Oh, yes sir, he does indeed. Mr. Lincoln was here in attendance twice just last month, I do believe." And Raybold touched his jaw; he did indeed seem to have some kind of pain on the side of his face, a toothache maybe. Jerry could sympathize. He wondered what the dentists were like here. Did they even have anesthetics? Suddenly he was in abject terror of being trapped.

When he had mastered the pang of fear, and could again be sure that his voice was steady, he asked, over the sound of Ned's hammer: "Will he be here Friday, do you suppose?"

"I've no reason to think so, Mr. Flint. Of course sometimes he and his lady decide to come to the theater on short notice. And then—" The ticket-seller looked suddenly doubtful.

"What is it?"

"Well, you were asking about box seats. And if Mr. Lincoln *were* to come on Friday night, we would be unable to honor tickets for any of the other boxes. Out of respect for the President. We'd give you other tickets in exchange, of course, here on the main floor. Or up there in the front of the dress circle if you'd prefer." He pointed upward.

Jerry craned his neck, trying to see up into the dark first balcony from here. He could use another look at that part of the auditorium. "Might we go up and take a look?"

"Of course."

A minute later, standing again at the front of the first balcony, he surveyed the scene with a slightly more knowledgeable eyes, thanks to Pilgrim's little lecture.

There were cane-bottomed chairs for the audience in this balcony, more than four hundred of them if Raybold had his numbers right. And it appeared that, in accordance with what Pilgrim had said, Booth would be compelled to pass this way to reach the President's box. On the right side of the dress circle, as you faced the stage, a narrow white door at the end of the front aisle gave access to the passageway that would run behind the two upper boxes on that side. That is, assuming the layout on the right was a mirror-image of the box seats Jerry had already visited on the left. Pilgrim had said it was. That white door was the one that Booth was going to block; the one that Jerry was going to have to get through before it closed behind the assassin.

"Do you mind," Jerry asked, "if I take a look into the boxes?"

"Certainly."

They went through the little white door, which opened inward and was unlocked. The lock looked broken; and Jerry could see no ready means of putting up a barricade. Inside was a gloomy passage just like the one on the other side of the stage where Jerry had met Pilgrim. The passage on this side led to the rear of Box 7 and Box 8. Here, as in the boxes on the opposite side, the gaslights over the stage shone in. The furnishings in the boxes were not impressive, except for a crimson sofa at the rear of Box 7.

Tom Raybold explained that when the President attended, and on certain other important occasions, the wooden partition dividing Boxes 7 and 8 was removed, converting them to one unit suitable for a large party. Then more comfortable chairs were brought in, some of them from Mr. Ford's own living quarters upstairs in the building. There was one particular rocking chair in which President Lincoln liked to sit.

There was no reason to prolong the tour any longer. Walking with Raybold back down to the lobby, Jerry announced, as if it had just occurred to him, that he thought he would take just two tickets for Friday night, in the dress circle, and organize his theater party some other time. Privately he decided that a man buying two tickets to any theater was less likely to attract attention that someone buying only one.

Aloud he explained that some of his companions might not be ready to go out for an evening of fun on Good Friday.

"And another thing," he added, "some of my friends have recommended a certain actor to me—John Wilkes Booth. I believe he has played here in the past?"

"Oh yes, certainly, a number of times. Everyone at Ford's knows Mr. Booth—he has his mail sent here sometimes. He's in town now, but he won't be on our stage Friday night. Can't say when he'll be in one of our plays again."

They had reached the ticket office, where there was no problem in buying two seats in the dress circle for Friday night—Jerry got the impression that the performance was a long way from being sold out.

As Raybold was showing him out of the theater, Jerry paused. "I would certainly like to meet Mr. Booth. When my sister back home heard that I was about to visit Washington, and that he might be here, she commissioned me to get his autograph."

Raybold smiled. "He's in town now. Staying at the National Hotel."

TWELVE

A minute later Jerry had got his directions from
Tom Raybold and was on his way again, still traveling on foot. Four blocks east and four blocks
south from Ford's Theater and he had found his
goal, a long, five-story building of pale brick at the
corner of Sixth and Pennsylvania.

The National was not quite as impressive a hotel
as Willard's, or as crowded, but still it was imposing. The air in the lobby was somewhat more
subdued and genteel, and when Jerry entered he
heard Southern accents on every side.

The desk clerk made no difficulty about giving
out the room number of John Wilkes Booth, and
said that yes, the actor happened to be in. Jerry
walked upstairs to find him.

When he stood before the door of the room, he

could hear low voices inside, but was unable to distinguish words. When he tapped on the door they quieted immediately.

Then the door was opened six or eight inches by a man perhaps two or three years older than Jerry, who was immediately reminded of Pilgrim. Not by face, but by attitude. The well-dressed man in the doorway had something of an actor's presence, immediately perceptible. He was not large, except perhaps for his hands. Only an inch or two taller than Jerry, but erect and handsome, with black hair and a black luxurious mustache that contrasted with his pale skin.

"Mr. Booth?"

"Yes sir?" The voice was an actor's too, as suave and practiced as Pilgrim's, and soft if not exactly Southern. His manner was at once arrogant and courtly.

Jerry said: "My name is Jeremiah Flint. I wonder if I might trouble you for an autograph. If now is not a convenient time, I can certainly come back later. The truth is, I'm a visitor in Washington, and my sister rather firmly laid the duty on me of not leaving the city until I had at least tried . . ."

Booth was smiling tolerantly at him now. The door swung halfway open. Now Jerry caught a glimpse of a second occupant of the room, a large, dark-haired, strong-looking youth seated at a table, on which he drummed his fingers as if waiting impatiently for the interruption to be over.

The actor in the doorway said to Jerry: "We must make every effort not to disappoint the ladies—have you something you wish me to sign?"

"Yes I do, Mr. Booth, thank you. A playbill, if

you don't mind." Jerry had picked it up before leaving Ford's, and produced it from his pocket now. "It would give Martha a great deal of pleasure. I know she has seen you on stage several times."

"Then we must do our best not to disappoint her. Step in, please."

Jerry entered the room, and followed Booth across to a small writing table, where the actor picked up a steel-nibbed pen and neatly opened a bottle of ink. Meanwhile the other man remained silently in his chair; when Booth glanced at him he immediately stopped drumming with his fingers.

Jerry watched the signing carefully. Booth's pale, well-manicured hands were large and strong, as if they had been meant for a man with a bigger body. A detail caught Jerry's eye; there were the tattooed initials, JWB, near the branching of the thumb and forefinger on the right hand. A strange decoration for an actor to wear, he thought.

Less than a minute after he had entered the room, Jerry was out in the corridor again, the autographed playbill in hand, and Booth's door closed behind him. Jerry moved a step closer to the door, listening intently for a moment, but heard nothing. He retreated down the corridor.

In the lobby, he hesitated briefly at the door leading to the street, and then turned back. Buying a newspaper, he settled himself to read, in a chair from which he would be able to keep an eye on the main stairway. He was also close enough to the desk to have a good chance of hearing any name callers might ask for.

Jerry didn't think the other man in Booth's room

was an autograph hound, and he certainly hadn't looked like an actor, at least not compared to Booth himself; too sloppy and somehow unkempt, though he had been well dressed. That, in Jerry's mind, left a great many possibilities open, including one in which the powerful-looking youth might be a co-conspirator. There might be other conspirators; damn it, he hadn't had the chance to go into any of that with Pilgrim. The two men up there now might be planning the assassination at this moment.

Jerry decided to hang around, on the chance that he might be able to learn something that would be of help. The fact was that he could think of nothing else to do just now that gave even the slightest promise of being useful.

Jerry lurked with his paper in the lobby for almost an hour before the tall, powerfully built man who had been with Booth appeared, coming downstairs alone. As Jerry had noted earlier, he was clad in respectable clothing, fairly new, but worn with a lack of attention to such things as fastenings and minor stains. Tall and muscular, moving with an unconscious catlike grace, Booth's companion looked neither to right nor left as he passed through the lobby, seeming totally unaware of Jerry watching him as he went straight out the door.

Jerry made himself wait for a count of three. Then he stood up and folded his paper, and, trying not to hurry, followed the other out of the lobby into the street. There was the tall form moving away from him.

Jerry followed. The effort might well, he supposed, be a complete and total waste of time, but still he was determined to give it a try, even though, for all he knew, he was tailing the president of the John Wilkes Booth fan club. Or perhaps a theatrical agent.

The quarry led Jerry up Pennsylvania to Seventh, then north for almost half a mile to H, then quickly around a corner.

Jerry followed without changing his pace, but now he was thinking furiously. Had the tall man realized he was being tailed; was this a ploy to shake his pursuer off, or draw him into a trap? He must have eyes in the back of his head if so, for he had never looked behind him.

Jerry in turn rounded the corner warily, just in time to see his quarry halfway up a long ascent of wooden stairs, about to enter the high first floor of a house of dingy brick. A young woman, a servant of some kind probably, was shaking a dustcloth out of a window on the ground floor of the house.

What now? Jerry could think of no reasonable excuse for stopping, so he kept on walking. He noted as he passed the house that the tall man had gone right in; and he noted the address also: 541 H Street. ROOMS TO LET, said a faded sign in another of the lower windows.

What now? Jerry didn't know. He made his way by a winding route back to his hotel, stopping in a couple of stores on the way to purchase a couple of new collars and shirts. How about a new suit? He could easily afford it. But he swore to himself that he was not going to be in this century long enough to need one.

Re-entering his hotel room after lunch, he half

expected to find Pilgrim lounging there, waiting for him. But there was no one. Jerry stood at the window looking out upon an alien world. Well, Pilgrim had said that communication between time-frames wasn't easy.

Presently Jerry went out again. He spent most of the afternoon walking restlessly through this peculiar world and thinking about it, trying to familiarize himself more thoroughly with the way of life of its inhabitants. Within a few blocks of the house where Lincoln lived he noted some former slave-auction facilities, still identified as such by painted signs, but deserted now. Thank God, no one was still doing that kind of business in the capital. Ignoring a threat of rain, he wandered around the large perimeter of the White House grounds, until he was brought to a halt by the foul-smelling canal along their southern boundary. In the twentieth-century, this area, Jerry seemed to remember, was occupied by a grassy mall.

He stood for a while beside the canal, marveling at the dismal stench of it, and how everyone around him put up with it so stoically. In summer it must be truly remarkable.

Presently he walked along the canal until he could cross it on a footbridge, and went to stand by the unfinished Washington Monument, observing that a kind of stockyard and open air slaughterhouse had been established at its base. Turning east, past grazing sheep, he looked at the red-roofed construction of the Smithsonian Institution, still confined here to one building, like some kind of vast elfin castle. He tried yet again to think of what else he might do to ready himself for Friday evening's confrontation, and he could think of nothing.

For variety, he dined away from Willard's. But shortly after dinner he was back in his room and sound asleep.

THIRTEEN

The next morning, Jerry awoke from a dreamless sleep thinking *this is Thursday, April thirteenth. There will be no Friday the thirteenth this month.*

Only then did he react to the sound that had awakened him, a rough knocking on the door of his room.

It was broad daylight, time he was up anyway. He sat on the edge of his bed, reaching for his pants. "Who is it?" he shouted.

"Porter." The answering voice was muffled.

"Just a second." For a moment he had dared to entertain a foolish hope that it was Pilgrim, come to take him home or at least to bring him lifesaving information. Half-dressed, Jerry shuffled to the door and pulled it open.

As soon as the latch released, a force from outside pushed the door open wide, and sent Jerry staggering back. Two large men in civvies burst into the room. Each of them had Jerry by an arm before he could start to react.

"You're under arrest."

"What for?"

"Shut up." His arms were forced behind his back, and the handcuffs went on his wrists, painfully tight. Miranda rights were a long way in the future.

"At least you could let me get dressed."

They grudgingly agreed with that. One man watched him, glowering, while the other closed the door of the room, and searched. Bedclothes, the garments Jerry hadn't put on yet, the stuff in his closet, all went flying. It was a violent effort but it didn't look all that efficient.

At least, he thought, I've already managed to lose my pistol. But that was a foolish consolation. In this world carrying a firearm was no crime, and the mere presence of one probably wouldn't make anyone suspicious.

He was patted down for weapons, then the cuffs were removed and he was allowed to get dressed before being handcuffed again. As he tucked his watch into its pocket in his vest, he said: "You've got the wrong man."

"No we ain't."

"What's this all about?"

The older man, who had a graying mustache, was doing the talking for the pair. "Just walk out with us quietly, it'll be easier that way."

"Sure. But where're we going? I still don't know what this is all about."

He wasn't going to find out now. As soon as he was dressed they pulled him out into the hall and started down the stairs. One of the men locked Jerry's room behind him, and brought the key along.

On the stairs a couple of passers-by looked at him and his escort curiously. As the three of them were passing swiftly through a corner of the lobby, on the way out a side door, a distraction at the other end of the lobby, near the front desk, turned all eyes in that direction. A wave of talk passed through the lobby.

"It's Grant!"

"General Grant is here!"

So much for the sophistication of the capital, that more or less took the presence of President Lincoln in stride; Jerry got the impression that Grant, the conquering hero, had rarely been seen in town before. What was he doing here now, away from his army? But why not, now that the war was virtually over. And was it possible that the General's presence in the city was going to have any effect on what happened at Ford's tomorrow night?

The only immediate effect on Jerry was that his departure from the hotel was probably noticed by no one at all.

Waiting just outside Willard's side entrance was a dark police wagon, with small windows of heavy steel mesh. Jerry was hustled immediately into it. A moment later the horses were being cursed and beaten into motion, and they were off. He could feel the wagon turn in the general direction of the Capitol.

The younger and larger of the prisoner's two escorts rode with him inside the wagon, and stared at him with heavy suspicion through the entire journey, saying nothing. Jerry responded by looking out the window, wondering how long the sudden emptiness in the pit of his stomach was going to last, how long it would take him to absorb his new reality. Maybe in a month, or even sooner, with the war officially at an end, Stanton—or whoever was having him arrested—would let him out of jail. He could set up selling petroleum, like Win Johnson back in Illinois. He—

Enough of that. He had an appointment he meant to keep at Ford's, tomorrow evening.

Pilgrim might be able to help. *Might.* Jerry had been warned against counting on any help at all from that direction. It was Pilgrim's fault that he was in this mess, and . . .

At this point it didn't really matter whose fault it was.

Jerry was seated on a wooden bench, and there was not much to see through the high windows of the wagon, except for some springtime treetops and the fronts of buildings. The ride took only a few minutes, and when Jerry was hustled out of the conveyance again at the end of it, he was able to catch a quick glimpse of the Capitol dome, quite near at hand.

The wagon had stopped very close beside one of city's many large stone buildings; this one, by its heavily barred windows, was obviously a prison or police station. He noticed that here too, for some reason, his escort preferred to use the side entrance, off the busy street.

Once inside the gloomy fortress, the prisoner was conducted through one locked door after another. He was searched again, by the same men who had arrested him, and everything taken out of his pockets, including of course his money and his watch. His hat, coat, tie, and boots were also confiscated.

Ignoring his protests, the two men silently thrust Jerry into a small solitary cell. The door slammed shut.

Their footsteps in the corridor outside died away. Otherwise there was quiet.

. His cell was lighted by one small window, more like a ventilator, too small for a man to squeeze through even if it had not been barred and positioned just below the eight-foot ceiling. For furniture there was a built-in wooden bench, and under the bench an empty bucket that smelled like what it was, an unsanitized latrine.

Jerry settled himself on the bench, stared at the door that was solid wood except for a small peephole, and waited for what might happen next. He was already convinced that it would be a waste of breath to send screams down the empty corridor outside.

He leaned his head back against the wall, realized it felt damp and slimy, and sat erect again. Presently he closed his eyes. Maybe when he opened them, Pilgrim would be sitting beside him on the bench, ready to give him another pep talk. Pilgrim gave the worst pep talks Jerry had ever heard, but he felt that he could use another one about now. But when Jerry opened his eyes again, he was still alone.

He wondered if the thugs who had arrested him were estimating the value of his watch, maybe arguing over who would get to keep it. Or did they plan to sell it and split the proceeds? Well, there was nothing that Jerry could do about it if they were. Nothing he could do about anything, not until someone opened the door to his cell. Which surely ought to happen soon.

The hours passed slowly in prison. The light from the window changed slightly, gradually, in its quality as the sun, somewhere on the other side of the building, made its unhurried way across the sky. He had until tomorrow night. Tomorrow night. Jerry warned himself to keep his nerve. Stanton—or whoever—couldn't possibly just leave him sitting here until then. Could he?

At a time Jerry judged to be somewhere around mid-afternoon, a jailer at last appeared, carrying a jug of water and two pieces of bread on a tin plate. The man was sullenly unresponsive to all questions, and disappeared again as soon as he had accomplished his delivery. Jerry drank gratefully, then chewed meditatively on the bread, thankful for his good, strong, heavily fluoridated twentieth-century teeth. As if drawn by the scent of food, a couple of mice now appeared in a far corner of the little cell, wriggling their noses. Maybe, their cellmate thought hopefully, the presence of mice was a sign that there would not be rats.

Maybe he was being too quiet, too stoic. When he had finished as much as he could chew of the bread, he went to the door with its half-open peephole and yelled at full volume down the hallway outside. From somewhere out there another series of maniacal yells echoed and mocked his own; evidently he was not, after all, the only prisoner in the building. But there was no other result.

He alternately paced his cell and sat down on the bench to rest. The hours passed. Nothing happened.

—and then Jerry, fallen asleep sitting on the wooden bench, awoke with a start in the darkness when a key rattled loudly in the lock of his cell's door. A moment later, the same two men who had arrested him came in, the younger of the two carrying a lantern.

Without a word of explanation Jerry was jerked to his feet, then hustled out of his cell and down the darkened corridor. The doors of other cells, whether occupied or empty, were all closed. The lantern made a moving, bobbing patch of light.

They took him down another dark stairway. Or maybe it was the same one by which he had been brought in, Jerry could not be sure.

When they had reached what Jerry thought was the ground floor, the two jailers brought him into an office, or at least a room containing some desks and chairs and filing cabinets. There was a notable absence of paperwork for a real office, and the place had a disused air about it. No one else was in the room. The lantern was put down on a desk which had an empty chair behind it, and Jerry was made to stand facing the desk.

On the wide, scarred wooden surface of the desk the things that had been taken from him had been laid out, except for the money, being notable only by its absence. There were Jim Lockwood's hat, and coat, and boots. There was Pilgrim's watch. When Jerry held his breath he was able to hear the timepiece ticking. There was the room key for his hotel, and there were his two theater tickets for tomorrow night.

When he stretched his neck just a little, he could see that the hands of the watch indicated a little after seven. The metal faceplate, though not the glass, had been swung open, as if someone had wondered whether something might be concealed inside.

For almost a minute after their arrival there was no sound in the room except for an occasional belch from one of the jailers, and the soft but substantial ticking of the watch. Presently a door behind the desk opened, and a man stepped through carrying a lighted lamp. He was hatless, dressed in dark, nondescript civilian clothes. In his late thirties, Jerry estimated. Sandy hair and beard. Only a little taller than Jerry but more powerfully built.

"Colonel," said one of the men behind Jerry. It was only a kind of verbal salute, for the sandy-haired one responded to it with a casual gesture of his right hand, after he had set down his lamp beside the lantern on the desk.

Unhurriedly the Colonel seated himself, adjusting both lamp and lantern so that he remained in comparative darkness, while a maximum amount of glare was directed toward the prisoner. The prisoner, accustomed to electric light, might under other circumstances have found laughable this attempt to make him squint.

Then the man behind the desk leaned forward in his chair, putting his blue-gray eyes and sandy whiskers in the light. When he spoke he came straight to the point. "Who're you really workin' for, Lockwood?"

"Sir, whoever you are, my name is Paul Pilgrim. I don't know why these men brought me—"

One of the men who was standing behind Jerry cuffed him on the back of the head, hard enough to make his ears ring. A hard voice behind him said: "Stow that. Give the Colonel a fair answer, or, by God, you'll wish you had."

The Colonel was smiling now, and this time his voice was confidential, almost warm and friendly. "Who're you workin' for?" he repeated. By this time Jerry had no doubt that this was Colonel Lafayette C. Baker. Right now Jerry was ready to settle for Stanton.

Jerry was also close enough to hysteria to imagine that he was able to see the humor in the situation. He had to laugh, and he did.

They let him laugh for a little while, the men standing behind him taking their cue from the appreciative grin on the Colonel's face. Jerry in turn appreciated their tolerance. After a while he got himself under control again and said: "I'm working for myself, if you want to know the truth."

Colonel Baker took his statement in good humor. "By God, ain't it the truth, though? Ain't we all doin' that?" He indulged in a chuckle of his own, then rubbed his bearded chin as if to mime the behavior of a deep thinker. "I'm all for adopt-

ing a philosophical viewpoint in these matters."
His voice had become less countrified, as if adjusting to match Jerry's. "Yes, I'll go along with that."
The Colonel's eyes altered. "Long as you realize,
in turn, I mean to have a little more out of you
than just philosophy."

"Oh, I'll tell you more than that," said Jerry,
not wanting to get hit again. But even as he promised information, he was wondering just what sort
he was going to provide. It certainly wasn't going
to be the truth. There would be no safety for him
in that.

"I know you will, son," said Baker in a kindly
way. "Sometime tonight . . . say, don't I know you
from somewhere? Ever been in San Francisco?"

"No sir."

"How 'bout the army?"

"No."

"Mebbe not. Don't suppose it matters." The
sandy-haired man squinted at Jerry a little longer,
then put out a hand on the desk and pushed most
of Jerry's property, the hat and coat and boots and
valuables, out of his way, toward one side. Then
from the cluttered desktop Baker's hand picked up
another item that Jerry had not noticed until now.
It was, Jerry saw, slightly flexible, long as a rolling
pin and almost as thick. The Colonel's fingers toyed
with this cross between a club and a blackjack,
turning it over, then rolled it gently back and forth
on the worn wooden surface.

Jerry began to wonder whether the special talents Pilgrim had talked about might really save
him if he was killed, or whether he and perhaps
Pilgrim had dreamed them up. Of course he might

come to wish he was dead, long before these people killed him.

The Colonel showed a few yellow teeth. Leering as if it might be the start of a dirty joke, he asked Jerry, "You know a woman calls herself Colleen Monahan?"

Jerry let himself think about that question. "No," he said at last, and wondered how long he was going to be able to stick to that.

"Goddam." The Colonel expressed an abstract kind of wonder, as if at some amazing natural phenomenon. "You're still thinkin' you can tell me lies and not get hurt for it." The man behind the desk marveled at such an attitude, as if he had never encountered any precedent for it. His manner and expression said that he was entering uncharted territory, and he was going to have to think a while before he could determine what best to do about it.

But of course there was only one thing to do about it, really. At last he took the truncheon in hand decisively and stood up and came around from behind the desk. Then he paused, as if suddenly aware that more thinking might be required. And then, meeting the eyes of his two henchmen and making a gesture, he silently indicated that he wanted them out of the room.

"Sir?" the one with the gray mustache questioned, doubtfully.

"Go on. I'll yell if I need help." And then without warning Baker swung his little club in a hard overhand stroke.

A perfect street-fighter's move; Jerry had just time to think. He also barely had time to get his arms up into a blocking position, fists clenched, forearms making a deep V, so that neither arm took quite the full force of the weighted weapon. The left arm took most of it, too much, high up near the wrist. Jerry felt first the numbing shock and then the pain; he was sure that a bone must have been broken. He collapsed helplessly to one knee, holding his wrist, eyes half-closed in a grimace of pain. *It's broken*, was all that he could think.

Dimly he was aware that the two henchmen, without further argument, had gone out of the room. Colonel Baker was locking the door behind them. Then he turned back to Jerry, as friendly-looking as ever.

"Now, Son Lockwood. Nobody but me is gonna hear it when you tell me who you and that bitch Monahan are really workin' for. I got my own reasons for confidentiality. Actually I know already, but I want to hear it from you. And I want to hear who else might be on my tail, workin' directly for the same person."

Jerry, gradually becoming able to see and think again, got to his feet. He backed away slowly as Baker advanced on him, gently swinging the club in his right hand.

There wasn't much room in this office to maneuver, forward, back, or sideways. And Jerry's left arm was useless whether it was actually broken or not. He couldn't, he absolutely couldn't, hit or grab or block anything with that arm just now. Not if his life depended on it.

He wasn't going to be able to block another

blow from that club, with either hand. He'd have to dodge instead. And then—

"You can't hide behind that desk, son. You can't hide at all. Know where I'm gonna put the next lick? Right in the kidneys. You'll piss blood for a month or so. And you'll *feel* the next one, too. That last one didn't hurt a-tall."

Jerry moved behind the desk, then out from behind it on the other side. The man was right, there was no use his attempting to hide behind the furniture. He shifted his feet, kicking aside a tobacco-stained little rug to make a smoother footing.

Baker, pleased to see this little preparation for some kind of resistance, was moving forward, supremely confident. "Tell you what, son—"

Jerry's roundhouse kick with the right foot came in horizontally under Baker's guard, at an angle probably unexpectable by any nineteenth-century American street-fighter. The ball of his foot took its target in the ribs. In practice Jerry had seldom kicked any inanimate target as hard as this; he thought from the feel of the impact that he might have broken bone.

Lafe Baker's bulging eyes bulged even more. The round red mouth above the ruddy beard opened wider, in an almost silent O of sheer astonishment.

Jerry stepped forward, shifting his weight, and fired his right hand straight at that bearded jaw. His victim was already slumping back, and down, and the punch connected under the right eye. Jerry could feel a pain of impact in his practice-toughened knuckles. Baker's backward movement accelerated. He hit his head on the side of his own desk as he went down, and his head clanged into the brass halo of the spittoon.

For a moment Jerry hovered over his fallen enemy, resisting the impulse to kick him again; the Colonel would not be getting up during the next five minutes. Baker's head rested against the side of the heavy desk, and the spittoon, half tipped over, made a hard pillow for him. The sandy beard was beginning to marinate in stale tobacco juice. Only an uneven, shuddering breathing showed the man was still alive.

A moment longer Jerry hovered over him indecisively, trying to think. Then he sprang to the desk and began to reclaim his belongings, putting on the clothes and stuffing the other items hastily into his pockets. No use, he thought, trying to find the money. The all-important watch was still ticking away serenely, and he kissed it before he tucked it into his watch pocket and secured the chain. And there, safely in his hands again, were the theater tickets for Friday night.

Now Jerry hesitated briefly once more. Was there something else?

On impulse he crouched over Baker once more, reaching inside the man's coat, coming up with a large, mean-looking revolver. He also discovered and abstracted a fat bunch of keys.

Dropping the keys in his own pocket, Jerry grabbed the Colonel by his collar and dragged him behind the desk where he would be a great deal less conspicuous. Then, with the revolver in his right hand held out of sight behind him, Jerry went to the door. He turned the lock—he found that he could use his left hand a little now, as long as he didn't think about it—and stuck his head out into the badly-lighted hallway.

A ragged black man carrying a mop and bucket went by, carefully seeing nothing. Two white men, leaning against the wall and chewing tobacco, looked at Jerry with real surprise.

Jerry looked back at them as arrogantly as he could and gave them a peremptory motion of his head. "He wants you both in here, right away."

The two of them filed in past Jerry, looking round them uncertainly for the Colonel, and Jerry closed the door on them when they were in. The two had reached a position near the desk by now, and in a moment they were turning around, about to ask him what the hell was going on.

At that point he let them see the revolver. "Just turn back and face the desk, gentlemen. That's it. Stand there. Just like that."

His blood was up, and he was acting with a ruthlessness that almost surprised himself. One after the other he tipped the men's hats forward from their heads onto the desk; one after the other he clubbed their skulls with the revolver barrel. The first victim, he of the gray mustache, sank to the floor at once. The younger man clung to the desktop, struggling against going down, and Jerry hit him again, a little harder this time.

He stuck the gun into his belt; he could hope that under his coat it would not be noticed. Then without looking back he let himself out of the room, and turned down the hallway to the left, in which direction he thought that he had glimpsed an exit. There was the black man with the mop, using it on the floor now, still seeing nothing. The pain in Jerry's left arm had abated to the merely severe, and he thought he might soon have feeling again in the fingertips. At best he was going to have one terrific lump on that forearm.

The back door of the prison was locked, with no latch to turn it open from inside; but one of the keys on Lafe's ring worked, letting Jerry easily out into the night. No one had taken note of his departure. It was still early in the evening, for the street lamps were still lighted.

There was the Capitol, its gaslighted dome glowing against the stars, to give a fugitive his bearings. His recovered watch ticked in his pocket. In a few hours Good Friday was going to begin.

Jerry started walking, anywhere to get away from the vicinity of the prison. One thing was sure, he couldn't go back to the hotel.

FOURTEEN

From now on Baker and his people were going to be hunting Jim Lockwood with all their energy. So would whatever forces Stanton and Colleen Monahan had available—and Stanton had armies at his command if he wanted to deploy them for that purpose. Jerry supposed that damned near everyone in the District of Columbia would be looking for him now, and he had to stay out of sight for approximately twenty-four hours before the play even started at Ford's. The task would be made no easier by the fact that every cent of his money had been taken from him. He swore under his breath, realizing only now that the men he had left unconscious would certainly have had some money in their pockets. Very likely *his* money. Well, it was too late now.

He had eased his left hand into a coat pocket, the better to nurse his throbbing wrist; he moved it again now, slightly, trying to find the easiest position. He was going to need help.

There was Pilgrim, of course. But Pilgrim had given him no active assistance at all up to this point, and Jerry saw no reason to expect that he would do so now. Nor was there any native of this century to whom Jerry could turn for help. He did not even know anyone here, unless he counted his new-made enemy Colleen Monahan . . .

But then Jerry, striding northward away from the prison, came almost to a full stop on the dark wooden sidewalk. It was true that he had formed no alliances or even acquaintances here that might serve him now. But it was not true that he knew no one. There was one man he did know here in Washington, an able and resourceful and determined man who was no friend of Colonel Baker, or Secretary Stanton either. A man whom Jerry had scarcely met, but of whom he nevertheless had certain, deep, and important knowledge. Not very thorough knowledge, true, but in a sense quite profound . . .

It was not yet eight o'clock of a cool April evening when Jerry found himself standing in front of the boarding house on H Street. His first impulse on thinking of John Wilkes Booth had been to go directly to the National Hotel, but he had promptly rejected that idea. Any halfway competent counterintelligence system operating in Washington, including Baker's and/or Stanton's, must have eyes and ears more or less continually present in each of the major hotels. He thought now that had been foolish to try to stay at Willard's when those people were looking for him. Not that he had had a whole lot of choice, but it was surprising that he had gotten away with it as long as he had.

Lights were showing in several windows of the rooming house on H Street. The front of the house was dark at ground level, and so Jerry approached the building from the rear, where a couple of saddled horses were tied at a hitching post. Pausing on a walk of loose planks that ran close beside the house, he was able to look at close range into a lighted kitchen where a woman sat doing something at a table. He tapped on the door.

She was only a girl, really, he saw when she came to investigate his knocking. Dark-haired, not bad looking, no more than seventeen or eighteen. She had jumped up eagerly enough to answer the door, but looked warily at the strange man when she saw him. Evidently someone else had been expected.

"What do you want?" she asked in a cautious voice.

Jerry took off his hat, letting the girl get an unshaded look at what he hoped was an innocent, trustworthy face. He said urgently: "I want to talk to John Wilkes Booth. You must help me, it's very important."

Her caution increased, her face becoming mask-like. "No one by that name lives here."

An older woman, small and rather grim-looking, came into the kitchen from the front of the house. Her lined face still bore a notable resemblance to the girl's. "What's going on, Annie?"

The girl turned with relief. "Ma, this man says he wants Wilkes Booth."

Jerry was leaning against the doorframe, letting his weariness and the signs of prison show. He appealed to them both: "Can you let me come in and sit down? I've been hurt." He raised his left forearm slightly, easing his hand out of the coat pocket, then let it hang down at his side.

The older woman studied him for a moment with shrewd calculating eyes. "Come in, then. Annie, get the gentleman a cup of water."

"Thank you, ma'am."

Seated at the kitchen table, Jerry could hear other voices, men's voices, coming from the front of the house, where they must be sitting talking in the dark. Annie put a tin cup of water on the table in front of him, and he drank from it thirstily.

Now another young woman appeared from the direction of the front room, to look briefly into the kitchen before retreating. She was succeeded in the doorway by a figure that Jerry somehow recognized—yes, it was the whiskey-marinated carpenter from Ford's. Tom Raybold in the auditorium had called this man Ned. The next face in the parade was even more quickly recognizable. It was that of the powerful, sullenly handsome youth who had been visiting Booth in his hotel.

This man shouldered his way forward into the kitchen, to stand close beside the table looking down at Jerry. His voice when he spoke to the visitor was southern-soft, though not as friendly as that of Colonel Baker: "Who are you? And why should you think that Wilkes Booth is here?"

"My name is Jeremiah Flint. I thought he came here sometimes."

"And if he did?"

"I have reason to think—to think that Mr. Booth might be disposed to help a gentleman who has got himself into some serious trouble with the abolitionists who are now in control of this city."

There was a silence in the kitchen. But it was not a shocked silence, Jerry thought. Not for nothing he had spent those long days and nights on railroad cars, listening to arguments among people of every shade of political persuasion.

The tall young man leaned forward suddenly, a move not exactly menacing but still pantherish, shot out a hand and extracted the pistol from Jerry's belt. "You won't be needin' that in here," he explained mildly.

"I trust I won't." Jerry spoke just as softly. He tried to smile. "I don't believe I find myself among the friends of Old Abe at the moment."

"There are no friends of tyrants here."

This was in a new voice, resonant and easy to remember. Jerry turned to face the doorway. There was the actor himself, elegantly dressed, standing with a hand on each side of the frame and regarding Jerry with a slight frown. Booth went on: "I believe I have encountered you somewhere before, sir."

"Jeremiah Flint of Texas, Mr. Booth. We met at your hotel yesterday, and you were good enough to autograph a playbill for my sister."

"Ah yes."

"I might have spoken to you of other matters then, but you were not alone; you were engaged

with this gentleman, whose identity I did not know."
Jerry nodded at the tall youth beside him. "Since
then I have been arrested. Early this morning, at
my own hotel, Willard's. Today I was kept all day
in prison. Beginning this evening I was questioned
by someone I believe to be Colonel Lafayette C.
Baker himself. I managed to get away, but not
without giving and receiving some slight damage."
He raised his left arm gingerly. When the sleeve
fell back a little, an empurpled lump the size of a
small egg showed on the side of his wrist. He
could feel another, smaller, on the back of his
head, and he was ready to present it as additional
evidence if needed.

"How could you get away?" This, in a disbeliev-
ing voice, came from the older woman.

Jerry turned to her with what he hoped was a
frank and open gaze. "It sounds incredible, I know.
They—Baker and two of his men—had me in a jail
somewhere near the Capitol. I was brought in
through a side entrance, and when the chance
came I walked out the same way. I have the
feeling that most of the people there did not know
of my presence, or the Colonel's either. I even
had the impression that he himself might have
been in that building secretly. We were quite
apart from the other officers and prisoners there."
He sipped at the cup of water the girl had now put
down in front of him.

"Were you followed here?" the woman demanded
sharply.

"Madam, I am certain that I was not."

"What did they want of you?" Booth asked. He

had folded his arms now, and his eyes were probing at Jerry relentlessly.

"The names of some of my friends in Texas. But
they learned nothing."

"And how did you manage to escape?"

"Baker—if it was he—sent his men out of the
room in which he had begun to ask me questions.
Evidently he hoped to hear from me something
that he wanted to keep secret even from his own
men. He thought he had already—disabled me."
Jerry raised his left arm gingerly. "But it turned
out he had not."

Something, a spontaneous mixture of envy, admiration, and despair, blazed for a moment in
Booth's face; but he masked his feelings quickly
and stood silent, thinking.

"I had heard," the older woman said, "that Lafe
Baker was currently in New York."

"What," asked Booth, "did this interrogator look
like?" When Jerry had described the man behind
the desk, the actor commented thoughtfully: "That
does sound like Lafe Baker himself. But I too had
heard that he was in New York." He paused,
creating a moment full of stage presence and effect. "So you are from Texas, Mr. Flint. May I
ask, without probing into any private matters, what
you are doing now in Washington?"

Jerry took a deep breath. He had anticipated
this question, but still he thought his answer over
carefully before he gave it. He was reasonably
sure that these people did not really believe his
story—yet. Much was going to depend upon his
answer, and he was trying to remember something
that Jan Chen had told him.

"I consider myself," he answered finally, "a soldier of the Confederacy, seeking upon my own responsibility to find what duty I can do here for my cause." And he dug in the side pocket of his coat—slowly and carefully, with the strong lad and Booth both watching—and brought out a heavy bunch of keys.

Jerry tossed them with a jingling thud onto the middle of the kitchen table. "Those," he added, "are Lafe Baker's. I have not examined them closely, but they may bear some evidence of ownership."

The strong man grabbed up the keys, then stood holding them in his hand, not knowing what to do next. Booth scarcely looked at the keys. His lips had parted slightly when he heard Jerry's answer. Again envy and admiration crossed the actor's face, this time mingled with awe rather than despair; it was as if he had just heard Revelation. Again the expression did not appear to have been calculated. He stood silent, staring at Jerry and making new assessments.

"Or else," said the older woman to Jerry, in a still-suspicious voice, "you are one of Pinkerton's agents. Or—" She had begun now to look closely at the keys in the young man's hand, and something about them evidently proved convincing. Her tone of accusation faltered.

"Pinkerton," said Booth sharply, "has been in New Orleans for a long time, out of the business more than a year. No, look at Mr. Flint's injury. I think he is an authentic hero for having achieved such an escape, and we cannot refuse to help him." He became courtly again. "Introductions have been delayed, but let us have them now. Mr.

Flint, this is Mrs. Surrat, the kindly landlady of this establishment. And this is her lovely daughter, Anna." Anna, flustered, tried to curtsy.

Next Booth nodded toward the powerful young man. "My good friend and associate, Lewis Paine."

Jerry's good right hand was almost crushed in a silent handshake from the youth. Meanwhile Booth went on: "And my acquaintance Mr. Ned Spangler, who works as a sceneshifter at Ford's. Mrs. Surrat, Anna—Mr. Flint deserves the best of hospitality. What is there to eat?"

"He's welcome to a supper." Mrs. Surrat began to bestir herself, then paused. "But he can't hide here. There's no place for him to sleep."

Booth started to frown, then appeared to be amused. "Very well, I'll find another place for him. Lewis, show the gentleman where he can wash up."

"Right, Cap'n."

Ten minutes later Jerry, having removed some of the scum of prison from his face and hands, was back at the table in the kitchen, whose windows were now securely curtained against any observation from outside. Pork chops and greens and fried potatoes were put before him on a tin plate, and he needed little urging to dig in. Paine leaned in a doorway, heavy arms folded, watching Jerry eat; Spangler and young Anna had both disappeared. Booth, an enameled cup of steaming coffee in front of him, rose from the chair opposite Jerry's to welcome him back.

"I suppose—" Booth began, then turned his head sharply, listening; held up a hand for silence.

Mrs. Surrat, at the sink, glanced at him but then went on rattling pans in water. Evidently the landlady here was used to conspiratorial maneuvers.

"Who was that?" Booth asked in a low voice of Spangler, who was just coming in from the front room.

"Only Weichmann." Ned stood blinkly at them all stupidly; he had brought fresh whiskey fumes into the kitchen with him.

"Who's Weichmann?" Jerry asked.

"A young War Department clerk," Booth informed him in low voice, turning back to face the table, "who boards here. I fear his sympathies are not with us, though he's an old friend of the landlady's son."

Mrs. Surrat turned from the sink, drying her hands on a towel, evidently willing to leave the dishes soaking until tomorrow when presumably there would be kitchen help. She looked at Jerry, and for the first time favored him with a trace of a smile. "You will wish to get out of Washington, I suppose."

"Yes. When I am satisfied that . . . that there is nothing more for me to do here, yes." Jerry nodded. He had turned to face Mrs. Surrat, but he was aware of Booth watching him keenly. *Only twenty-four hours*, Jerry was thinking. *I must have that much more time, free, here in the city. When I am through at Ford's, whatever the outcome there, then all of these people can go—*

Mrs. Surrat asked him: "Where will you want to go?"

Jerry allowed his face to show the weariness he

felt. "A good question. I'm afraid that I no longer have any country left."

Lewis Paine, leaning in the doorway, shook his head in gloomy agreement. Booth actually let out a small cry, as of pain; but when Jerry turned to look at him the actor, his face a study in tragedy, was nodding agreement too. "Now that Lee has surrendered . . ." Booth allowed his words to trail off.

What would another good Confederate fanatic say to that? "Lee could not help it," Jerry protested. "He had to surrender, to save his men from useless slaughter."

Booth was looking at Jerry as intently as before, as if hoping against hope to hear from him words that would mean salvation. "I know he could not help it; but now his army has disappeared. Richmond is lost, the government dissolved. Where will you go?"

"I mean to find General Johnston," Jerry declared stoutly. "In Carolina. We can go on fighting in the mountains."

Booth looked as if he might be envious of this heroic dedication. Certainly he was moved by it—though evidently not to the extent of being ready to emulate it himself. "I wish I could come with you," the actor announced wistfully, and for a moment Jerry feared that his stratagem might after all be about to damage history beyond repair.

But only for a moment. Booth continued: "But alas, I cannot. Matters of even greater moment hold me here."

"I'm sure they do, sir." Jerry's reply was so

promptly spoken and came with such obvious sincerity that Booth was gratified.

The actor sipped at his coffee, made a face, and stood up suddenly. "I will write you a note," he declared, "to present to a friend of mine. When you are finished, come into the dining room." But then he suddenly changed his mind and resumed his seat. "Never mind," he amended. "Take your time. When you have eaten, I will take you there myself."

Young Anna had returned now, with warm water in a basin, and a collection of bandages and unlabeled jars containing what Jerry presumed were household remedies. She began tending to his arm, which required that he first take off his coat. The old knife-cut in the sleeve, usually inconspicuous, became for the moment plainly visible.

Booth impulsively got to his feet, taking his own coat off. "If you would honor me, sir, by wearing mine. We appear to be of a size."

"That's not necessary, Mr. Booth."

"I repeat, I would be honored, sir, to have you accept it from me." There was a proud, almost threatening urgency in the actor's voice.

"In that case, sir, I shall be honored to accept."

FIFTEEN

Soon after Jerry had finished his supper, and thanked his hostess with what he hoped was sufficient courtesy, he and Booth set out upon the darkened street. Dogs in nearby yards barked at them mindlessly, undecided between offering greetings or challenge. Jerry now had an evil-smelling poultice bandaged to his left wrist, and was wearing Booth's coat. The garment, of some beautiful soft tan fabric, was a little loose in the shoulders but otherwise fit its new owner well enough. Booth meanwhile had somewhat gingerly put on Jerry's coat.

Hardly had the kitchen door of Surrat's boarding house closed behind them when Jerry recalled that the man called Paine, inside, was still in possession of his, or rather Baker's, pistol. But

Jerry said nothing. He wasn't going to go back and ask for the weapon; he had never really trusted himself with firearms and in fact was rather relieved to be without it.

"It is only a few blocks to your lodging for the night," Booth had informed him courteously when they had reached the street. "If you are quite able to walk?"

"Food and rest have marvelously restored me. Food and rest, and a sense of being among friends once again. Please lead on."

They trudged west on H Street, Booth whistling a slow tune softly, and soon passed the imposing structure of the Patent Office. A conversational silence grew. Jerry kept expecting to be asked more details of his escape, but it was not to be. Perhaps Booth was jealous of the daring feat; or, perhaps, absorbed in his own plans.

Just when they had left the Patent Office behind, the streetlights dimmed suddenly, brightened again briefly, dimmed and then went out.

"Nine o'clock," Booth commented succinctly, striding on. There was still some faint light from the sky, and the occasional spill of illumination from the window of a house. Enough light to see where you were going, generally, if you were not too particular about what your boots stepped in.

Somewhere, not too far away, black-sounding voices were raised in a hymn. The April night was very mild. Summer here, thought Jerry, must be ungodly hot. He could remember it that way from his trip in the nineteen-seventies.

Now Booth as he walked was pulling something out of his pocket, passing it to Jerry. "Brandy?"

"Thank you," Jerry took a small nip and passed the flask back. They walked on, Jerry listening, thinking, or trying to think. Tomorrow night, less than twenty-four hours from now, he was quite possibly going to have to do something nasty to this generous assassin who walked beside him now. Or Booth would do something nasty to him. He, Jerry, would not be able to do much to anyone else in Ford's Theater tomorrow, he supposed, without derailing history.

Now Booth was saying in a low confiding voice: "Tomorrow, when you have rested, I should like to have a confidential talk with you. On the subject of what the true duty of a Confederate ought to be, at this time, in this city."

"I shall be glad to have that talk, Mr. Booth. But I shall be better able to give it the attention it deserves if I get some sleep first."

"Of course." They paced on another quarter of a block before Booth added: "It is difficult, in this city, for a man who has a great enterprise in mind to find someone reliable to work with."

Jerry made an effort to change the subject. "Where are we going?"

"To a certain house on Ohio Street, where they know me well. I am sure any friend of mine will be graciously received there."

They had passed Ninth Street by now and had come to Tenth, where Booth turned left. Ahead, the street was bright with private gaslights; Jerry realized that the path the actor had chosen for them was going to take them directly past Ford's Theater.

Tonight's performance was evidently not over

yet, for both sides of the street in the vicinity of the theater were solidly parked with waiting carriages. A couple of taverns in the same block were doing a good business, various drivers and servants passing the time inside while they waited for their employers.

"Perhaps I will be recognized here," Booth muttered, as if to himself. "But it doesn't matter." He squared his shoulders and strode on bravely in Jerry's soiled and knife-torn coat, which fit him imperfectly.

Two more blocks south on Tenth Street, and they had passed the theater, without any sign of Booth's being recognized. At that point Jerry's guide crossed the Avenue, then turned right. Again Jerry had caught a glimpse of the White House in its park; again it seemed to him that nothing of any consequence in this city could be more than a few blocks from anything else.

Booth as he walked resumed his grumbling about his associates, still without naming any names. He could find one bright spot, though. "Paine, of course, has demonstrated his coolness and ability. He rode with Mosby in the valley, before he was captured and had to give parole."

Jerry could vaguely recall hearing of a Confederate guerrilla leader named Mosby. "Yes, Paine struck me as one who might be counted on in a pinch."

"Yes." Booth was sad again. "O'Laughlin—you haven't met him yet—is the only other one of the group with any military experience, and that no more than trivial."

Still it must be more than you have yourself,

thought Jerry. The actor was obviously young, healthy, athletic. Jerry had seen and heard enough in this world to be sure that no one was kept out of the army—any army—for any such triviality as a perforated eardrum, say. So Booth could have been with Lee if he'd wanted to. Or he could be still fighting at this moment, with Johnston. But he had obviously chosen to remain a well-paid civilian, living and working in the North. An interesting point, but certainly not one that Jerry was going to bring up aloud.

A few more blocks and they had reached their goal, a large wooden structure on Ohio Street, set back in a deep, wide lawn behind an iron fence, and surrounded by tall trees already leafed for spring. Jerry, looking at the size of the building and the number of lighted, red-curtained windows it possessed, remembered suddenly that Booth had spoken of their destination as a "house". Now Jerry realized that the actor hadn't meant a home.

They entered the house—how else, thought Jerry?—through an inconspicuous side door. Farther back there stood a long hitching rail where enough horses were currently parked to outfit a squadron of cavalry. The music of a violin, playing something quick and sprightly, could be heard from somewhere inside.

A middle-aged woman elaborately gowned and made up, greeted Booth as an honored old friend. On second glance the proprietress was considerably younger than a first impression indicated, the cosmetics being evidently a kind of badge of office deliberately intended to add years.

Booth squeezed the lady's right hand in both of

his. "Bella, I would be happy if you could do something for a friend of mine, Mr. Smith here. He finds himself for one reason and another—it is altogether too long and tedious a story to tell it now—he finds himself, I say, temporarily but drastically bereft of lodging. It would be a fine and Christian act if you were to provide him with a bed for the night—on my account, of course."

Jerry, increasingly dead on his feet after a day of imprisonment, fight and flight, had taken off his hat and stood looking around him numbly. On a sideboard nearby lilacs, in a crystal bowl with other flowers, helped to fight off the presence of the nearby canal.

"Only a bed?" Bella wondered aloud, looking Jerry over and automatically taking a professional attitude. She could hardly have failed to notice that Mr. Smith and Mr. Booth had switched coats, but she was not going to say anything about it.

Booth was lighting a cigar, forgetting his manners so far as not to offer Jerry—or Bella—one. "A bed," said the actor, "is a minimum requirement. You will have to ask Mr. Smith what else he might enjoy. All on my account, as I have said."

"Of course." Bella, having come to a decision, smiled at them both, and patted an arm of each. "Leave everything to me."

They were still in the entry hall. A stair with a gilded rail ascended gracefully in candlelight nearby, and now someone, a blond young woman in a silvery gown, was coming down that stair. The actor's eyes lighted, and he bowed gravely at her approach.

"I thought I heard a voice I recognized," the

blond woman almost whispered, resting a hand familiarly on Booth's shoulder. Then she brushed at the shoulder, frowning as a wife might frown at some domestic disaster. "Wilkes, what's happened to your coat?"

"Later we can discuss that, my dear Ella." Booth patted her hand in an almost domestic way. "Mr. Smith, I shall call for you in the morning, when you have rested." He gave Jerry a meaningful look, and a hard, parting handgrip upon the shoulder—thoughtfully remembering that the right arm was the good one. "There is much that we have to discuss."

Jerry mumbled something in the way of thanks. Then the proprietress had him by the arm and was steering him away toward the rear of the house, giving orders to black servants as she passed them, in the way that someone of the late twentieth century might punch buttons on a computer.

Now he was given into the care of the servants, who sized him up, welcomed him with professional sweetness, and worked on him efficiently, without ever seeming to look at him directly. In a matter of seconds they were leading him into a room where a hot bath waited, that seemed to have been prepared for him on miraculously short notice. He wondered if they kept a steaming tub ready at all times, in case a customer should feel the need of cleansing.

Two teenaged black girls wearing only voluminous white undergarments—voluminous at least by twentieth-century standards—introduced themselves as Rose and Lily. The pair, who looked enough alike to be twins, helped Jerry get his clothes off, and saw him installed in the tub. Lily, who helped him ease off his coat and shirtsleeves, shook her head at the sight of his arm. Frowning at Anna Surrat's amateurish poultice, she peeled it off and threw it into a slop jar. The lump on his wrist was bigger and uglier than ever, and the arm still pained him all the way down into the fingers, but Jerry was beginning to hope that it wasn't really getting worse; the injury might not be all that much worse, really, than some batterings his forearms had received in practice.

With a show of modest smiles and giggles his attendants helped him—he didn't need help but he was too tired to argue—into the tub, where he sat soaking his hurts away, along with the smell and feel of prison. Presently Lily went out, she said, to get some medicine. Meanwhile Rose dispatched another servitor with orders to bring Jerry a platter of cold chicken and asparagus spears, along with a glass of wine.

Waiting for food and medicine, he leaned back in the tub, eyes closed.

Delicate fingers moved across his shoulder and his chest. Rose evidently viewed him as a professional challenge. "Like me t' get in the tub and scrub you back? Bet ah could fit right in there with you. Might be jes' a little tight."

He opened his eyes again. "Ordinarily I would like nothing better. Tonight . . . I think not."

She rubbed his shoulders therapeutically. "If you change yoah mind, honey, just say the word."

Jerry closed his eyes again. All he could think about was what was going to happen tomorrow night, when someone was very likely to get killed.

If he looked at it realistically, he himself was a good candidate. Probably the best, besides Lincoln himself. Perhaps the best of all. Oh, of course, he had been assured that he had his special powers. What had Pilgrim said? *Not ordinary danger, even of the degree that you confronted on the train. It might be more accurate to say that only death itself can activate them.* Getting killed would be hardly more than a tonic stimulus. He wished he could believe that.

He ducked his head under the water and began to wash his face and hair. Lily, back again, giggling, rinsed his head with warm water from a pitcher. Then Jerry's food arrived, the tray set down on a small table right beside the tub, and he nibbled and sipped. His spirits rose a little.

After a little while, when the water had begun to cool, he made motions toward getting out of the tub. The two girls, who were still hovering as caretakers, surrounded him with a huge towel. When they were sure he was dry, the one playing nurse anointed his arm again, with something that at least smelled much better than the previous ointment.

Having put on the most essential half of his clothing, Jerry gathered the rest under his arm, making sure as unobtrusively as possible that he still had his watch and theater tickets with him. He bowed slightly to his two attendants. "And now, if you would be so kind as to show me where I might get some rest?"

It was nearly midnight by Pilgrim's watch when they escorted him to a small room, with a small bed. There was some tentative posing in the doorway by his attendants on their way out, but he let his eyelids sag closed and shook his head. When the door had closed he opened his eyes and found himself alone.

There was the bed. Jerry lay down with his boots on, meaning to rest for just a moment before he undressed. Somewhere the violin was playing, almost sadly now.

He awoke in pale gray dawn to the sound of distant battering upon a heavy door and angry voices shouting that the police were here.

SIXTEEN

Jerry rolled out of bed, looking groggily for his boots. Only when his feet hit the floor did he realize that he still had the boots on; hastily he donned shirt and coat—Booth's coat. He had slept through most of the night without taking off anything that he had put on after his bath. He picked up his hat now from where it had fallen on the floor, and put it on his head.

The banging and the shouting from below continued, augmented now by several octaves of screaming female voices. Jerry thought he could recognize Lily's generous contralto. Most of the noise was coming from the front of the house.

Taking stock of the situation, Jerry decided that if he were in charge of conducting a police raid, he'd surely have people at the back door before he started banging on the front. Dimly realizing that he was somehow not quite the same Jeremiah Flint who had driven into Springfield looking for a job, he concluded that with a house as tall as this one, and with so many trees around it, quite possibly all was not lost. Jerry was already opening the single window of his room. A moment later he had stepped out over the low sill, onto a sloping section of shingled roof, his appearance startling a pair of frightened robins into flight. Peering over the edge of the roof at shrubs and grass below, he confirmed that he was about three stories over the back yard.

There were plenty of tree branches within reach; the only question was which one of them to choose. In a moment Jerry had got hold of a limb that looked sturdy enough to support him, and had swung out on it. He had left the roof behind before it occurred to him to wonder whether his left wrist was going to be able to support its share of his weight. He looked down once; his wrist, impressed on a cellular level by the distance to the ground, decided it had no choice but to do the job.

Hand over hand Jerry progressed painfully toward the trunk. He wasn't going to look down again. He shouldn't have looked down even once. Instead he would concentrate on something else. What kind of tree was this, an elm?

Eventually, after six or eight swings, alternating handholds, he was close enough to the trunk to be able to rest his feet upon another branch. Now he could look down again, and did. Men in derby hats, three or four of them or maybe more with pistols in their hands, were swarming through the yard below. They appeared to be running from front to back and back to front again. So far the raiding party seemed to be trying everything but looking up. The new spring leaves sprouting between those men and their potential victim in the tree were thin and fragile, and so was the screen they made; silently Jerry urged them to grow quickly.

Edging his way toward the trunk, he reached it at last and went around it—this far above the ground the stem was slender enough for him to embrace it easily. The next step was to choose a direction and start out, one booted foot after another, along another branch, meanwhile still gripping upper branches to keep his balance. His chosen course was going to take him toward the alley that ran in back of the house, and was divided from the back yard by a tall wooden fence. The fence had a long wooden privy butting up against it, the planks of both constructions being freshly whitewashed, as if Tom Sawyer lived here.

Now, with a sinking feeling, Jerry became aware of the fact that there were people sitting on horses out there in the alley, their faces upturned in his direction.

This discovery made him pause, but, after considering the alternatives, he pressed on. One of the people who so silently observed his progress was a chestnut-haired young woman, wearing trousers underneath her full skirt, who sat astride her horse like a man.

The branch under Jerry's boots grew ever more slender the farther he got from the trunk, and bent ever lower with his weight. The higher branches that he clutched at with both hands were bending too. Now Jerry's boots were no more than five feet or so above the slanting, tar-papered privy roof. A goat, tethered in the yard near the back fence, was looking upward with deep interest at Jerry's acrobatics.

By now the branches bearing his weight had sagged enough so that he was partially screened, by tall hollyhocks and bushes, from the back door of the house. In that direction cries of triumph and screams of outrage signalled that the police had at last managed to force entry. With relief Jerry released his hold on the branches, half-stepping, half-falling to the roof of the outhouse. He would not have been surprised to put a leg through the roof of the privy and get stuck, or—God forbid—plunge to the very depths. But no, the wood beneath his boots was solid.

And a good thing, too. He had just begun his next move, a vault over the fence and into the weed-grown alley when a gunshot sounded from the direction of the house, and a bullet went singing over his head.

Then he was on his feet in the alley. Colleen Monahan and two men, all three of them mounted, were with him, and someone was urging an unoccupied horse in front of him. All Jerry could remember about riding was that for some reason you had to get on from the left side; not that he had ever tried to get aboard a horse before. He wasn't doing very well at it now.

"He's hurt," Colleen was saying sharply, mistaking his clumsiness for weakness or physical disability. "You, give him a hand!"

Somehow Jerry was pulled and pushed up into the saddle. He had barely got his feet into the stirrups when they were off, heading down the alley at what felt to him like a gallop. More gunshots sounded, somewhere behind them.

Another horse and rider were close beside Jerry on each flank, and someone was holding his mount's reins for him. Bouncing fiercely up and down, he clung to the front of the saddle, where there was supposed to be a horn, wasn't there?—no, he had read somewhere that only western saddles were so equipped.

Coming out of the alley, the four riders thundered southeast on Ohio Avenue, then across one of the iron bridges that crossed the foul canal, leading them into the half-wild Mall. To the west, on their right, the truncated Washington Monument rose out of the morning fog, balanced by the bizarre towers of the Smithsonian a few hundred yards to the east. Fog was rolling north from the Potomac now, coming in dense billows, and once they were a hundred yards into the Mall Colleen called a halt.

The small party sat their horses, listening for immediate pursuit. One of the men with Colleen was black and one was white. Both were young and poorly dressed; Jerry decided that he had never seen either of them before.

"Nobody comin'," the black man said after they had been silent a while. He appeared to be unarmed, though the white youth had a pistol stuck in his belt. The horses snorted and shifted weight restlessly, ready for more early morning exercise.

"They'll be looking," said Colleen. Her frivolous little lady's hat had fallen back off her head with the riding, but was still held by a delicate cord around her sturdy throat. She looked at Jerry with what he read as a mixture of sympathy and despair. "How bad are you hurt? Did they hit you back there?"

He realized she was talking about the gunshots, and shook his head. "I'm bruised, that's all. From talking to Lafe Baker. But I don't think I can ride very far."

"All right." She gave the white youth a commanding stare. "Ben, ride back to the War Department, learn what you can—then report back to me."

The young man—he really was very young, maybe sixteen, Jerry saw now—nodded. He started to speak, evidently found himself inarticulate, and departed with a kind of half-military salute to her and Jerry.

Colleen turned to the young black. "Mose, take the rest of these horses and put 'em away. Then return to your regular job. Baker's people will be looking for a mounted group, so Jim and I will travel on foot."

She swung down out of her saddle, the long skirt immediately falling into place to cover up her trousers. Jerry dismounted also, without waiting to be urged. It proved to be a lot easier than getting on.

"Yas'm." Mose looked Jerry in the face steadily for a long moment, as if he were seeking to memorize his features, or perhaps to find something; it was the most direct gaze Jerry had received from a black person since his arrival in this era. Then Mose dismounted too, gathering all of the horses' bridles into his hands.

With a motion of her head Colleen led Jerry eastward through the mist. When they had walked twenty yards through the long grass of the Mall, Mose and the horses were already invisible behind them.

"So it's bruised you are, is it?" she asked, looking sideways at him as they moved on. "I hear that Lafe Baker himself is bruised this morning, a great black shiner underneath one eye."

"I expect he is. But how did you find out?"

"I have my ways of knowing things. Men, you may have noticed, often don't take a woman seriously. The colonel might have gone back to New York by now, I don't know. Well, you're a strange man, Jim Lockwood, but it appears that in some ways you can be a marvel."

"You'd better watch out for Baker," Jerry warned her grimly. "He asked me if I knew you. I told him no, but . . ."

"I've got my eye on him, never fear. When I heard he was planning to raid Bella's this morning, I thought it just might have something to do with you. And if anything happens to me, Mr. Stanton'll know who to blame. Let's try going this way."

For a moment Jerry wondered if he had been followed after all. But he was sure he'd gotten away unnoticed. One of Booth's people? He gave the problem up as unsolvable.

The single impressive building of the Smithsonian

was close before them now, a dream-castle of reddish stonework rising out of mist, longer than a football field and topped by a profusion of mismatched towers. Here paths had been built up with gravel above the level of the ubiquitous mud. In this area the grass was shorter and better cared for, and spring flowerbeds surrounded the building with early blooms.

A bench loomed out of the fog. Jerry sighed. "No one's chasing us right now. How about sitting down for a minute? I suspect I'm going to have to do a lot of running yet today."

"And I suspect you're right."

They settled themselves on the park bench, side by side, as any strolling couple might. "Colleen. Why did you think the raid on Bella's might have something to do with me?"

"Wilkes Booth's doxy lives there, when he's not entertaining her at his own hotel. She's Bella's sister, by the way. And for some reason he's also in thick with those folk at Surrat's boardinghouse. I know you went there, but I don't know why. Are you going to tell me?"

"You knew I went there? How?"

"I tell you, I can find out things. What were you doing mixed up with those people? Someone in the War Department, I'm told, had a report six weeks ago that they might be up to no good."

Jerry leaned back on the bench, groaning quietly, trying to think. He could feel the history he was supposed to protect slipping out of his grasp like a handful of water. And he was acutely aware that Colleen was watching him intently.

When he spoke it was without looking at her. "Sorry about running out on you like that."

"I was wondering when you would get around to an apology. And I'm lookin' forward to hearing the best story you can come up with to explain what you did."

"And I don't know if I can explain something else to you. I mean why I was there at Bella's—"

"Don't try to change the subject." Colleen's anger was becoming more apparent in her voice. "I know why men go to brothels. I'm tired of lookin' forward, I'd like to hear the reason now, why you ran out on me."

He turned his head, hopelessly meeting her accusing stare. He shrugged. "There was another mission that I had to perform," he said at last.

"Another mission, more important than seeing Stanton, bringing him the facts he needs about Lafe Baker? Come on, now! If it weren't for several things that identify you as Jim Lockwood, I'd say—but that's no good, you *have* to be Jim Lockwood!"

"Yes, I do, don't I?" He thought again, then said: "All I can tell you is this—there's something, a job I'm charged with, that even Stanton doesn't know about. I couldn't tell you any more than that if you were to pull out a gun and threaten to shoot me for refusing."

Having said that much, Jerry waited. He had already seen this particular young lady pull out a gun and shoot.

For a long moment Colleen only stared at him, apparently suspended between rage and sympathy. Then the latter, for some reason, won. "Oh,

you madman!" she cried out softly. She put out a
hand and gripped his right arm—fortunately not
his left—where it lay extended along the back of
the bench; she squeezed his arm and shook it, as if
he were her brother and she was trying to shake
some sense back into him.

"You madman! If Stanton hadn't been so busy that
I didn't have to tell him the whole story, he'd
probably have *me* locked up by now. I told him that
I'd got you back to Washington safely, and—he just
brushed me off and told me I'd have to make a full
report later! With the war ending, he has even
more worrisome matters than Colonel Baker on
his mind. He'll be wanting to get back to that
problem soon, though. I'm going to bring you to
him this morning, before you disappear again."

"I don't think I ought to see him," said Jerry,
leaning back again and closing his eyes.

"You're into something, aren't you? Something
that's against the law. And you're going to tell me
what it is. You can't be a Secesh agent. You *can't*,
not now, when there's no Secesh government left.
What is it, then? Smuggling?"

"Nothing."

"Liar. I'm bringing you to Stanton. Unless of
course," said Colleen's voice, a new thought bringing both hope and alarm, "we'd both be worse off
if he did see you."

Jerry sat up and opened his eyes again. Then he
got out his—Pilgrim's—neatly ticking watch, flipped
open the lid, and looked at the position of the
hands. Twenty minutes after seven in the morning. The show at Ford's started at eight in the
evening. Some time after that hour—exactly at

what moment Jerry had never yet been able to determine—Wilkes Booth would enter Lincoln's box and kill the President. Promptly at eight, still almost thirteen hours from now, he, Jerry, had to be in his seat at Ford's, and free of interference.

"Where's Stanton now?" he asked.

Colleen looked hopeful at so sane a question. "Last night he and General Grant were working together at Stanton's house. They're almost busier now that the war is ending than they were when it was going on. I suppose there are a lot of things to be decided—the size of the peacetime army, and so forth."

"I suppose so."

"Officially, Stanton is supposed to be at the War Department at nine this morning. If we're there then we can insist on seeing him. Until then, we'd better keep out of sight."

"I'll agree with that last part." Jerry looked around them. The fog was only beginning to lift. As far as he could see, they had the whole Mall, and the Smithsonian, to themselves. "This looks like about as good a place as any to kill some time."

In the distance somewhere a military voice was shouting orders; some routine drill, evidently, for Colleen took no notice of it.

"The truth is," said Jerry, breaking a brief silence, "I can't see Stanton until tomorrow."

"Whyever not?"

"I told you I had another mission, that came first."

"Holy Mary. A mission for the Union?"

"Of course. Who else?"

"And who gave you this other mission?"

"I can't tell even you that."

"And where do you do this other job, and when?"

Jerry was silent.

"You're a stubborn man, James Lockwood. Stubborn as my husband was, God rest his soul, and I suppose it was his stubbornness in not letting himself be captured by the rebels that killed him at the last." There were tears in Colleen's brown eyes as she brought her hand out of the pocket of her dress. There was a derringer in it.

SEVENTEEN

"I'll tell you the truth then," said Jerry. "I'm not Jim Lockwood."

Colleen's gun-hand twitched, but she couldn't very well shoot him, if that was her intention, with that statement unexplained. Instead she blinked back tears. "Then where is he?"

"You're crying for him?"

"For you and me, you idiot. Mostly for me. For thinking you and I might . . . where is he?"

"Oh. Oh. I'm pretty sure he's dead, back in Missouri, or Illinois. *I* didn't kill him, understand. I'm trying to complete the job he started."

"And your real name is what?"

"Flint. Jeremiah Flint. People who know me usually call me Jerry."

"People who know you well must call you a

good many things. But you *are* a Union agent? Stanton's man?"

"I'm Union, yes, all the way. You might even say I'm a strong Abolitionist. The trouble is, though, Stanton will be expecting the real Lockwood and he won't know me from Adam."

"Who hired you, then, if you're not Stanton's man? Who gave you your orders?"

Jerry was silent.

"The only authority higher than the Secretary of War is the President himself."

Jerry said nothing.

"Holy Mother. I'm going to take you to Stanton myself, and show you to him. You tell him what you've told me."

"I tell you, as soon as he sees I'm not Jim Lockwood, he'll lock me up."

"You'll tell him the whole story, of how Lockwood died. You can't refuse to tell him, even if you can't tell me."

Jerry, furiously trying and failing to think, looked at her. "I can't argue with that," he said at last. That at least was the truth; he was out of arguments and lies, and he would have to settle for getting her to put the gun away if he could.

She did put it away, and Jerry heaved a silent sigh of relief.

"The fog is lifting, we can't stay here much longer." She had the tears firmly under control now. "We are going to hide somewhere until a quarter to nine. Then we walk to the War Department."

"All right." Jerry turned his head toward the Smithsonian, where he could now see figures moving within the thinning mist. "Some people are going in over there."

"There are people who live there, the director and his family. Also some of the learned men who come there to work."

"I didn't know that."

"Still, the Colonel's men will not be likely to look for us in there, I think. We'll go in, if we can."

They rose from their bench and walked to the building. At the front door a sign informed them that visitors were not admitted until eight.

To kill the half hour or so remaining, they strolled among the flower beds. Conversation was limited. Jerry, stealing glances at his companion's face, her hair, her throat, found himself beginning to think what he considered were crazy thoughts. But he went on thinking them anyway.

Colleen passed some money to Jerry so he would be able to pay for their admission when the time came. At eight o'clock a dour ticket-seller let them into the museum, the day's first visitors. The building looked new, but the dim, cavernous rooms were already dusty and had the smell of age. These people, he thought, badly needed lessons in museum management, along with a great many other things.

On impulse he took Colleen's hand, but she pulled it free, saying: "Look at your fine watch now and then. Don't let's dally here past a quarter to nine."

"All right."

The two of them walked among endless glass cases with dark wood frames, arrayed with endless labeled trays of arrowheads and fossil teeth. They looked at skeletons and fosils in cabinets, and had time to stick their noses into the library.

It appeared that Colleen could not remain totally angry at him for long. "Are you a reading man, Jerry?"

"I used to be. I'll be one again, when this is over. The war, I mean—and everything. And what about you, Colleen Monahan? Is that your real name?"

"Colleen's mine. And Monahan's my maiden name, though I've used others." She sighed. "And oh, yes, I would like to be a reader. Sit in a cozy parlor and drink tea and read." She ran her hand along a row of books. "Some day . . ."

"Listen, I . . ." And then Jerry ran out of words altogether. It was a crazy thing to do, but he put his hands on her shoulders and turned her to face him fully, and kissed her. How odd that she had to turn her face up at an angle. He always thought of her, somehow, as being the same height he was, and here she was several inches shorter.

Some time passed before she pulled away.

"Colleen, I—"

"No. Say nothing about it now."

"I just—"

"Say nothing, I tell you. Not now. Later."

Hand in hand, now, they continued to tour the exhibits, though Jerry at least looked at them without really seeing anything.

He was certain that the minutes must be racing by swiftly. There were moments when Jerry was almost able to forget his evening appointment at Ford's. He pretended to himself to hope that Colleen had forgotten about Stanton.

"Jerry? The time?"

He pulled out his watch and looked at it. No use trying to stretch things out here any longer. "Quarter to nine," he admitted.

"Time to go, then."

"Time to go."

He could feel her reluctance, along with her determination, as they left the museum. Like an ordinary strolling couple, they walked along the Mall toward Washington's unfinished shaft. A few more people were about now. The sun was well up now, the morning fog completely burned away. High cloudiness clung to the sky. Jerry kept expecting Lafe Baker's men to burst into view somewhere, on horseback with guns drawn like a gang of rustlers in an old-time movie. But things weren't done that way in the city, not in the daytime anyway. If for no other reason, there was always too much cavalry around, ready to take a hand in any disturbance.

Colleen led him north on the Fourteenth Street bridge over the canal. From the north end of the bridge it was only one block to the southeast corner of the President's Park. A narrow footpath between the canal and the fence guarding the Park brought them to Seventeenth Street where they turned north again. In minutes they were approaching the main building of the War Department from its publicly accessible side. Now they moved among the usual daytime throng of people.

Colleen knew her way in through the outer obstacles posed by armed uniformed sentries and plainclothes guards. In a crowded vestibule it took her two minutes to learn that Mr. Stanton was seeing no one this morning, being again closeted in his office with General Grant. Jerry, enjoying the temporary reprieve, could imagine the questions the two men were deciding on how was the great war effort to be shut down: what military contracts should be canceled, and so on. And what size was the peacetime army going to be? That last would depend, of course, on what policy should be adopted toward the conquered South. Probably it would depend to some extent on who was President next week, next year.

Colleen and Jerry waited in the lobby of the War Department, at last finding a place to sit on a bench in a relatively remote hall. Few words passed between them; they had plenty to talk about but none of it was suitable for public discussion. Colleen made sure that from where she sat she could see the door that Stanton would ordinarily use, going in and out. Several times she sprang to her feet, evidently having picked up some hint that the Secretary might be about to appear. But these were false alarms.

At eleven o'clock she went to a desk to try again. Jerry meditated trying to sneak out while she was thus engaged, thus putting an effective end to the possibility of any relationship but enmity. But it would really be better that way, wouldn't it? For both of them? But he held back. There were still nine hours or more before his appointment, and he had no idea of where he would go if he left this building now. Anyway, Colleen kept turning round to smile at him—it was a bitter, knowing smile, not tender at all. He wouldn't have more than a few seconds' start—and, anyway, if he ran out now, and Colleen did not invoke a swift and effective pursuit—or merely shoot him in the back—there would still be Lafe Baker to deal with.

This time when Colleen came back to him from the desk, even her false smile had disappeared; she was fuming. "Mr. Secretary Stanton has gone to the White House. Cabinet meeting. Never mind, maybe we can catch him there. The President is going to want to take a look at you anyway, when he hears your story." She smiled at Jerry wickedly and added softly: "Sneak out on me again, and I'll scream bloody treason. If I do that in here, or in the White House, you may be punctured by a bayonet or two, but you won't run far."

Jerry smiled the best smile that he could muster, and did as he was told.

As they were walking across the broad lawn that separated War Department from White House, Colleen asked him quietly: "How did you get Lockwood's key for the safe-deposit box in Chicago?"

"The two of us were friends, out west. I—owed him something. Before he died he had my word for it that I would see to it that the job he had begun got finished." Jerry had now been long enough in the nineteenth century to feel some hope that a claim like that might be accepted.

"And what about the signature at the bank?"

"I did the best I could to copy the way his signature looked on the page. I don't think the clerk really looked at it anyway."

"Whenever *I* signed, he only looked at me. Leered at me is more like it." She sighed faintly. "Well, Jeremiah. It's a great mess you've put us both into. But now that the war is over I suppose we might manage to come out of it alive. If this new story that you're tellin' me is true."

"Oh, it's true, right enough."

Now she was looking at Jerry's vest, looped by a silvery chain. "The watch is Jim's too, I suppose."

"The watch? No, it's my own."

"I see." He couldn't tell if that question and answer had really meant anything or not.

There were a dozen people, more or less, hanging around the north entrance to the White House, the door directly below the window from which Lincoln had given his speech on Tuesday night. The gathering right at the door included a couple of guards, and a couple of men arguing with one of the guards. The others present, white and black, well-dressed and poor, were loitering in the background.

Colleen ignored them all, and marched right in with Jerry following. But just inside they had to stop. The aged doorkeeper, addressed familiarly by Colleen as "Edward", informed her that Mr. Stanton was in a Cabinet meeting upstairs. Edward could not, he said, allow her and her companion to go up the office stairs to the upper floor, and Mr. Stanton would be unable to see them anyway.

"We'll wait," said Colleen, though that did not appear to be a promising course of action, judging by the numbers of people who were already doing it. Once more Jerry allowed himself to relax a little.

Edward's attention was soon engaged with what appeared to be a group of tourists, come like their twentieth-century descendants, but very much more casually, to see what they could of the old house. As soon as the doorkeeper had turned away, Colleen, who evidently knew her way around in here, quietly gestured to Jerry to follow her. She led him down a wide hall toward the western end of the ground floor. At the end of the hall a broad staircase went up.

At a landing whose window gave a magnificent view of the distant Potomac, entrenched among spring-clad hills, the stairs reversed direction west to east. A moment later Jerry and Colleen were at the top of the processional stairs, at the west end of a hallway just as broad and even longer than the one downstairs.

They were getting closer to the business center of the Executive Mansion; there were twice as many loungers here as outside the front door. Here the men standing about and leaning against the walls tried to look busy and important, even as they waited in hope of being able to talk to those who truly were.

But the style of management here was not quite as casual and informal as it looked at first sight. When they reached a gate in a low wooden railing near the eastern end of the hall, Colleen was recognized by a guard and allowed to proceed a little farther; Jerry had to wait for her among the office-seekers and other petitioners.

He leaned against the wall, obscured for the moment in the cigar smoke and chuckling conversation of a knot of idlers. The pendulum of his fear was starting to swing back. Colleen was one resourceful and determined woman, and he would not be at all surprised if she did somehow get herself and Jerry ushered into the Cabinet meeting. Suppose she did return in a moment, take him by the sleeve, and march him in to see Stanton, maybe with Lincoln himself sitting in the same room. Maybe it wasn't really rational to think she could break in on a cabinet meeting like that, but just suppose . . .

Jerry was sweating. Colleen might be turning her head to look for him as before, but she couldn't see him; there were too many bodies in between. Now was his chance, if he was truly going to do what he had to do. There was really no choice— and in the long run she'd be better off as well.

Lounging nonchalantly along the hall in the direction away from the crowded office, he noticed a black servant open a door and pass through, and he also noticed, beyond the door, what must be a service stairway, going down.

In a moment Jerry had slipped through the door himself and was on his way downstairs. Blessing the sloppy security he came out at ground level, and soon regained the main hall, where he could hear old Edward the doorkeeper shouting at some other difficult visitor. A moment after that, Jerry had successfully attached himself to one of the groups of gawking tourists, just as they began to file into the huge East Room, directly under the offices above.

A few minutes later, the tourist contingent was outside again, back on the Avenue, where Jerry bid them a fond though quiet farewell.

EIGHTEEN

In getting away from the White House, Jerry walked side streets in a loop that brought him back to the Avenue just opposite Willard's. From that point he headed east, under an overcast sky. The atmosphere felt clammy and somehow oppressive. He had no better plan than to get back to where a concentration of markets, stores, and hotels promise throngs of people. It was not quite noon yet, and he still had to avoid capture for more than eight hours before the curtain rose at Ford's.

He bought a newspaper and went into a tavern for something to eat. With a fatalistic lack of surprise he read the front-page notice announcing that General Grant was expected to attend Ford's with the President tonight. Pilgrim had said there'd be a party of four. Again it was the unfamiliar General and not the President who was really the big news.

Without knowing why Jerry turned his head and glanced toward the window. An expressionless black face was looking in through the glass at him. He recognized Colleen's companion Mose.

The man seemed to be in no particular hurry to rush off and report Jerry's whereabouts to Colleen, or Stanton, or whoever. Jerry finished his lunch and paid his bill—Colleen had either not noticed or not cared about the denomination of the bill she had given him earlier—by which time Mose's face had disappeared from the window. Putting the paper under his arm, Jerry walked unhurriedly, but very alertly, out into the street.

As he walked east again, a glance over his shoulder told him that Mose was following, ten steps or so behind.

In an open-air market just off the Avenue, Jerry turned aside and stopped, as if he were considering some seafood. In front of a group of noisy men who were busily cleaning fish he stopped to talk with Mose, who approached to stand before him in the attitude of a servant receiving instructions.

"Mose, why are you following me?"

The black man's voice was too low for anyone else to hear. His accent was not gone, but greatly modified. "I had thought, Mistah Lockwood, that you were to be speaking to Mistah Stanton at this hour. I wish to see to it that no harm comes to you before you have the chance to do so." *There*, his look seemed to say to Jerry. *Damn me if you will for speaking like a human being, but I have gained the power, and I intend to use it.*

"Mose. I'm going to have to trust you."

"Yes, sah?"

Jerry looked about him, like a man about to take a plunge. Which indeed he was. He said: "I have just come from the White House. There is something I must do that even Miss Monahan must not know about. Not just yet."

Mose waited, silent, watching, judging. He was bigger than Jerry.

Jerry did his best. "She has probably told you how important my work is, though not exactly what it is."

"Yes sah. She has said something to that effect."

"I was supposed to meet someone here—near here. But something has gone wrong. Miss Monahan will be putting herself in danger if she tries to help me directly now, and . . . the fact is I would much rather that she not."

Mose nodded slowly, reserving judgment; anyone watching would see only a servant painfully trying to make sure he had his instructions right.

Jerry pressed on. "The problem is that I must hide somewhere until dark. Somewhere where Baker's men, in particular, will not be able to find me. Several of them know what I look like."

"That could well be a problem, Mistah Lockwood."

"Mose, will you help? Do you know someplace where I can hide? I must have until midnight tonight."

The black youth confronted what was evidently a new level of responsibility for him in the Secret Service game. Finally he grappled with it. "Lord

God, Mistah Lockwood. Follow me. We gone out this market by the back way."

Jerry followed Mose north, with alternations east and west, along one side street after another. At intervals Jerry nervously checked his pockets, making sure that his theater tickets and his watch were still secure.

He wondered hopefully if Pilgrim might be looking for a chance to contact him as well. There was still an enormous amount of information that Jerry needed for tonight but did not have. He might have to be alone for Pilgrim to be able to get through . . . there was no use worrying about it.

Mose led him up an alley near Tenth Street, right past the rear of Ford's Theater. Jerry observed this without surprise. There were black-inhabited shacks here; Jerry could deduce the color of the inhabitants before he saw them, from the mere intensity of the squalor.

Mose came to a stop in front of one shack, of a size that would have made an ample children's play-hut back in twentieth-century suburban Illinois. The youth took a quick look around then tapped on the unpainted wall beside the heavy curtain that did duty as a front door. A moment later he stuck his head inside, and Jerry heard words exchanged. A moment after that, he was bidden to enter.

The interior was a single dirt-floored room with a back doorway that opened onto a shallow closet or shed. The only light entered through a single small translucent window of what Jerry supposed might be oiled paper. Two or three small children

were underfoot; at the potbellied stove in one
corner a black woman of indeterminate age, shabby
and barefoot, her hair tied up in a kerchief like
that of Scarlett O'Hara's Mammy, turned to the
visitor a face stoic in its wrinkles.

Mose and the woman—Jerry could not tell if
she was his mother, or what—conversed briefly.
Jerry thought he could catch an English word at
intervals, but most of the dialogue, at least to his
perception, was truly in some other language.

Presently Mose turned back to him. "You can
stay here, Mistah Lockwood. For a few hours anyway. I shall be back when it gets dark, if not
before."

"Thanks. If you see Colleen—well, she will be
safer if she does not know where I am."

Mose looked troubled, but he nodded.

"Thank you for your help, Mose. This will be a
very great help to me indeed."

The youth, turned suddenly inarticulate, nodded again. Then he was gone.

Jerry retreated into the hut, and sat down on
one end of the only bed; he couldn't see anything
else to sit on, except a small table that was fully
occupied at the moment, with pots and pans that
looked as if they might have been salvaged from a
scrap pile. He smiled tentatively at the woman,
and tried to speak to her, but she remained dead-
pan silent.

Time passed. Eventually slow footsteps were
heard outside the curtain, which was pushed back.
The woman hurried to greet the new arrival, a
graying man as ageless as herself who was carrying

a rusty shovel. The new arrival was not as poker-faced as she, and his expression on seeing Jerry went through a whole actor's repertory of responses.

The two held conversation in what sounded to Jerry like the same dialect used by the woman and Mose. At length the graying man put down his shovel and went out. He returned in a few minutes, bringing water in a battered bucket, and offered Jerry a dipperful.

"Thank you." Jerry reached for the dipper, while his host and hostess smiled and nodded welcome. Jerry was thirsty, and the water tasted good—though the look of the pail and dipper suggested the possibility of typhoid. That, thought Jerry, would probably be among the least of his problems, even if he caught it. Meanwhile the man had produced a chair from somewhere and invited the guest to sit in it. There seemed to be a general reluctance on the part of the householders to speak to him at all; it was hard for Jerry to believe they could not manage something close to white folks' English if they tried. But now that he was here, and his presence had been acknowledged by the offering of water, they seemed to prefer to ignore him. Not a bad attitude, Jerry realized on second thought, to take with regard to a guest who must be some-how involved in intelligence work. Only the tiny children, grandchildren here probably, two of them entirely naked except for shirts that had once been cloth bags, interrupted their play now and then to stare at him with frank curiosity. At last he had to smile at them; and felt in his pockets, only to be reminded that his only money was the small amount remaining from what Colleen had given him. Only

a little more than two dollars, and he might en-
counter some unforeseen expense in the five hours
remaining before show time. Still he decided that
he could spare a penny for each child.

Whatever the reason for the shy silence of the
adults, he was willing to respect it. Sitting in the
hard chair, he took out Pilgrim's watch and flipped
the lid—a quarter after three. Jerry imagined the
ticking was getting louder. The air in the hut was
beginning to turn oppressively close. Little light
and air came in through the innumerable crevices
in the walls. His left arm was beginning to ache
again.

Soon the woman began cooking something on
the stove, boiling potatoes with some kind of
greens—the man, coming back into the shack from
one of his trips outside, offered Jerry a plate, but
he turned it down with thanks, thinking from the
looks of the cookpot that he had eaten more for
lunch than these people were likely to get today
altogether. He drank another dipper of water, and
asked his host about an outhouse. Reminding Jerry
with a grim look that he was supposed to be in
hiding, the old man brought him a chipped chamber pot, and pointed him through the back door
into the attached shed.

Between distractions, Jerry did the best he could
to lay his plans for the evening. He decided that a
few minutes before eight o'clock, when he judged
a more or less steady flow of people would be
arriving for the play, he would slip down the alley
to Tenth Street, go to the door of the theater,
present his ticket as inconspicuously as possible,

and walk in. He could think of no reason why anyone should be looking for him at Ford's, unless Pilgrim had come up with another nasty surprise for him. And somehow the day passed. At a quarter to seven by Jerry's watch the sun was setting.

The curtain was supposed to go up at eight on *Our American Cousin*. A few minutes before that time, Jerry said quiet thanks to his hosts and eased out of his hiding place. Trying his best to be inconspicuous, he made his way among the shanties, through the alley, and out onto Tenth Street. Men equipped with ladders, and long candles shielded in metal cans, were going about lighting the streetlamps. Near the theater there was, as he had hoped, already a crowd, with wagons and carriages drawing up in the street, and people walking toward the theater.

Jerry had a two-days growth of beard, and his clothes, except for the coat, itself unchanged since Thursday morning, were neither neat nor clean. Still the standards of the time were not that demanding, and he thought he could get by. As he walked toward Ford's, trying to appear the casual theatergoer, he did his best to confront his situation realistically.

On the plus side, Booth would not expect anyone to know his purpose. And Jerry was armed with Pilgrim's exotic hardware, whatever that might prove to be worth. On the minus side . . . well, on the minus side was just about everything else.

First, there was his lack of knowledge. Not only about the timing of the attack, but about other aspects of the situation as well, such as the possible presence of Booth's confederates in the theater or just outside.

And what about General Grant? The newspaper had said that Grant was going to be here too. That certainly ought to draw a crowd; no one in the city had seen that much of Grant, while the President was a semi-familiar face.

No one interfered with Jerry as he approached the theater. Baker's people had missed the boat again, it would appear, and so had Colleen Monahan's, if indeed she had any agents beside Mose still in the field. Quite likely, Jerry supposed, she was by now herself in a woman's cell somewhere. Having to do that to her hurt him more than he thought it would, but there had been no help for it if he was to have any chance at all.

With a stream of other playgoers Jerry passed into the theater and through the busy lobby. The whole interior of the building was now well-lighted, a clean and well-decorated place.

As Jerry climbed the stairs to the dress circle, where his two seats were in row D, the farthest front. The seats throughout the auditorium were filling rapidly. Horns and fiddles were making the usual preliminary sounds; the theater lacked an orchestra pit, and musicians were occupying the space directly in front of the stage.

Jerry settled himself in one of his two seats. From here, now that the lights were on, he had an excellent view of the inconspicuous white door through which Booth intended to pass to reach the Presidential box. The only other way to get in would seem to be by the use of a ladder, climbing from the stage itself, and Jerry thought he could dismiss any such scheme as that.

There was no doubt as to where the Lincoln party would be. The arched openings of the double box seat at Jerry's upper right had now been decorated with thickly draped red, white and blue bunting and a picture of George Washington. Jerry supposed that by this time the fancy chairs mentioned by Raybold had been moved into the box as well.

But there was no way for an occupant of Jerry's seat, or of almost any other in the theater, to get a good look into the Presidential box. Leaning over the vacant chair to his right, he asked his neighbor in that direction, a stout, bureaucratic-looking gentleman: "Have the President and General Grant arrived yet?"

Maybe the man was a judge; he gave the question serious thought. "No sir, I don't believe so."

Though neither President nor General had yet appeared by eight o'clock, the houselights dimmed in unison quite punctually. Jerry realized that the gas supply for the lights must be under some central control.

He was aware, a minute later, of the curtain going up, and of actors appearing on the stage. But after that he was barely conscious of what they might be doing there. The President was late. Was that usual? Or was history already twisted out of shape? Had he, Jerry, done something already that was going to wreck the world? Had his strange behavior finally worried someone, someone important enough to take precautions to protect the President? He, Jerry, was going to be trapped

here in this dreary time for the rest of his life—
probably only a few years of miserable existence.
Or was it possible—

From time to time the laughter of his fellow
playgoers rose and fell around him, distracting
him from his worries, so that he supposed the
show was meant to be a comedy. Its characters
had names like Asa Trenchard, Mrs. Mountchessington, Lord Dundreary, and Florence Trenchard—
that part was played by Laura Keene. Jerry could
tell by the applause when she first appeared.

Jerry pulled out Pilgrim's watch but failed to
register the time before his nervous hand had put
the watch away. Then he pulled the timepiece
out to look at it again.

It was almost eight-thirty when Jerry heard a
sharp murmur run through the audience. Heads
were turning. He looked up and saw Abraham
Lincoln, six feet four and wearing a tall stovepipe
hat, walking almost directly toward him along the
aisle that ran from the stairs to the Presidential
box. A small party of people followed the President in single file. First came a short man in
shabby civilian clothes, who looked as if he was in
doubt as to whether he ought to hurry ahead of
Lincoln or not. That could not possibly be General
Grant. Was history slipping? Jerry couldn't worry
about it; he could only press ahead.

After the shabby man came a woman Jerry supposed had to be Mrs. Lincoln in a low-cut gown,
looking younger and more attractive than Jerry
had for some reason expected her to be. Following
the President's wife came a youthful couple Jerry
did not recognize, obviously aglow with the excite-

ment of a very special occasion. And bringing up the rear, a male attendant carried what looked like a folded shawl or robe.

Behind Jerry a man's voice whispered to a companion: "Looks like Grant couldn't make it. Who are they? The younger couple?"

"Why, that's Clara Harris, the senator's daughter. Her escort is a Major Rathbone, I believe." The young man was in civilian clothes.

The tall figure of the President passed right in front of Jerry, almost within arm's length, plodding on with a peculiar, flat-footed gait, huge hands swinging on long arms, nodding and smiling to right and left in acknowledgement of the growing applause. Now he removed his tall hat, carrying it in his right hand, and he waved it to and fro in a kind of continuous salute. Everyone in the theater was standing now. The band had struck up *Hail to the Chief*.

On stage, one of the actresses who was playing the part of a semi-invalid had just said something about her need to avoid drafts. "Do not be alarmed," ad-libbed the young man playing opposite. "For there is no more draft!" The applause in the theater built briefly to almost deafening volume.

The President had now arrived at the white door, which someone was holding open for him. In a moment his entire party had followed him through, and the door was closed again. In a matter of seconds the hesitant plainclothes attendant—if he was a bodyguard, Jerry was not impressed—emerged from the white door again, and took his seat beside it, in a small chair with his back to the box seats, facing the rest of the audience.

Booth, or anyone else who wanted to approach Lincoln, was evidently going to have to get past that guard. Using violence to do so, thought Jerry, would be sure to alert everyone else in the theater before the assassin—or Jerry—could get close enough to the chosen victim to do anything effective.

And he, Jerry, was going to have to get past that guard post somehow. Since his tour of the theater on Wednesday had entertained no hope of being able to sneak in early and lie concealed until the proper moment right in the box, or in the inner passage. There simply was no place in there for anyone to hide, and anyway the guard tonight had presumably inspected the site before Lincoln and his party settled in.

Now the white door was opening again, and Jerry stared as someone else came out. It was the attendant who had been carrying the shawl or blanket. Empty-handed now, the man moved toward the stairs and vanished in the direction of the lobby.

The play went on, and people laughed at it. Jerry sat on the edge of his seat, watching the door and the guard, and waiting. John Wilkes Booth was going to appear from somewhere tonight, sooner or later, as sure as fate itself, and make his move. Unless history had already been derailed, and Jerry was already doomed to die before the invention of the automobile. No, he couldn't accept that. Booth would come. But exactly how and when . . .

And then a familiar form was walking along the

aisle toward him. But it wasn't Booth. Colleen Monahan, elegantly dressed for the theater, smiled at Jerry and took the seat beside him as confidently as if he had been saving it for her all along.

"This seat is not taken, is it, sir?" she whispered politely. Back deep in her brown eyes an Irish harpy danced, waiting her turn to come forward.

"It *is* taken," Jerry whispered back desperately.

"Indeed sir, it is now. By me." And Colleen gave every appearance of settling in with pleasure to watch the play.

NINETEEN

And what could Jerry do about it? Absolutely nothing. He sat there holding his tall hat in his lap, his young lady companion beside him, her attention brightly on the stage as if nothing more momentous than this play had ever entered her silly head. It was eight-forty now. And it seemed miraculous to Jerry that the play should still be going on, the performers calling out their lines as confidently as if their world itself was in no danger of having the curtain rung down in the middle of this act, the parts of all the actors on its stage drastically rewritten. As if—

There was a burst of laughter, somewhat louder than usual, from the audience. Abruptly the shabby guard shifted in his seat beside the white door, then arose briefly from his chair to peer around the edge of the wall that otherwise prevented him from seeing the stage. He gave the impression of regretting more and more being stuck in a place from which he was unable to see the show. But after a moment he resumed his seat.

Beside Jerry, Colleen, her eyes bright, her lips smiling, was still watching the show, as if she had no other care in the world but this.

About ten more minutes passed. Then the guard—looking at that man closely now, Jerry would not have wanted to rely on him for anything—repeated his earlier performance, getting up to glance fleetingly at the stage once more, then resuming his seat.

Eight fifty-five. The guard got up unhurriedly out of his chair, stretched with his arms over his head, put on his hat, and with one more glance in the direction of the stage—the play seemed, after all, not such a big attraction—walked leisurely out of the auditorium.

Lincoln, as far as Jerry could see, had now been left totally unguarded.

So that's how it works. The guard is in on the plot, thought Jerry. At least that meant one possible difficulty had been removed for Jerry himself. His legs were quivering now from the long tension, his muscles on the verge of hurling him from his chair. Somehow he forced his body to relax.

Colleen was looking at him. Not steadily, but he was sure that she was studying him, a bit and a moment at a time, out of the corner of her eye. And her pretense of interest in the play was fading. A professional agent, she could not fail to be aware of the ongoing tension in the man beside her. And it must be striking her as odd that he was not offering explanations, that he was so intent on—something else—that he had almost completely ignored her.

Now it was nine-ten by Pilgrim's faithful watch, and Booth had not yet appeared. That would seem to argue against collusion by the guard. Maybe the guard had only gone out for a smoke, or a quick drink in the saloon next door. Maybe he would soon be back, to complicate Jerry's situation further.

But the shabbily dressed man who had been posted to sit by the white door did not come back. Jerry waited, staring past Colleen at the empty chair.

There was applause around them. With a start he looked back toward the stage and realized that the curtain was going down and the houselights were brightening. Was the play over? Had Lincoln been saved only because Jerry had introduced some distraction that kept Booth from ever coming to the theater? Might such a result possibly be good enough for Pilgrim, or did it mean that history had been mangled, and the helpless time-traveler trapped after all?

Then belatedly Jerry realized that this could be, must be, only a between-acts intermission. Colleen was looking at him. The tiny triumphant smile she had worn on her arrival had faded, had to be replaced by a look of wary concern.

Around them people were standing up and stretching, chatting about the play. They moved in the aisles, but not with the purposeful attitude of a crowd starting out for home. Many of the audience were looking toward the Presidential box, though with the draperies in place it was impossible for anyone elsewhere in the theater to get more than the tiniest glimpse of its august occupant.

Jerry stood on tired, quivering legs, and Colleen got up to stand beside him. "Well, Mr. Lockwood. Will you escort me to the lobby? I believe there might be some refreshment available there." When he hesitated, she added in the same voice: "Or would you prefer to end this now?"

He didn't know exactly what she meant, but he was afraid she would blow a whistle and bring plainclothesmen swarming from God knew where. Anyway, Lincoln wasn't shot during intermission; Jan Chen, Pilgrim, or someone had told Jerry that the play was in process when the crime occurred.

He nodded and offered her his arm. Numbly he descended to the lobby, Colleen beside him on the stair holding his arm lightly, as a hundred other ladies in sight were walking with their men. The hum of voices was genteel; in the lobby itself were mostly ladies, while the gentlemen appeared to have moved outside *en masse*. Wisps of blue cigar and pipe smoke wafted in through the open doors leading to the street. It had been a long time since Jerry had seen an expanse of carpeted floor the size of the lobby without spittoons.

"Would it be too much trouble, Mr. Lockwood, to get me a lemonade?"

"Not at all."

He visited the genteel bar on one side of the lobby, and was back with her drink a moment later.

"And for yourself? Nothing to drink? I won't be

offended if you choose something stronger. For that you'll have to go to the tavern next door." Colleen's voice was brittle and strained; the more she spoke, the more unnatural she sounded.

Jerry started to reply, then simply nodded. Now was not the time for him to take a drink; but he could certainly use a moment to himself, away from Colleen at least, to try to regroup.

The intermission was evidently going to be a long one, for the men outside in front of the theater, and in Taltavul's next door, gave no sign of drifting back to the theater.

On entering the bar, Jerry recognized among the crowd the guard who had been sitting outside of Lincoln's box. Was the man really in on the conspiracy, then?

While Jerry was wondering if he should take a short beer after all, a couple of gulps just to heal the dryness in his throat, a name was called nearby in a familiar voice. Turning, responding more to the voice than to the name—which had been Smith—Jerry with relief saw John Wilkes Booth, dressed in dark gray, standing at the bar with a bottle of whiskey and a glass in front of him.

Booth's dark eyes were almost twinkling, as if with a great secret. "Mr. Smith—will you have a drink with me?"

Jerry, filled with a vast relief, accepted. "Gladly, Mr. Booth, gladly."

Relief was short lived. Jerry wondered if Booth might now have given up his murderous plan, and decided to spend the evening getting sloshed instead.

Would that, could that, possibly satisfy Pilgrim? Jerry didn't know, but he felt grave doubts. Pilgrim had, after all, specifically enjoined him against merely warning Lincoln.

"Are you enjoying the show?" Booth asked. Having obtained a glass for Jerry by gestures, he was pouring delicately to fill it.

"Oh yes." Jerry couldn't think of anything better to say. He lifted his glass and sipped at it as delicately as it had been poured.

"Be sure to see the rest," Booth was gazing now into the mirror behind the bar. "There is going to be some rare fine acting."

Someone down the bar, six or eight customers distant, was calling the actor's name, trying to get his attention. Booth and Jerry looked, to see a man evidently trying to drink a toast.

"—to the late Junius Booth. Wilkes, you are a good actor, yes. But you'll never be the man your father was."

Booth drank to his father without hesitation. But for a moment a small smile seemed to play under his mustache. He shook his head in disagreement: "When I leave the stage, I will be the most famous man in America."

A few moments later, Jerry took his leave of the people in the bar. Colleen appeared actually surprised when he came back into the lobby. She said: "This one time I *expected* you to disappear— and you did not."

"No, I did not. Shall we go back to our seats? The play will be starting soon."

Silently she took his arm. Her face was turned

toward him, her eyes studying his face, as they climbed the stairs from the lobby.

Soon they were back in the dress circle. She was not smiling now, nor pretending. When she spoke her voice was still so low that the people around them would have trouble hearing it; but it was no longer the voice of a lady who had come to watch a play.

"Damn you. Damn you, man. Do you still think you can brazen this out, whatever it is? Do you know how far I've stuck out my neck for you already? I had convinced myself that—what happened between us on the train was . . . is it that you're ready to die to be rid of me, or what?"

"Colleen." He could feel and hear the sheer hopelessness in his own voice. "It meant something to me, what happened between us. But I can't argue about it . . . not now. How did you know that I was here?"

Her voice sank further. "One of the girls in the brothel reports to me too. She went through your pockets while you were there." She stared at him in anger a moment longer; then she walked briskly away, not looking back.

The gaslights had brightened again when the intermission began. When Colleen left Jerry got out of his seat again to pace back and forth in the aisle, stretching and soothing muscles that cried for either rest or action. He kept watching the white door. Would the President feel the urge to stretch his long legs too, and emerge from seclusion?

Almost ten o'clock, and the play had not yet resumed. And now a man, a middle-aged well-dressed civilian Jerry had never seen before, was coming along the aisle in front of Jerry, approaching the white door with a piece of paper folded in his hand.

This visitor certainly was not Booth. Who was he, then? A possible confederate? Certainly not one of the group from Surrat's boarding house. Jerry stared, holding his breath, on the verge of pulling the trigger of his watch and charging forward, yet knowing that he must not, until he knew that Booth himself had begun to make his move.

The man with the paper in his hand conferred briefly with two military officers in uniform who happened to be the members of the audience who nearest to the post abandoned by the guard. Then with a nod he opened the door and walked in calmly.

Within a minute the messenger, for such he seemed to be, had emerged again, without his paper. Looking rather well satisfied with himself and his importance, the man retreated in the direction of the stairs.

Almost as soon as he had disappeared, the house-lights dimmed again, warning patrons to return to their seats. Jerry crouched in his chair again. Shortly the play resumed.

Jerry had just looked at his watch for the hundredth time, and had somehow managed to retain the information it provided, and so he knew that it was ten minutes after ten when Booth at last appeared in the auditorium. When Jerry saw him first the actor, well dressed in dark, inconspicuous clothing, was standing at the top of the short series of steps leading down from the main exit to the aisle that ran across the front of the dress circle. Jerry could see Booth hesitate there for a moment, looking in the direction of the Presidential box, as if he were surprised to discover that his victim was essentially unguarded.

Now Jerry had the watch clutched in his left hand. And the great moment, the one he had rehearsed in a thousand waking and sleeping dreams since his last talk with Pilgrim, had come at last. He snapped open the glass cover—so much he had done before, in resetting the watch to local time at Washington—and moved both hands to twelve o'clock.

But now he took the stem in the fingers of his right hand, and pulled on it, feeling the click, making the change that was supposed to activate the first stage of the device. He felt and heard one sharp click, small but definite, from the machine.

Now he had pulled on the stem, seconds were passing, but nothing had really happened. No. He realized that something *was* happening, though it was a slower and subtler effect than anything he had expected.

Around Jerry, time was altering.

TWENTY

When he saw Booth, poised at the top of the few steps leading down to the dress circle aisle, Jerry opened the face of his watch and set both hands to twelve. Booth had started down those steps before Jerry pulled out the stem to the first stop. Now, many seconds later, the actor was still descending those few steps; in Jerry's eyes, he was moving like a slow-motion instant replay.

Now Jerry realized that since he pulled out the stem of the watch all sounds in the auditorium had been transformed: the speech of the actor on stage had slowed tremendously, and his voice was lowering from a tenor toward a drawling baritone. The background noise of audience whispers, coughing, breath and movement had taken on a deep, sepulchral timbre.

Concomitant with these changes the light was fading and taking on a reddish hue, moderate but unequivocal; for a moment Jerry thought that Booth must have found an accomplice to turn down the gas in the theater, dimming all the lights, on stage and off, at the crucial moment. But no one else in the theater appeared to notice anything. In fact, the audience seemed strangely calm—posed and almost motionless.

On stage, the voice of the actress who played Mrs. Mountchessington, confronting Harry Hawk as Asa Trenchard, was now prolonging each syllable grotesquely as the tone slid down, down and down the scale, descending to an improbable bass. Half-hypnotized, Jerry watched and listened as if his own mental processes had been slowed down by the transformation in the world around him.

At last Booth reached the bottom of the stairs and was approaching Jerry, following in the footsteps of Lincoln and his party almost two hours earlier. Each of the widely spaced footfalls of the actor was marked by a very faint sound, a fading rumble hard to identify, following the dull subterranean thump of heel impact. When Jerry realized that rumbling sound would have been a jingle were it not so slow and deep, he remembered that Booth was wearing spurs. Of course; there was a getaway horse waiting for him in the alley.

Paradoxically, despite the enormous elongation of each moment in Jerry's own almost-hypnotized time-frame, Booth's slow and steady walk was already carrying the actor past him. For the briefest of moments Booth's eye caught Jerry's, and a slow change, a kind of half-recognition, began its passage across the actor's face. But Booth had no thought to spare now for anything but his purpose, and he did not pause in his determined progress. His eyes—shifting slowly as Jerry saw them—looked forward again. If anything Booth walked a little faster.

Jerry got to his feet, realizing as soon as he willed the movement that time for him had not been slowed down. Stepping into the aisle, he felt that he was moving at normal speed in a slow-motion universe. Intent on overtaking Booth, he shot past seated rows of nearly frozen matrons and distinguished gentlemen, their applauding hands suspended before their faces, past army officers with mustached mouths and ladies with rouged lips, all stretched open in distorted laughter at the doings of the actors.

He realized that Pilgrim's device must have caused more than a mere difference in speed. The thousand eyes that were fixed with anticipation on the stage did not see Jerry. The swiftness of his speeding passage did not stir their feathers or ruffle their gowns. Activating the watch-stem to its first stop had partially disconnected him from the world around him, rendered him somehow out of phase with it. But not out of phase with Booth . . . could their mutual counter-purposes be somehow linking them? Or had the effect, whatever it was, merely not kicked in yet? In any event, so far as others were concerned, Pilgrim's little device was concealing him as well as giving him a few precious seconds of advantage. If only he could learn how to use that advantage before it was too late!

Unchallenged, John Wilkes Booth had reached

the white door and opened it. Before Jerry caught up with him he was already three-fourths of the way through the doorway. The actor had turned a sidelong glance at the two army officers seated nearest to the door, but both of them were watching the play, and ignored Booth. Now already the actor was closing the door behind him, and if what Pilgrim had told Jerry was correct, in another moment that door would be blocked solidly from the inside—

Jerry, his fear rapidly mounting toward panic, sprinted forward so that to himself he seemed to float amid a frozen waxwork audience. At the last moment he shot through the gradually narrowing aperture of the white door, past Booth and into the small blind hallway that ran behind the boxes.

But his passage was not entirely a clean one. Trying to slide past the door even as Booth was pushing it closed from inside, Jerry caromed at high speed off the actor's shoulder, to go spinning on into the dark little vestibule. There Jerry bounced off a wall and collapsed to the floor.

At the moment of the physical collision, the time-distortion effect ceased to operate. Once past Booth, Jerry found himself suddenly conscious of his extra burden of momentum. It was more than he ought to have been able to achieve by running, more as if he had jumped from a speeding automobile. First Booth's shoulder and then the wall, with stunning impact, absorbed the burden from him.

Jerry's sudden materialization also took Booth by surprise, and the grazing collision knocked Booth down; but the actor, having absorbed only a small part of Jerry's momentum, and mentally braced for violent interference at any moment, recovered from the collision while Jerry still sprawled at the end of the little vestibule. Booth picked up a wooden bar that had been lying inconspicuously on the dark floor. Not to use as a weapon; instead Booth jammed the piece of wood into place behind the white door, which he had finally managed to get completely closed. A notch to hold the bar had already been cut into the plaster of the wall.

Now there could be no further interference from outside the Presidential box; not until it was too late.

And Booth had no need of any wooden bar to fight with; a long knife appeared in his left hand as he faced Jerry; there was already a small pistol in his right. In the gaze he turned on Jerry was the bitter contempt of a man terribly betrayed.

"No one shall stop me now," the actor declared. His soft voice, for once out of control turned harsh and broke on the last word.

Jerry was already sickeningly conscious of total failure as he regained his feet. Already someone was knocking on the blockaded door leading to the auditorium. The voices of the people on stage, in Jerry's ears restored to normal pitch and speed, were going on, the speakers still oblivious that the hinges of history were threatening to come loose twelve feet above them.

A great roar of laughter went up from the audience, at the words of the character Asa Trenchard, now alone on stage. Booth's derringer was still unfired, the President still breathed. History was already running a few seconds late.

But maybe all was not yet totally lost.

Jerry faced Booth. "I don't want—" Jerry was beginning, when suddenly the door immediately on Booth's left, leading into the Presidential box, swung open. The face of Major Rathbone appeared there, displaying, even above civilian clothes, the keen look of command.

'What is going on—" the Major began; then his eyes widened as he saw the knife in Booth's hand. The look of command vanished. Rathbone's lungs filled. "Help!" he bellowed. "Assassins!"

Booth, evidently determined to save the single bullet in his derringer for Lincoln, at once plunged his knife into Rathbone's chest; the wounded man fell back.

Now Jerry was moving forward, Pilgrim's timepiece once more gripped in his left hand, the fingers of his right hand reaching for the stem. He had to get within three meters. Because within a very few seconds the fatal shot—

Booth, inevitably convinced that Jerry meant to stop him, turned on Jerry with the knife, now held in his right hand. Even as Jerry managed to grip the wrist of the hand that drove that weapon toward him, he knew his own damaged left wrist was not going to be able to take the strain.

In terror of his life now, all other purposes forgotten, Jerry screamed for help. Then he could no longer hold back the arm that held the knife. He saw and felt it come plunging into his chest, cold paralyzing steel that brought the certainty of death . . .

He fell. Through a thickening haze of red and gray, Jerry saw Booth re-open the door into the box. Through a cottony fog, Jerry heard the assassin's pistol fire.

"Thus ever to tyrants!" Someone shouted in the distance. The words were followed by a sound as of cloth ripping, and then a crashing fall. Jerry realized that Booth, almost on schedule, had gone over the railing onto the stage.

"The President has been shot!" Someone was crying out the words.

Jerry could do nothing but sit slumped against the wall. People were trying to break in through the blocked door. There was an uproar of pounding and shouting all around him, but it seemed to have less and less to do with him, with each beat of his failing heart. He looked down at the watch he had been forced to drop. Still held to him by its chain, it lay on his bloodied waistcoat. He tried to reach for the stem of the device, but could not move his hands. He felt himself trying, failing, falling, dying—

—and then he was sitting alert and unbloodied in his wicker chair in the dress circle as Mrs. Mountchessington declaimed loudly to Asa Trenchard. Jerry's breathing and pulse were normal. He was not even sweating, much less drenched in his own gore, but as he sat he could feel his pulse begin to race. The watch, ticking methodically, stem still unactivated, was resting in his left hand in his lap, and when he looked down at the familiar painted face of the timepiece he saw that the hands stood at ten minutes after ten.

. . . *will you be able to do it three times? I don't know. I expect you can do it once or twice, and that will be your limit.*

He had failed, had wasted the one chance afforded him by Pilgrim; but his own special power of backing away from death had evidently given him another.

Ten minutes after ten, the watch said. Jerry raised his eyes sharply and turned his head.

John Wilkes Booth, plainly dressed in dark clothing, booted and spurred for riding, had just come into sight at the top of the little set of steps. The actor hesitated there for just a moment, as if he were surprised to find the Presidential box unguarded.

Automatically Jerry's hands moved, opening the glass face of Pilgrim's little device. Jerry's right forefinger set—or re-set—the hands to twelve exactly. Next his forefinger and thumb pulled the stem out to the first position.

And as before, time changed for him, relative to time in the auditorium around him.

Once again the houselights appeared to dim around him, sounds deepened, and all movements but his own slowed down. But this time he got to his feet at once, not waiting for Booth to pass his chair. This time he got out into the aisle ahead of Booth. As before, no one in any of the surrounding seats seemed to be aware of Jerry's passage.

Nor did Booth. The actor, approaching, paused for just an instant in the aisle, to stare at the chair Jerry had just vacated—as if a moment ago Booth had been aware of someone sitting there, and that now there was no one.

This time Jerry, unseen and unheard by his opponent, was waiting, flattened against the wall beside the white door when Booth reached for its knob and swung it open. And this time Jerry got in first.

Still undetected, he retreated speedily to the far end of the narrow vestibule. From there, only a few feet away, he watched while Booth, moving in slow motion, blockaded the white door with the wooden bar, and then put his hand on the knob of the door of Box 7. Jerry could hear the breathing of the assassin, who was unaware of anyone near him in the confined space.

As soon as Booth reached for the knob of the door in front of him, Jerry opened the other door to the box, the one farthest from the auditorium—Box 8.

The solid contact of his hand with the doorknob was not a collision. But the instant he moved the door, Jerry was jarred out of his accelerated state again, and back into the time-frame shared by everyone around him. Lights, sound, normal voices and motion, all flooded back.

Now he was standing in the Presidential box itself, and saw the four people there, seated more or less in a row with their backs to him—Major Rathbone's dark wavy hair, on Jerry's far right as he stood behind them; next young Clara Harris, daughter of a Senator; then Mrs. Lincoln, who had just let go of her husband's hand; and finally Lincoln himself, sitting relaxed in a rocking chair, enjoying the play.

Lincoln's head turned to the right, not with alarm, not yet, but curiosity. He had seen Jerry enter, though the President was not at first aware of the entry of Booth, who had come in a second or two after Jerry, to stand immediately behind the President.

But Mrs. Lincoln saw her husband's head turn to the right. Turning her own head to see what Abraham was looking at, she did see Booth, and let out a loud scream at the sight of the weapon in his hand.

And on hearing this Lincoln took alarm and turned his whole body in his seat.

Rathbone had already risen. Moving faster than Jerry had expected, the major had thrown himself on Booth, so that the pistol discharging sent its ball harmlessly into the wall at the rear of the box.

But the dagger in Booth's left hand sliced into the major's chest and sent him sagging backward.

Jerry was fumbling with his watch, his fingers trying to hold the stem. It was all he could do to keep from dropping the device again as one of the combatants bumped into him.

The pounding on the outer door, the blocked door, begun only moments ago, had already grown to the proportions of a real assault.

Now Booth turned on the President and raised the knife again.

Abraham Lincoln had had time to turn fully around and gain his feet, kicking the encumbering rocking chair away. His huge left hand enfolded the wrist that held the knife. The other hand had seized Booth somewhere by his dark gray coat. The frontier wrestler's body turned, the long arms of the railsplitter levered. The knife fell from Booth's grip. The smaller body of the actor rose in an arc that would have graced a twentieth-century judo *dojo*, and went soaring over the railing, launched head first toward the stage twelve feet below.

Jerry never heard the ignominious crash of the landing. Far on the other side of the stage, deep in the shadows of the left-hand upper box, an orange flash appeared. He never heard the sound of the shot, but he felt the staggering, numbing impact of the bullet, somewhere around the inner end of his right collarbone—

—and he was sitting in the dress circle, uninjured, breathing calmly, his body still physiologically unaroused, listening to Mrs. Mountchessington declaim. One more try, at least, was to be granted him. One more, or an infinity of hopeless tries, perhaps.

—*it is possible to get caught up in something like a closed programming loop*—

Who had told him that?

And where was Booth?

—Booth had already passed Jerry's seat in the dress circle, was going on into the white door—

Jerry loped after the actor, got through the door into the vestibule before it closed and locked. This time Jerry waited, invisible, until Booth had peered through the bored hole at his victim, then stood up and opened the door behind the seated President.

Then Jerry followed Booth through the same door into the Lincoln box.

This time by touching nothing but the floor, coming into hard contact with nothing movable in his environment, Jerry preserved his invisibility for a relatively long time. Holding his watch ready, fingers on the stem, Jerry saw—and felt that he had seen it a thousand times before—Booth's derringer raised in the pale tattooed hand, the little hammer of the pistol drawn back. The hammer drawn back, and then falling, endlessly falling.

Jerry pulled the stem of the time-watch, activating the beacon.

And now, he watched the dull-bright curve of the leaden ball as it emerged from the truncated barrel of the little pistol. A fine spray of gas and unburnt powder, at first almost invisible, came escaping past the bullet, preceding it across the few inches between the muzzle and the target.

But in the last moment before that impact, two new figures had instantaneously become visible to him. They hung in midair, apparently unsupported, one of them on each side of Lincoln's rocking chair. Even with the blurring of the world Jerry could recognize, or thought he could, the figure on his left as that of Pilgrim. The figure on the right was some stunted alien presence, much smaller than Pilgrim, and utterly grotesque.

He felt no worry about that now. The leaden ball had emerged completely from the muzzle of the derringer now, with a gout of flame and thicker smoke bursting forth behind it, continuing to force the missile forward on its deadly path.

But the two figures flanking the President were now moving even more quickly than the pistol ball. During the long subjective second during which Jerry was able to watch the bullet's passage, they lifted Lincoln up out of his rocking chair between them. Then it appeared to Jerry that the President's long body had slipped from their grasp—or else that they were abandoning their effort, as if in the realization that it was useless. It seemed that between them, Pilgrim and the monster pushed Lincoln down into his chair again. Then the two mysterious presences were gone.

Jerry saw the head of Abraham Lincoln jerk forward violently under the impact of Booth's bullet, the shaggy dark hair rising and falling in a momentary flutter.

And with that event, time came back to normal with a rush. This time he got to his feet at once, not waiting for Booth to pass his chair.

But this time, before the acceleration could progress very far, the whole scene before him jerked to a stop, like the last freeze-frame of a motion picture. There was Lincoln, slumped already. Beside him, his wife, still unaware, her own nerves and brain not yet reacting to the pistol's bark. There were the other two legitimate occupants of the box, seated with their attention still on the figure of Asa Trenchard who at the moment occupied the stage alone. There was Booth, death looking out of his wide dark eyes fixed upon his victim. The smoke from the derringer was still only beginning to fill the space inside the box.

And then the freeze-frame faded. And with the fading of the last light to darkness, silence descended also, and Jerry knew the quiet and the blackness of the grave.

TWENTY-ONE

Light came reaching into darkness, sure-footed as death, pushing aside even the gloom of death itself. Strange that after what had happened to him Jerry, with the light growing outside his eyelids, could hear the song of robins, and inhale the scent of lilacs. Once—it must have been a hundred years ago, on a quiet night in Springfield— Jan Chen had quoted a line of Walt Whitman to him: *When lilacs last in the dooryard bloomed—*

Then full memory returned in a rush of what had happened in Ford's Theater, the fighting and dying and living there, as accurate and immediate as if intervening sleep or unconsciousness had never wiped it away.

"We failed," he moaned aloud, and opened his eyes wide at the same moment. He spoke before he knew where he was, or whether or not he was alone.

Then he saw that he was alone. This time he was lying on no corn-husk pallet. Nor was this the fine but too-soft mattress he had enjoyed at Willard's Hotel. This bed was clean and firm and rather institutional. Something about the subtle coloration of the walls, the light, perhaps the air said twentieth century to him even before he turned his head. The curtains on the window were partially drawn back, and Jerry could look out the window of the converted farmhouse to see electric wires fastened to a pole outside.

He recognized this room, right enough. Jerry turned over in the brass bed with its white modern sheets, and discovered that he was still wearing his nineteenth-century underwear, and nothing else. The outer garments of Jim Lockwood—and the coat of John Wilkes Booth—all looking considerably the worse for wear, were scattered in various places around the room, some on a floor, some on one article of furniture or another. There were dried brownish bloodstains on the torn sleeve of a dirty shirt.

Jerry's beard was coming along nicely, three days' worth of it at least, he thought. On his left forearm he could feel the tug of modern bandages. Someone had done a neat job there with tape and gauze. Had Booth's dagger nicked him again at the end of that last rewrite of reality?

Only the small wounds require bandaging. Perhaps death can safely be ignored. It needs no healing attention, whether it comes in the form of a knife-wound from a crazy actor, or in the form of a gunshot from—

The door leading to the hallway opened without any preliminary knock, and Jan Chen came through it. She was wearing white and khaki, looking rather like what Jerry supposed a nurse in a field hospital ought to look like.

"No," she said, positively and without preamble, shaking her head at him. Obviously she had heard his outcry upon awaking. "No, Jerry, we did not fail. Most specifically, you did not. You managed to activate the beacon perfectly on your third try."

Pilgrim, wearing a white lab coat open over his usual hiker's clothing, had come into the bedroom right after her, and now he raised a hand in a kind of benediction. "Well done, Jeremiah."

Jerry sat up in bed and found that his sense of outrage and thoughts of revenge had been left behind somewhere. "I think I got killed at least twice," he said.

"You did. You died by blade and bullet, ultimately to very good effect."

"You mean that the last time, it worked?"

"It worked indeed. Lincoln is safe and history as you know it is intact."

"The last thing I remember seeing is Lincoln getting shot."

"You could not see everything that happened. And I trust the other members of Ford's audience saw much less than you did."

Jerry sank back on his good elbow. "Then tell me what I missed. Was it you who shot me from across the way?"

Pilgrim raised an eyebrow. "I thought you understood that I could take no such direct part in those affairs of eighteen sixty-five. Instead it was I who pulled you off stage, as it were, and bandaged your most recent wound. When you had completed your most difficult role, successfully."

"You mean that after I saw Lincoln shot I somehow time-walked again and—"

"No, I think you had reached the limit of your resilience. There was danger of a closed loop establishing itself, or—but never mind. The people in the theater believe also that they saw the President shot, and the history books record the dark deed just as before. But the head that took the bullet was not Lincoln's." Pilgrim smiled.

Jerry could only look in confusion from one of his visitors to the other.

Pilgrim made a gesture with both hands, as if unveiling something. "It was the head of a simulacrum. An organic dummy, a duplicate down to the proper location and color of each hair, the last little scar, dressed in replicas of clothing Lincoln wore that night—which is all a matter of historical record. Your job was to signal us the exactly proper time and place of the substitution, which would otherwise have been a disastrous failure."

"A—dummy?"

"Nothing so crude as the image that word must evoke for you. It did the job nicely. Nothing was required of it beyond breathing and bleeding for a few hours with a bullet in its brain. Death was officially announced at a little after seven on Saturday morning, with the victim never having regained consciousness."

"The victim," Jerry said. "An organic dummy?"

Pilgrim was shaking his head, in response to

something in Jerry's face. "No, Jeremiah. We sacrificed no human victim. Oh, to the eye of the doctors at the autopsy in the White House the blood and brains looked quite convincing—they are not, but the science of the mid-nineteenth century was incapable of making the distinction. I believe you may have had a brief look at our simulacrum, on the night you left us. It was then resting in the bed in the next room."

Jerry had sat up again, and now he was starting to get out of bed. His left arm was sore and he felt a little weak, but on the whole he was doing well enough. Very well indeed, considering all the things he could remember happening to him. Jan was holding a robe for him and he put his arms into the sleeves, being careful with the injured one. He looked at the clothes of Jim Lockwood, that he was never going to wear again. He looked at the stained coat of John Wilkes Booth, and tried to analyze what he felt. He decided his chief feeling was of relief that he was not still wearing it.

Nor was he ever going to see Colleen Monahan again.

Fastening the belt on the robe, he looked from Jan Chen to Pilgrim, and asked them: "Who did shoot me? On that second try?"

Jan looked at Pilgrim, letting him answer. He said: "Whoever it was really did you a favor, you know."

"Yes, I know. I was wondering whether that was what they had in mind."

"I would doubt it."

"It wasn't you, then, or any of your agents?"

"It was not."

"Then I suppose it was Colleen Monahan."

"In fact it was."

"And she was really trying to kill me."

"Oh, undoubtedly. What she had seen, and had heard from you, convinced her that you were involved in a plot to kill the President. You and Booth came bursting into the Presidential box together. She was there in the theater, you see, upon her own initiative—"

"I know about that. I just wish I'd had the chance to try to explain . . . never mind." He paused. "What happened to her, historically?"

Pilgrim appeared to be trying to remember. "She created only a negligible ripple in the flow of history. After the assassination, she kept quiet about any suspicions she might have had. Married a Union veteran in eighteen sixty-six. Died of yellow fever, as I recall, in eighteen sixty-seven."

"Oh." But Jerry was not, he was not, going to think about that woman now. She had been dead for almost a century before Jerry Flint was born.

Jerry drew a deep breath and changed the subject. Something of his old anger was returning. "On the night I left here, the figure I saw in the next room moved."

"Yes, of course," Pilgrim admitted. "The simulacrum. As a sleeper might move, no more than that. Am I correct?"

"Correct," Jerry admitted.

"The simulacrum had bones and muscles—even nerves, of a sort. No real brain, I assure you. Gray organic boilerplate, lacking the potential for consciousness."

"I thought it—he—was asleep." Jerry shook his

head, marveling. "I thought I had seen *Abe Lincoln* sleeping in the room next to mine. I mean—an *absolute* dead ringer. I thought I was going crazy. Or you were trying to drive me nuts."

"I hope you will be careful," said Jan Chen, sounding vaguely horrified. "He doesn't like to be called Abe. Even by old friends, which you really are not."

"He?"

"Mr. Lincoln. The former President. He's sleeping in the next room now, under mild sedation."

It took Jerry a moment to grasp what she was saying. "And the simulacrum is . . . ?"

"Buried," said Pilgrim, "under twelve tons of concrete and a lot of granite and bronze statues, in Oak Ridge Cemetery."

Jerry turned away from both of them and went to the window. The curtains were half closed, and he drew them wide. He looked out past nearby lilac bushes in spring bloom, across muddy fields to where a tractor was laboring in the distance, pulling new machinery.

Something, a distorted, smaller-than-adult-human figure, ran across the yard on two legs and disappeared. He thought it had been wearing some kind of helmet.

Then Jerry turned back to face the two people who were in the room with him. "All right," he said. "You've brought me back to the twentieth century. And you've brought yourself back. I suppose you'd be able to bring Lincoln too, once he wasn't—needed there any more. What happens to him now? Why are you doing this? Who are you? And what is that damned thing that just now ran across your yard?"

"That 'damned thing', as you describe it," said Pilgrim cooly, "is one of my shipmates. The name by which you know me is not my original *nomen*, but neither is it a random choice, believe me. I am a poor wayfaring stranger in this world, and my one wish is to go home."

"Go home. And where is that?"

"Long ago, as the saying has it, and far away. So remote in time and space from where we are now that even to begin the explanation would involve another story entirely."

Jerry swiveled his gaze to Jan Chen. "And you?"

"Just a local recruit," she told him, almost shyly. "Twentieth-century American, like yourself. When I was offered the chance of really meeting Lincoln— well, I would have killed to get this job." Jerry, somehow, found it easy to believe her.

"As for what we are really going to do with Lincoln, as you put it," Pilgrim continued, "I am going to present him with a set of choices."

"Oh?"

"Yes. And when he understands the facts, I do not think his lawyer's mind will conclude that he was kidnapped, or blame us for pulling him out of the bullet's path.

"One of his choices will be to proceed to the twenty-third century, where some of his country- men are anxious to meet him. Mr. Helpman— remember?—is their representative. Indeed, it is their opinion that they need your sixteenth Presi- dent desperately."

Jan Chen took over the explanation. "In return

for our bringing Mr. Lincoln to them," she added brightly, "they're providing Dr. Pilgrim with something he needs for his ship. In order to get home. Olivia—you remember the lady you talked with before you left?—is sort of like a social worker, helping him get home. That's how she explained it to me," she added quickly, when Pilgrim turned a look on her.

" 'Social worker' " Pilgrim repeated, bemusedly.

"Parole officer?" Jan ventured timidly.

"I remember Olivia," said Jerry, and closed his eyes and rubbed them. "Where does she come from?"

"You wouldn't know the place," Pilgrim muttered. " 'Social worker', " he repeated under his breath, as if he found that description fascinating.

"So," Jerry asked, "why do these twenty-third century people think that they need Lincoln? Can't they solve their own problems?" Again he saw that tired, sallow, bearded face, as he had seen it several times at close range. There had been a definite contentment in that countenance despite its weariness; the satisfaction of a man who was finishing a long race and now expected to be able to rest.

"Their reasons," said Pilgrim, "will be for Mr. Lincoln to hear—when he is ready—and for him to evaluate. I am not free to tell you about them. I will say that I expect the President to find their offer extremely interesting. At any rate, he is here in the twentieth century now and cannot go back to Ford's Theater. Will you help us welcome him to his new life? It should give you valuable practice."

"Practice?"

"In teaching nineteenth-century folk about the marvels of the twentieth."

"And why should I need practice in that?"

"Oh, did I forget to mention it?" Pilgrim's eyes gleamed wickedly. "We decided to bring out another person, too, before we removed our probes from Ford's Theater. A young lady whose violent behavior would otherwise have created some problems taking the form of paradox, threatening to undermine our results. Only a couple of years' future for her anyway in the nineteenth century and no demand at all in the twenty-third. Perhaps you would do me one more favor, my young friend, and help her to find a niche in this one?—but easy, easy, you may see her presently. She needs her sleep right now. But Mr. Lincoln I think is ready to wake up."

No more than a minute later the three of them, Jerry, Pilgrim, and Jan Chen, were walking into the next bedroom. Unlike the room in which Jerry had awakened, this one had been elaborately refurnished since the night of his departure. Here the furnishings, including even some new panelling on the walls, had been chosen to recreate a reasonably authentic room of the nineteenth century.

Abraham Lincoln was lying in the old brass-framed bed, most of his body under a white coarse sheet and a handmade quilt. He was wearing a white nightshirt, and he appeared to be in the first stages of a gradual awakening.

The sixteenth President raised himself a little, rubbing his dark-graying tousled hair with a powerful hand, and looked in a puzzled way at the three people who had entered the room to stand respectfully at the foot of the bed. He seemed to be waiting for one of them to speak.

It was Jerry, acting on impulse, who opened his mouth first. "Good morning, Mr. President. Last night an attempt was made upon your life. But you are safe now. We are your friends."

THE END

Rob a Pharaoh and you've made an enemy
not just for life . . . but for *all time.*

FRED SABERHAGEN

PYRAMIDS

Tom Scheffler knew that his great uncle,
Montgomery Chapel, had worked as an Egyptologist
during the 1930s, and after that had become a
millionaire by selling artifacts no one else could
have obtained. Scheffler also knew that the old
man, fifty years later, was still afraid of some
man—some *entity*—known only as Pilgrim. But
what did that mean to Scheffler, an impoverished
student with the chance to spend a year "house-
sitting" a multi-million-dollar condo?

What Scheffler didn't know—and would learn
the hard way—was that Pilgrim was coming back,
aboard a ship that traveled both space and time,
headed for a confrontation in a weirdly changed
past where the monstrous gods of ancient Egypt
walked the Earth. And where Pharaoh Khufu,
builder of the greatest monument the world had
ever known, lay in wait for grave robbers from
out of time . . .

JANUARY 1987 • 65609-0 • 320 pp. • $3.50

Here is an excerpt from the new collection "MEN HUNTING THINGS," edited by David Drake, coming in April 1988 from Baen Books:

IT'S A LOT LIKE WAR

A hunter and a soldier on a modern battlefield contrast in more ways than they're similar.

That wasn't always the case. Captain C.H. Stigand's 1913 book of reminiscences, HUNTING THE ELEPHANT IN AFRICA, contains a chapter entitled "Stalking the African" (between "Camp Hints" and "Hunting the Bongo"). It's a straightforward series of anecdotes involving the business for which Stigand was paid by his government—punitive expeditions against native races in the British African colonies.

Readers of modern sensibilities may be pleased to learn that Stigand died six years later with a Dinka spear through his ribs; but he was a man of his times, not an aberration. Richard Meinertzhagen wrote with great satisfaction of the unique "right and left" he made during a punitive expedition against the Irryeni in 1904: he shot a native with the right barrel of his elephant gun—and then dropped the lion which his first shot had startled into view.

It would be easy enough to say that the whites who served in Africa in the 19th century considered native races to be sub-human and therefore game to be hunted under a specialized set of rules. There's some justification for viewing the colonial overlords that way. The stringency of the attendant "hunting laws" varied from British and German possessions, whose administrators took their "civilizing mission" seriously, to the Congo Free State where Leopold, King of the Belgians, gave the dregs of all the world license to do as they pleased—so long as it made him a profit.

(For what it's worth, Leopold's butchers *didn't* bring him much profit. The Congo became a Belgian—rather than a personal—possession when Leopold defaulted on the loans his country had advanced him against the colony's security.)

But the unity of hunting and war went beyond racial attitudes. Meinertzhagen was seventy years old in 1948 when his cruise ship docked in Haifa during the Israeli War of Independence. He borrowed a rifle and 200 rounds—which he fired off during what he described as "a glorious day!", increasing his personal bag by perhaps twenty Arab gunmen.

Similarly, Frederick Courteney Selous—perhaps the most famous big-game hunter of them all—enlisted at the outbreak of World War One even though he *wasn't* a professional soldier. He was sixty-five years old when a German sniper blew his brains out in what is now Tanzania.

Hunters and soldiers were nearly identical for most of the millennia since human societies became organized enough to wage war. Why isn't that still true today?

In large measure, I think, the change is due to the advance of technology. In modern warfare, a soldier who is seen by the enemy is probably doomed. Indeed, most casualties are men who *weren't* seen by the enemy. They were simply caught by bombs, shells, or automatic gunfire sweeping an area.

A glance at casualties grouped by cause of wound from World War One onward suggests that indirect artillery fire is the only significant factor in battle. All other weapons—tanks included—serve only to provide targets for the howitzers to grind up; and the gunners lobbing their shells in high arcs almost never see a living enemy.

The reality isn't quite *that* simple; but I defy anybody who's spent time in a modern war zone to tell me that they felt personally in control of their environment.

Hunters can be killed or injured by their intended prey. Still, most of them die in bed. (The most likely human victim of a hungry leopard or a peckish rhinoceros has always been an unarmed native who was in the wrong place at the wrong time.) Very few soldiers become battle casualties either—but soldiers don't have the option that hunters have, to go home any time they please.

A modern war zone is a terrifying place, if you let yourself think about it; and even at its smallest scale, guerrilla warfare, it's utterly impersonal.

A guerrilla can never be sure that the infra-red trace of his stove hasn't been spotted by an aircraft in the silent darkness, or that his footsteps aren't being picked up by sensors disguised as pebbles along the trail down which he pads. Either way, a salvo of artillery shells may be the last thing he hears—unless they've blown him out of existence before the shriek of their supersonic passage reaches his ears.

But technology doesn't free his opponent from fear—or give him personal control of the battlefield, either. When the counter-insurgent moves, he's likely to put his foot or his vehicle on top of a mine. The blast will be the only warning he has that he's being maimed. Even men protected by the four-inch steel of a tank know the guerrillas may have buried a 500-pound bomb under *this* stretch of road. If that happens, his family will be sent a hundred and fifty pounds of sand—with instructions not to open the coffin.

At rest, the counter-insurgent wears his boots because he may be attacked at any instant. Then he'll shoot out into the night—but he'll have no target except the muzzle flashes of the guns trying to kill him, and there'll be no result to point to in the morning except perhaps a smear of blood or a weapon dropped somewhere along the tree line.

If a rocket screams across the darkness, the counter-insurgent can hunch down in his slit trench and pray that the glowing green ball with a sound like a steam locomotive will land on somebody else instead. Prayer probably won't help, any more than it'll stop the rain or make the mosquitos stop biting. But nothing else will help either.

So nowadays, a soldier doesn't have much in common with a hunter. That's not to say that warfare is no longer similar to hunting, however.

On the contrary: modern soldiers and hunted beasts have a great deal in common.

APRIL 1988 * 65399-7 * 288 pp * $2.95

WILL *YOU* SURVIVE?

In addition to Dean Ing's powerful science fiction novels—*Systemic Shock, Wild Country, Blood of Eagles* and others—he has written cogently and inventively about the art of survival. **The Chernobyl Syndrome** is the result of his research into life after a possible nuclear exchange . . . because as our civilization gets bigger and better, we become more and more dependent on its products. What would *you* do if the machine stops—or blows up?

Some of the topics Dean Ing covers:
* How to *make* a getaway airplane
* Honing your "crisis skills"
* Fleeing the firestorm: escape tactics for city-dwellers
* How to build a homemade fallout meter
* Civil defense, American style
* "Microfarming"—survival in five acres
    And much, much more.

Also by Dean Ing, available through Baen Books:

ANASAZI
Why did the long-vanished Anasazi Indians retreat from their homes and gardens on the green mesa top to precarious cliffside cities? Were they afraid of someone—or some*thing*? "There's no evidence of warfare in the ruins of their earlier homes . . . but maybe the marauders they feared didn't wage war in the usual way," says Dean Ing. *Anasazi* postulates a race of alien beings who needed human bodies in order to survive on Earth—a race of aliens that *still* exists.

FIREFIGHT 2000
How do you integrate armies supplied with bayonets and ballistic missiles; citizens enjoying Volkswagens and Ferraris; cities drawing power from windmills and nuclear powerplants? Ing takes a look at these dichotomies, and more. This collection of fact and fiction serves as a metaphor for tomorrow: covering terror and hope, right guesses and wrong, high tech and thatched cottages.

Order Dean Ing's books listed above with this order form. Simply check your choices below and send the combined cover price/s to: Baen Books, Dept. BA, 260 Fifth Avenue, New York, New York 10001.

THE CHERNOBYL SYNDROME • 65345-8 •
    320 pp. • $3.50   ———
ANASAZI • 65629-5 • 288 pp. • $2.95   ———
FIREFIGHT 2000 • 65650-X • 252 pp. • $2.95 ———

ROBERT A. HEINLEIN

"Heinlein knows more about blending provocative scientific thinking with strong human stories than any dozen other contemporary science fiction writers."
—*Chicago Sun-Times*

"Robert A. Heinlein wears imagination as though it were his private suit of clothes. What makes his work so rich is that he combines his lively, creative sense with an approach that is at once literate, informed, and exciting."
—*New York Times*

Seven of Robert A. Heinlein's best-loved titles are now available in superbly packaged new Baen editions, with embossed series-look covers by artist John Melo. Collect them all by sending in the order form below:

REVOLT IN 2100, 65589-2, $3.50 ☐

METHUSELAH'S CHILDREN, 65597-3, $3.50 ☐

THE GREEN HILLS OF EARTH, 65608-2, $3.50 ☐

THE MAN WHO SOLD THE MOON, 65623-6, $3.50 ☐

THE MENACE FROM EARTH*, 65636-8, $3.50 ☐

ASSIGNMENT IN ETERNITY**, 65637-6, $3.50 ☐

SIXTH COLUMN***, 65638-4, $3.50 ☐

HE'S OPINIONATED

HE'S DYNAMIC

HE'S LARGER THAN LIFE

MARTIN CAIDIN

Martin Caidin is a bestselling novelist, pilot *extraordinaire*, and expert on America's space program. *He's also a prophet of technological change.* His ability to predict future trends verges on the psychic, as when he wrote *Cyborg* (the novel which became "The Six Million Dollar Man") and *Marooned* (which precipitated the American-Soviet Apollo-Soyuz linkup mission). His tense, action-filled stories are based on personal experience in fields such as astronautics, aviation, oceanography and the military.

Caidin's characters also know their stuff. And they take on real life, because they're based on real people. Martin Caidin spent a stint as a merchant seaman in Europe and Africa, worked for Air Force Intelligence in the U.S. and Asia, and has flown his own planes to many parts of the world. His adventures can be yours in these novels from Baen Books.

--- --- --- --- --- --- --- ---

EXIT EARTH—Just as the US and the USSR have finally settled their differences, American scientists discover that the solar system is about to pass through a cloud of cosmic dust that will incite the Sun to a paroxysm of fury. All will die. There can be no escape—except, possibly, for a very few. *This is their story.* 656 pp. • 65630-9 • $4.50 _____

KILLER STATION—Earth's first space station *Pleiades* is a scientific boon—until one brief moment of sabotage changes it into a terrible Sword of Damocles. 55996-6 • 384 pp. • $3.50 _____

THE MESSIAH STONE—"An unusual thriller . . . not only in subject matter, but in the fact that the author claims that the basic idea behind the book is real! [THE MESSIAH STONE] concerns the possession of a stone; the person who controls the stone rules the world. The last such person is rumored to be Adolf Hitler. . . . Harrowing adventure and nonstop action."—*Science Fiction Review.* 65562-0 • 416 pp. • $3.95 _____

ZOBOA—It started with the hijacking of four atomic bombs, and ended with the Space Shuttle atop a pillar of fire. . . . "From the marvelous, cinematic opening pages, Caidin sweeps the reader along in a raucous, exciting thriller."—*Publishers Weekly* 65588-4 • 448 pp. • $3.50 _____

To order these Baen Books, check each title selected and return with a check or money order for the combined cover price. Send to Baen Books, 260 Fifth Avenue, New York, N.Y. 10001.

Distributed by Simon & Schuster
1230 Avenue of the Americas • New York, N.Y. 10020

Here is an excerpt from Vernor Vinge's new novel, Marooned in Realtime, *coming in June 1987 from Baen Books:*

The town nestled in the foothills of the Indonesian Alps, high enough so that equatorial heat and humidity was moderated to an almost uniform pleasantness. Here the Korolevs and their friends had finally assembled the rescued from all the ages. At the moment the population was less than two hundred, every living human being. They needed more; Yelén Korolev knew where to get one hundred more. She was determined to rescue them.

Steven Fraley, President of the Republic of New Mexico, was determined that those hundred remain unrescued. He was still arguing the case when Wil Brierson arrived. ". . . and you don't appreciate the history of our era, madam. The Peacers came near to exterminating the human race. Sure, saving this group will get you a few more warm bodies, but you risk the survival of our whole colony, of the entire human race, in doing so."

Yelén Korolev looked calm, but Wil knew her well enough to recognize the signs of an impending explosion: there were rosy patches on her cheeks, yet her features were otherwise even paler than usual. She ran a hand through her blond hair. "Mr. Fraley, I really do know the history of your era. Remember that almost all of us—no matter what our present age and experience—have our childhoods within a couple hundred years of one another. The Peace Authority"—her lips twitched in a quick smile at the name—"may have started the general war of 1997. They may even be responsible for the terrible plagues of the early twenty-first century. But as governments go, they were relatively benign. This group in Kampuchea"—she waved toward the north—"went into stasis in 2048, when the Peacers were overthrown. That was before decent health care was available. It's entirely possible that none of the original criminals are present."

Fraley opened and closed his mouth, but no words

came. Finally: "Haven't you heard of their 'Renaissance' scheme? In '48 they were ready to kill by the millions again. Those guys under Kampuchea probably got more hell-bombs than a dog has fleas. That base was their secret ace in the hole. If they hadn't screwed up their stasis, they'd've come out in 2100 and blown us away. And you probably wouldn't even have been born—"

Yelén cut into the torrent. "Hell-bombs? Popguns. Even you know that. Mr. Fraley, getting another hundred people into our colony will make our settlement just big enough to survive. Marta and I haven't spent our lives setting this up just to see it die like the undermanned attempts of the past. The only reason we postponed the founding of Korolev till megayear fifty was so we could rescue those Peacers when their bobble bursts."

She turned to her partner. "Is everybody accounted for?"

Marta Korolev had sat through the argument in silence, her dark features relaxed, her eyes closed. Her headband put her in communication with the estate's autonomous devices. No doubt she had managed a half dozen fliers during the last half hour, scouring the countryside for any truant colonists the Korolev satellites had spotted. Now she opened her eyes. "Everybody's accounted for and safe. In fact"—she caught sight of Wil standing at the back of the amphitheater and grinned—"almost everyone is here on the castle grounds. I think we can provide you people with quite a show this afternoon." She either hadn't followed or—more likely—had chosen to ignore the dispute between Yelén and Fraley.

"Okay, let's get started." A rustle of anticipation passed through the audience. Many were from the twenty-first century, like Wil. But they'd seen enough of the advanced travelers to know that such a statement was more than enough signal for spectacular events to happen.

From his place at the top of the amphitheater, Wil

had a good view to the north. The forests of the higher elevations fell away to a gray-green blur that was the equatorial jungle. Beyond that, haze obscured even the existence of the Inland Sea. Even on the rare, clear day when the sea mists lifted, the Kampuchean Alps were hidden beyond the horizon. Nevertheless, the rescue should be visible; he was a bit surprised that the bluish white of the northern horizon was undisturbed.

"Things will get more exciting, I promise." Yelén's voice brought his eyes back to the stage. Two large displays floated behind her.

"As Mr. Fraley says, the Peacer bobble was supposed to be a secret. It was originally underground. It is much further underground now—somebody blundered. What was to be a fifty-year jump became something . . . longer. As near as we can figure, their bobble should burst sometime in the next few thousand years; they've been in stasis fifty million years. During that time, continents drifted and new rifts formed. Parts of Kampuchea slid deep beneath new mountains." The display behind her lit with a multicolored transect of the Kampuchean Alps. The surface crust appeared as blue, shading into yellow and orange at the greater depths. Right at the margin of orange and magma red was a tiny black disk—the Peacer bobble, afloat against the ceiling of hell.

Inside the bobble, time was stopped. Those within were as they'd been at that instant of a near-forgotten war when the losers decided to escape to the future. No force could affect a bobble's contents; no force could affect its duration—not the heart of a star, not the heart of a lover.

But when the bobble burst, when the stasis ended . . . The Peacers were about forty kilometers down. There would be a moment of noise and heat and pain as the magma swallowed them. One hundred men and women would die, and a certain endangered species would move one more step toward final extinction.

The Korolevs proposed to raise the bobble to the

surface, where it would be safe for the few remaining millennia of its duration. Yelén waved at the display. "This was taken just before we started the operation. Here's the ongoing view."

The picture flickered. The red magma boundary had risen thousands of meters above the bobble. Pinheads of white light flashed in the orange and yellow that represented the solid crust. In the place of each of those lights, red blossomed and spread, almost—Wil winced at the thought—like blood from a stab wound. "Each of those sparkles is a hundred-megaton bomb. In the last few seconds, we've released more energy than all mankind's wars put together."

The red spread as the wounds coalesced into a vast hemorrhage in the bosom of Kampuchea. The magma was still twenty kilometers below ground level. The bombs were timed so there was a constant sparkling just above the highest level of red, bringing the melt closer and closer to the surface. At the bottom of the display, the Peacer bobble floated, serene and untouched. On this scale, its motion towards the surface was imperceptible.

Wil pulled his attention from the display and looked beyond the amphitheater. There was no change: the northern horizon was still haze and pale blue. The rescue site was fifteen hundred kilometers away, but even so, he'd expected something spectacular.

The elapsed-time clock on the display showed almost four minutes. The Korolev pattern of bomb bursts was still thousands of meters short of the surface.

President Fraley rose from his seat. "Madame Korolev, please. There is still time to stop this. I know you've rescued all types, cranks, joyriders, criminals, victims. But these are *monsters*." For once, Wil thought he heard sincerity—perhaps even fear—in the New Mexican's voice. *And he might be right*. If the rumors were true, if the Peacers had created the plagues of the early twenty-first century, then they were responsible for the deaths of billions. If they had succeeded with their Renaissance Project, they would have killed most of the survivors.

Yelén Korolev glanced down at Fraley but didn't reply. The New Mexican stiffened, then waved abruptly to his people. One hundred men and women—most in NM fatigues—came quickly to their feet. It was a dramatic gesture, if nothing else: the amphitheater would be almost empty with them gone.

"Mr. President, I suggest you and the others sit back down." It was Marta Korolev. Her tone was as pleasant as ever, but the insult in the words brought a flush to Steve Fraley's face. He gestured angrily and turned to the stone steps that led from the theater.

The ground shock arrived an instant later.

320 pp. • 65647-3 • $3.50

To order any Baen Book by mail, send the cover price plus 75 cents for first-class postage and handling to: Baen Books, Dept. B, 260 Fifth Avenue, New York, N.Y. 10001.